Wolfville

Alfred Henry Lewis

Adapted by Ariel Fernández C.

ABOUT THE AUTHOR

American investigative journalist, lawyer, Western novel writer, editor, and short story writer.
During the late 19th century, he wrote muckraker articles for Cosmopolitan. As an investigative journalist, Lewis wrote extensively about corruption in New York politics.
He also wrote biographies about Richard Croker and Andrew Jackson.
As a writer of genre fiction, his most successful works were in his Wolfville series of Western fiction.

PREFACE.

These tales by the Old Cattleman have been submitted to perhaps a dozen people. They have read, criticised, and advised. The advice was good; the criticism just. Some suggested a sketch which might in detail set forth Toffville; there were those who wanted something like a picture of the Old Cattleman; while others urged an elaboration of the personal characteristics of Old Man Enright, Doc Peets, Cherokee Hall, Moore, Tutt, Boggs, Faro Nell, Old Monte, and Texas Thompson. I have, how-ever, concluded to leave all these matters to the illustrations of Mr. Remington and the imaginations of those who read. I think it the better way- certainly it is the easier one for me. I shall therefore permit the Old Cattleman to tell his stories in his own fashion. The style will be crude, abrupt, and meagre, but I trust it will prove as satisfactory to the reader as it has to me.

A. H. L.
New York, May 15,1897.

CHAPTER I.

WOLFVILLE'S FIRST FUNERAL.

"These yere obsequies which I'm about mentionin'," observed the Old Cattleman, "is the first real funeral Wolfville has."

The old fellow had lighted a cob pipe and tilted his chair back in a fashion which proclaimed a plan to be comfortable. He had begun to tolerate—even encourage—my society, although it was clear that as a tenderfoot he regarded me with a species of gentle disdain.

I had provoked the subject of funeral ceremonies by a recurrence to the affair of the Yellowhouse Man, and a query as to what would have been the programme of the public-spirited hamlet of Wolfville if that invalid had died instead of yielding to the nursing of Jack Moore and that tariff on draw-poker which the genius of Old Man Enright decreed.

It came in easy illustration, as answer to my question, for the Old Cattleman to recall the funeral of a former leading spirit of Southwestern society. The name of this worthy was Jack King; and with a brief exposition of his more salient traits, my grizzled raconteur led down to his burial with the remark before quoted.

"Of course," continued the Old Cattleman, "of course while thar's some like this Yallerhouse gent who survives; thar's others of the boys who is downed one time an' another, an' goes shoutin' home to heaven by various trails. But ontil the event I now recalls, the remainders has been freighted east or west every time, an' the camp gets left. It's hard luck, but at last it comes toward us; an' thar we be one day with a corpse all our'n, an' no partnership with nobody nor nothin'.

"'It's the chance of our life,' says Doc Peets, 'an' we plays it. Thar's nothin' too rich for our blood, an' these obsequies is goin' to be spread-eagle, you bet! We'll show Red Dog an' sim'lar villages they ain't sign-camps compared with Wolfville.'

"So we begins to draw in our belts an' get a big ready. Jack King, as I says before, is corpse, eemergin' outen a game of poker as sech. Which prior tharto, Jack's been peevish, an' pesterin' an' pervadin' 'round for several days. The camp stands a heap o' trouble with him an' tries to smooth it along by givin' him his whiskey an' his way about as he wants 'em, hopin' for a change. But man is only human, an' when Jack starts in one night to make a flush beat a tray full for seven hundred dollars, he asks too much.

"Thar ain't no ondertakers, so we rounds up the outfit, an' knowin' he'd take a pride in it, an' do the slam-up thing, we puts in Doc Peets to deal the game unanimous.

"'Gents,' he says, as we-alls turns into the Red Light to be refreshed, 'in assoomin' the present pressure I feels the compliments paid me in the seelection. I shall act for the credit of the camp, an' I needs your help. I desires that these rites be a howlin' vict'ry. I don't want people comin' 'round next week allowin' thar ain't been no funeral, an' I don't reckon much that they will. We've got the corpse, an' if we gets bucked off now it's our fault.'

"So he app'ints Old Monte an' Dan Boggs to go for a box for Jack, an' details a couple of niggers from the corral to dig a tomb.

3

"'An' mind you-alls,' says Peets, `I wants that hole at least a mile from camp. In order to make a funeral a success, you needs distance. That's where deceased gets action. It gives the procession a chance to spread an' show up. You can't make no funeral imposin' except you're plumb liberal on distances.'

"It all goes smooth right off the reel. We gets a box an' grave ready, an' Peets sticks up a notice on the stage-station door, settin' the excitement for third-drink time next day. Prompt at the drop of the hat the camp lets go all holds an' turns loose in a body to put Jack through right. He's laid out in splendid shape in the New York Store, with nothin' to complain of if he's asked to make the kick himse'f. He has a new silk necktie, blue shirt an' pearl buttons, trousers, an' boots. Some one—Benson Annie, I reckons—has pasted some co't plaster over the hole on his cheek-bone where the bullet gets in, an' all 'round Jack looks better than I ever sees him.

"'Let the congregation remove its hats,' says Peets, a-settin' down on a box up at Jack's head, 'an' as many as can will please get somethin' to camp on. Now, my friends," he continues, "thar ain't no need of my puttin' on any frills or gettin' in any scroll work. The objects of this convention is plain an' straight. Mister King, here present, is dead. Deceased is a very headstrong person, an' persists yesterday in entertainin' views touchin' a club flush, queen at the head, which results in life everlastin'. Now, gents, this is a racket full of solemnity. We wants nothin' but good words. Don't mind about the trooth; which the same ain't in play at a funeral, nohow. We all knows Jack; we knows his record. Our information is ample that a-way; how he steals a hoss at Tucson; how be robs a gent last fall at Tombstone; how he downs a party at Cruces; how that scar on his neck he gets from Wells-Fargo's people when he stands up the stage over on the Lordsburg trail. But we lays it all aside to- day. We don't copper nary bet. Yesterday mornin', accompanied by the report of a Colt's forty-five, Mister King, who lies yere so cool an' easy, leaves us to enter in behind the great white shinin' gates of pearl an' gold, which swings inward to glory eternal. It's a great set back at this time thar ain't no sky-pilot in the camp. This deeficiency in sky-pilots is a hoss onto us, but we does our best. At a time like this I hears that singin' is a good, safe break, an' I tharfore calls on that little girl from Flagstaff to give us "The Dyin' Ranger."

"So the little Flagstaff girl cl'ars her valves with a drink, an' gives us the song; an' when the entire congregation draws kyards on the last verse it does everybody good.

> "'Far away from his dear old Texas,
> We laid him down to rest;
> With his saddle for a pillow,
> And his gun across his breast.'

"Then Peets gets out the Scriptures. 'I'm goin' to read a chapter outen these yere Testaments,' he says. 'I ain't makin' no claim for it, except it's part of the game an' accordin' to Hoyle. If thar's a preacher yere he'd do it, but bein' thar's no sech brand on this range I makes it as a forced play myse'f.'

"So he reads us, a chapter about the sepulcher, an' Mary Magdalene, an' the resurrection; an' everybody takes it in profound as prairie- dogs, for that's the lead to make, an' we knows it.

"Then Peets allows he'd like to hear from any gent onder the head of 'good of the order.'

"'Mister Ondertaker an' Chairman,' says Jim Hamilton, 'I yields to an inward impulse to say that this yere play weighs on me plumb heavy. As keeper of the dance-hall I sees a heap of the corpse an' knows him well. Mister King is my friend, an' while his moods is variable an' oncertain; an' it's cl'arly worth while to wear your gun while he's hoverin' near, I loves him. He has his weaknesses, as do we all. A disp'sition to make new rooles as he plays along for sech games of chance as enjoys his notice is perhaps his greatest failin'. His givin' way to this habit is primar'ly the cause of his bein' garnered in. I hopes he'll get along thar, an' offers a side bet, even money, up to five hundred dollars, he will. He may alter his system an' stand way up with the angels an' seraphs, an' if words from me could fix it, I'd shorely stack 'em in. I would say further that after consultin' with Billy Burns, who keeps the Red Light, we has, in honor of the dead an' to mark the occasion of his cashin' in, agreed upon a business departure of interest to all. This departure Mister Burns will state. I mournfully gives way to him for said purpose.'

"'Mister Peets, an' ladies an' gents,' says Burns, 'like Mister Hamilton, who I'm proud to meet yere as gent, citizen, an' friend, I knows deceased. He's a good man, an' a dead-game sport from 'way back. A protracted wrastle with the remorseless drinks of the frontier had begun to tell on him, an' for a year or so he's been liable to have spells. Referrin' to the remarks of Mister Hamilton, I states that by agreement between us an' in honor to departed, the quotations on whiskey in this yere camp, from now on, will be two drinks for two bits, instead of one as previous. We don't want to onsettle trade, an' we don't believe this will. We makes it as a ray of light in the darkness an' gloom of the hour.

"After this yere utterance, which is well received, we forms the procession. Doc Peets, with two buglers from the Fort, takes the lead, with Jack an' his box in one of the stage coaches comin' next. Enright, Tutt, Boggs, Short Creek Dave, Texas Thompson, an' me, bein' the six pallbearers, is on hosses next in line; an' Jack Moore commandin' of the rest of the outfit, lines out permiscus.

"'This is a great day for Wolfville," says Peets, as he rides up an' down the line. 'Thar ain't no camp this side of St. Looey could turn this trick. Which I only wishes Jack could see it himse'f. It's more calculated to bring this outfit into fav'rable notice than a lynchin'.'

"At the grave we turns in an' gives three cheers for King, an' three for Doc Peets; an' last we gives three more an' a tiger for the camp. The buglers cuts loose everythin' they knows, from the 'water- call' to the 'retreat,' an' while the niggers is a-shovelin' in the sand we bangs away with our six-shooters for general results delightful. You can gamble thar ain't been no funeral like it before or since.

"At the last Peets hauls outen the stage we uses for Jack, a headboard. When it's set up it looks like if Jack ain't satisfied, he's shorely hard to suit. On it in big letters is:

JaCK KinG
LIfE AiN'T
IN
HOLDiNG A GOOD HAND
BUT
In PLAYiNG A PORE HANd
WeLL.

"'You sees, we has to work in a little sentiment,' says Doc Peets.

"Then we details the niggers to stand watch-an'-watch every night till further orders. No; we ain't afraid Jack'll get out none, but the coyotes is shore due to come an' dig for him, so the niggers has to stand gyard. We don't allow to find spec'mens of Jack spread 'round loose after all the trouble we takes."

CHAPTER II.

THE STINGING LIZARD.

"Thar's no sorter doubt to it," said the Old Cattleman after a long pause devoted to meditation, and finally to the refilling of his cob pipe, "thar ain't the slightest room for cavil but them ceremonies over Jack King, deceased, is the most satisfactory pageant Wolfville ever promotes."

It was at this point I proved my cunning by saying nothing. I was pleased to hear the old man talk, and rightly theorized that the better method of invoking his reminiscences just at this time was to say never a word.

"However," he continued, "I don't reckon it's many weeks after we follows Jack to the tomb, when we comes a heap near schedoolin' another funeral, with the general public a-contributin' of the corpse. To be speecific, I refers to a occasion when we-alls comes powerful close to lynchin' Cherokee Hall.

"I don't mind on bosomin' myself about it. It's all a misonderstandin'; the same bein' Cherokee's fault complete. We don't know him more'n to merely drink with at that eepock, an' he's that sly an' furtive in his plays, an' covers his trails so speshul, he nacherally breeds sech suspicions that when the stage begins to be stood up reg'lar once a week, an' all onaccountable, Cherokee comes mighty close to culminatin' in a rope. Which goes to show that you can't be too open an' free in your game, an' Cherokee would tell you so himse'f.

"This yere tangle I'm thinkin' of ain't more'n a month after Cherokee takes to residin' in Wolfville. He comes trailin' in one evenin' from Tucson, an' onfolds a layout an' goes to turnin' faro- bank in the Red Light. No one remarks this partic'lar, which said spectacles is frequent. The general idee is that Cherokee's on the squar' an' his game is straight, an' of course public interest don't delve no further into his affairs.

"Cherokee, himse'f, is one of these yere slim, silent people who ain't talkin' much, an' his eye for color is one of them raw grays, like a new bowie.

"It's perhaps the third day when Cherokee begins to struggle into public notice. Thar's a felon whose name is Boone, but who calls himse'f the 'Stingin' Lizard,' an' who's been pesterin' 'round Wolfville, mebby, it's a month. This yere Stingin' Lizard is thar when Cherokee comes into camp; an' it looks like the Stingin' Lizard takes a notion ag'in Cherokee from the jump.

"Not that this yere Lizard is likely to control public feelin' in the matter; none whatever. He's some onpop'lar himself. He's too toomultuous for one thing, an' he has a habit of molestin' towerists an' folks he don't know at all, which palls on disinterested people who has dooties to perform. About once a week this Lizard man goes an' gets the treemers, an' then the camp has to set up with him till his visions subsides. Fact is, he's what you-alls East calls 'a disturbin' element,' an' we makes ready to hang him once or twice, but somethin' comes up an' puts it off, an' we sorter neglects it.

"But as I says, he takes a notion ag'in Cherokee. It's the third night after Cherokee gets in, an' he's ca'mly behind his box at the Red Light, when in peramb'lates this Lizard. Seems like Cherokee, bein' one of them quiet wolves, fools up the Lizard a lot. This Lizard's been hostile an' blood-hungry all day, an' I reckons he all at once recalls Cherokee; an', deemin' of him easy, he allows he'll go an' chew his mane some for relaxation.

"If I was low an' ornery like this Lizard, I ain't none shore but I'd be fooled them days on Cherokee myse'f. He's been fretful about his whiskey, Cherokee has,—puttin' it up she don't taste right, which not onlikely it don't; but beyond pickin' flaws in his nose- paint thar ain't much to take hold on about him. He's so slim an' noiseless besides, thar ain't none of us but figgers this yere Stingin' Lizard's due to stampede him if he tries; which makes what follows all the more impressive.

"So the Lizard projects along into the Red Light, whoopin' an' carryin' on by himse'f. Straightway he goes up ag'inst Cherokee's layout.

"I don't buy no chips," says the Lizard to Cherokee, as he gets in opposite. "I puts money in play; an' when I wins I wants money sim'lar. Thar's fifty dollars on the king coppered; an' fifty dollars on the eight open. Turn your kyards, an' turn 'em squar'. If you don't, I'll peel the ha'r an' hide plumb off the top of your head."

"Cherokee looks at the Lizard sorter soopercillus an' indifferent; but he don't say nothin'. He goes on with the deal, an', the kyards comin' that a-way, he takes in the Lizard's two bets.

"Durin' the next deal the Lizard ain't sayin' much direct, but keeps cussin' an' wranglin' to himse'f. But he's gettin' his money up all the time; an' with the fifty dollars he lose on the turn, he's shy mebby four hundred an' fifty at the close.

"'Bein' in the hole about five hundred dollars,' says the Lizard, in a manner which is a heap onrespectful, ' an' so that a wayfarin' gent may not be misled to rooin utter, I now rises to ask what for a limit do you put on this deadfall anyhow?'

"'The bridle's plumb off to you, amigo,' says Cherokee, an' his tones is some hard. I notices it all right enough, 'cause I'm doin' business at the table myse'f at the time, an' keepin' likewise case on the game. `The bridle's plumb off for you,' says Cherokee, 'so any notion you entertains in favor of bankruptin' of yourse'f quick may riot right along.'

"'You're dead shore of that?' says the Lizard with a sneer. `Now I reckons a thousand-dollar bet would scare this puerile game you deals a-screechin' up a tree or into a hole, too easy.'

"'I never likes to see no gent strugglin' in the coils of error,' says Cherokee, with a sneer a size larger than the Lizard's; `I don't know what wads of wealth them pore old clothes of yours conceals, but jest the same I tells you what I'll do. Climb right onto the layout, body, soul, an' roll, an' put a figger on your worthless se'f, an' I'll turn you for the whole shootin'-match. You're in yere to make things interestin', I sees that, an' I'll voylate my business principles an' take a night off to entertain you.' An' yere Cherokee lugs out a roll of bills big enough to choke a cow.

"'I goes you if I lose,' says the Stingin' Lizard. Then assoomin' a sooperior air, he remarks: 'Mebby it's a drink back on the trail when I has misgivin's as to the rectitood of this yere brace you're dealin'. Bein' public-sperited that a-way, in my first frenzy I allows I'll take my gun an' abate it a whole lot. But a ca'mer mood comes on, an' I decides, as not bein' so likely to disturb a peace- lovin' camp, I removes this trap for the onwary by merely bustin' the bank. Thar,' goes on the Stingin' Lizard, at the same time dumpin' a large wad on the layout, 'thar's even four thousand dollars. Roll your game for that jest as it lays.'

"'Straighten up your dust,' says Cherokee, his eyes gettin' a kind of gleam into 'em, 'straighten up your stuff an' get it some'ers. Don't leave it all spraddled over the scene. I turns for it ready enough, but we ain't goin' to argue none as to where it lays after the kyard falls.'

"The rest of us who's been buckin' the game moderate an' right cashes in at this, an' leaves an onobstructed cloth to the Stingin' Lizard. This yere's more caution than good nacher. As long as folks is bettin' along in limits, say onder fifty dollars, thar ain't no shootin' likely to ensoo. But whenever a game gets immoderate that a-way, an' the limit's off, an' things is goin' that locoed they begins to play a thousand an' over on a kyard an' scream for action, gents of experience stands ready to go to duckin' lead an' dodgin' bullets instanter.

"But to resoome: The Stingin' Lizard lines up his stuff, an' the deal begins. It ain't thirty seconds till the bank wins, an' the Stingin' Lizard is the wrong side of the layout from his money. He takes it onusual ugly, only he ain't sayin' much. He sa'nters over to the bar, an' gets a big drink. Cherokee is rifflin' the deck, but I notes he's got his gray eye on the Stingin' Lizard, an' my respect for him increases rapid. I sees he ain't goin' to get the worst of no deal, an' is organized to protect his game plumb through if this Lizard makes a break.

"'Do you—all know where I hails from?' asks the Stingin' Lizard, comin' back to Cherokee after he's done hid his drink.

"'Which I shorely don't;' says Cherokee. 'I has from time to time much worthless information thrust upon me, but so far I escapes all news of you complete.'

"'Where I comes from, which is Texas,' says the Lizard, ignorin' of Cherokee's manner, the same bein' some insultin', `they teaches the babies two things,-never eat your own beef, an' never let no kyard- thief down you:

"'Which is highly thrillin',' says Cherokee, 'as reminiscences of your yooth, but where does you-all get action on 'em in Arizona?'

"'Where I gets action won't be no question long,' says the Lizard, mighty truculent. 'I now announces that this yere game is a skin an' a brace. Tharfore I returns for my money; an', to be frank, I returns a-shootin':

"It's at this p'int we-alls who represents the public kicks back our chairs an' stampedes outen range. As the Lizard makes his bluff his hand goes to his artillery like a flash.

"The Lizard's some quick, but Cherokee's too soon for him. With the first move of the Lizard's hand, he searches out a bowie from som'ers back of his neck. I'm some employed placin' myse'f at the time, an' don't decern it none till Cherokee brings it over his shoulder like a stream of white light.

"It's shore great knife-work. Cherokee gives the Lizard aige an p'int, an' all in one motion. Before the Lizard more'n lifts his weepon, Cherokee half slashes his gun-hand off at the wrist; an' then, jest as the Lizard begins to wonder at it, he gets the nine- inch blade plumb through his neck. He's let out right thar.

"'It looks like I has more of this thing to do,' says Cherokee, an' his tone shows he's half-way mournin' over it, ` than any sport in the Territory. I tries to keep outen this, but that Lizard gent would have it.'

"After the killin', Enright an' Doc Peets, with Boggs, Tutt, an'
Jack Moore, sorter talks it over quiet, an' allows it's all right.

"'This Stingin' Lizard gent,' says Enright, has been projectin' 'round lustin' for trouble now, mebby it's six weeks. It's amazin' to me he lasts as long as he does, an' it speaks volumes for the forbearin', law-abiding temper of the Wolfville public. This Lizard's a mighty oppressive person, an' a heap obnoxious; an' while I don't like a knife none myse'f as a trail out, an' inclines to distrust a gent who does, I s'pose it's after all a heap a matter of taste an' the way your folks brings you up. I leans to the view, gents, that this yere corpse is constructed on the squar'. What do you-all think, Peets?'

"'I entertains ideas sim'lar,' says Doc Peets. 'Of course I takes it this kyard-sharp, Cherokee, aims to bury his dead. He nacherally ain't look. in' for the camp to go 'round cleanin' up after him none.' "That's about how it stands. Nobody finds fault with Cherokee, an' as he ups an' plants the Stingin' Lizard's remainder the next day, makin' the deal with a stained box, crape, an' the full regalia, it all leaves the camp with a mighty decent impression. By first-drink time in the evenin' of the second day, we ain't thinkin' no more about it.

16

"Now you-all begins to marvel where do we get to the hangin'   of Cherokee Hall? We're workin' in towards it now.

"You sees, followin' the Stingin' Lizard's jump into the misty beyond—which it's that sudden I offers two to one them angels notes a look of s'prise on the Stingin' Lizard's face as to how he comes to make the trip-Cherokee goes on dealin' faro same as usual. As I says before, he ain't no talker, nohow; now he says less than ever.

"But what strikes us as onusual is, he saddles up a pinto pony he's got over to the corral, an' jumps off every now an' then for two an' three days at a clatter. No one knows where he p'ints to, more'n he says he's due over in Tucson. These yere vacations of Cherokee's is all in the month after the Stingin' Lizard gets downed. "It's about this time, too, the stage gets held up sech a scand'lous number of times it gives people a tired feelin'. All by one party, too. He merely prances out in onexpected places with a Winchester; stands up the stage in an onconcerned way, an' then goes through everythin' an' everybody, from mail-bags to passengers, like the grace of heaven through a camp-meetin'. Nacheral, it all creates a heap of disgust. "'If this yere industrious hold-up keeps up his lick,' says Texas Thompson about the third time the stage gets rustled, `an' heads off a few more letters of mine, all I has to say is my wife back in Laredo ain't goin' to onderstand it none. She ain't lottin' much on me nohow, an' if the correspondence between us gets much more fitful, she's goin' p'intin' out for a divorce. This deal's liable to turn a split for me in my domestic affairs.' An' that's the way we-alls feels. This stage agent is shorely in disrepoot some in Wolfville. If he'd been shakin' up Red Dog's letter-bags, we wouldn't have minded so much.

"I never does know who's the first to think of Cherokee Hall, but all at once it's all over camp Talkin' it over, it's noticed mighty soon that, come right to cases, no one knows his record, where he's been or why he's yere. Then his stampedin' out of camp like he's been doin' for a month is too many for us.

"'I puts no trust in them Tucson lies he tells, neither,' says Doc Peets. 'Whatever would he be shakin' up over in Tucson? His game's yere, an' this theery that he's got to go scatterin' over thar once a week is some gauzy.'

"'That's whatever,' says Dan Boggs, who allers trails in after Doc Peets, an' plays the same system emphatic. An' I says myse'f, not findin' no fault with Boggs tharfor, that this yere Peets is the finest-eddicated an' levelest-headed sharp in Arizona.

"'Well,' says Jack Moore, who as I says before does the rope work for the Stranglers, 'if you-alls gets it settled that this faro gent's turnin' them tricks with the stage an' mail-bags, the sooner he's swingin' to the windmill, the sooner we hears from our loved ones at home. What do you say, Enright?'

"'Why,' says Enright, all thoughtful, 'I reckons it's a case. S'pose you caper over where he feeds at the O.K. House an' bring him to us. The signs an' signal-smokes shorely p'ints to this yere Cherokee as our meat; but these things has to be done in order. Bring him in, Jack, an', to save another trip, s'pose you bring a lariat from the corral at the same time.'

"It don't take Moore no time to throw a gun on Cherokee where he's consoomin' flapjacks at the O. K. House, an' tell him the committee needs him at the New York Store.

Cherokee don't buck none, but comes along, passive as a tabby cat.

"'Whatever's the hock kyard to all this?' he says to Jack Moore. 'Is it this Stingin' Lizard play a month ago?'

"'No,' says Moore, "t'ain't quite sech ancient hist'ry. It's stage coaches. Thar's a passel of people down yere as allows you've been rustlin' the mails.'

"Old Man Rucker, who keeps the O. K. House, is away when Moore rounds up his party. But Missis Rucker's thar, an' the way that old lady talks to Enright an' the committee is a shame. She comes over to the store, too, along of Moore an' Cherokee, an' prances in an' comes mighty near stampedin' the whole outfit.

"'See yere, Sam Enright,' she shouts, wipin' her hands on her bib, 'what be you-alls aimin' for to do? Linin' up, I s'pose to hang the only decent man in town?'

"'Ma'am,' says Enright, 'this yere sharp is 'cused of standin' up the stage them times recent over by Tucson. Do you know anythin' about it?'

"'No; I don't,' says Missis Rucker. 'You don't reckon, now, I did it none, do you? I says this, though; it's a heap sight more likely some drunkard a-settin' right yere on this committee stops them stages than Cherokee Hall.'

"'Woman's nacher's that emotional,' says Enright to the rest of us, 'she's oncapable of doin' right. While she's the loveliest of created things, still sech is the infirmities of her intellects, that gov'ment would bog down in its most important functions, if left to woman.'

19

"'Bog down or not,' says Missis Rucker, gettin' red an' heated, 'you fools settin' up thar like a band of prairie-dogs don't hang this yere Cherokee Hall. 'Nother thing, you ain't goin' to hang nobody to the windmill ag'in nohow. I has my work to do, an' thar's enough on my hands, feedin' sech swine as you-alls three times a day, without havin' to cut down dead folks outen my way every time I goes for a bucket of water. You-alls takes notice now; you don't hang nothin' to the windmill no more. As for this yere Cherokee, he ain't stopped no more stages than I be.'

"'But you sees yourse'f, ma'am, you hasn't the slightest evidence tharof,' says Enright, tryin' to soothe her down.

"'I has, however, what's a mighty sight better than evidence,' says
Missis Rucker, 'an' that's my firm convictions.'

"'Well, see yere,' says Cherokee, who's been listenin' all peaceful, 'let me in on this. What be you-alls doin' this on? I reckons I'm entitled to a look at your hand for my money.'

"Enright goes on an' lays it off for Cherokee; how he's outen camp every time the stage is robbed, an' the idee is abroad he does it.

"'As the kyards lay in the box,' says Cherokee, 'I don't reckon thar's much doubt but you-alls will wind up the deal by hangin' me?'

"'It's shorely five to one that a-way,' says Enright. 'Although I'm bound to say it ain't none decisive as yet.'

"'The trooth is,' says Cherokee, sorter thoughtful, 'I wasn't aimin' to be hung none this autumn. I ain't got time, gents, for one thing, an' has arranged a heap diff'rent. In the next place, I never stands up no stage.'

"'That's what they all says,' puts in Boggs, who's a mighty impatient man. 'I shorely notes no reason why we-alls can't proceed with this yere lynchin' at once. S'pose this Cherokee ain't stood up no stage; he's done plenty of other things as merits death. It strikes me thar's a sight of onnecessary talk yere."

"'If you ain't out working the road,' says Doc Peets to Cherokee, not heedin' of Bogg's petulance, 'them stage-robbin' times, s'pose you onfolds where you was at?"

"Well, son, not to string this yere story out longer'n three drinks, yere is how it is: This Cherokee it looks like is soft-hearted that a-way,—what you calls romantic. An' it seems likewise that shovin' the Stingin' Lizard from shore that time sorter takes advantage an' feeds on him. So he goes browsin' 'round the postmaster all casooal, an' puts questions. Cherokee gets a p'inter about some yearlin' or other in Tucson this Stingin' Lizard sends money to an' makes good for, which he finds the same to be fact on caperin' over. It's a nephy or some sech play. An' the Stingin' Lizard has the young one staked out over thar, an' is puttin' up for his raiment an' grub all reg'lar enough.

"'Which I yereafter backs this infant's play myse'f,' says Cherokee to the barkeep of the Oriental Saloon over in Tucson, which is the party the Stingin' Lizard pastures the young one on. 'You're all right, Bill,' goes on this Cherokee to the barkeep,' but now I goes back of the box for this infant boy, I reckons I'll saw him off onto a preacher, or some sharp sim'lar, where he gets a Christian example. Whatever do you think?'

"The barkeep says himse'f he allows it's the play to make. So he an' Cherokee goes surgin' 'round, an' at last they camps the boy—who's seven years comin' grass—on the only pulpit-sharp in Tucson. This gospel-spreader says he'll feed an' bed down the boy for some sum; which was shore a giant one, but the figgers I now forgets.

"Cherokee gives him a stack of blues to start his game, an' is now pesterin' 'round in a co't tryin' to get the young one counter- branded from the Stingin' Lizard's outfit into his, an' given the name of Cherokee Hall. That's what takes him over to Tucson them times, an' not stage-robbin'.

"Two days later, in fact, to make shore all doubts is over, Cherokee even rings in said divine on us; which the divine tells the same story. I don't reckon now he's much of a preacher neither; for he gives Wolfville one whirl for luck over in the warehouse back of the New York Store, an' I shore hears 'em as makes a mighty sight more noise, an' bangs the Bible twice as hard, back in the States. I says so to Cherokee; but he puts it up he don't bank none on his preachin'.

"'What I aims at,' says Cherokee, 'is someone who rides herd on the boy all right, an' don't let him stampede off none into vicious ways.'

"'Why don't you keep the camp informed of this yere orphan an' the play you makes?' says Enright, at the time it's explained to the committee,—the time they trees Cherokee about them stages.

"'It's that benev'lent an' mushy,' says Cherokee, 'I'm plumb ashamed of the deal, an' don't allow to go postin' no notices tharof. But along comes this yere hold-up business, an', all inadvertent, tips my hand; which the same I stands, however, jest the same.'

"'It's all right,' says Enright, some disgusted though; 'but the next time you makes them foundlin' asylum trips, don't walk in the water so much. Leave your trail so Wolfville sees it, an' then folks ain't so likely to jump your camp in the dark an' take to shootin' you up for Injuns an' sim'lar hostiles.'

"'But one thing more,' continues Enright, an' then we orders the drinks. Jack Moore is yereby instructed to present the compliments of the committee to Rucker, when he trails in from Tucson; which he also notifies him to hobble his wife yereafter durin' sessions of this body. She's not to go draggin' her lariat 'round loose no more, settin' law an' order at defiance durin' sech hours as is given to business by the Stranglers."

CHAPTER III.

THE STORY OF WILKINS

"No; I don't reckon I ever cuts the trail of this yere Wilson you mentions, once. If I does, the fact's done pulled its picket-pin an' strayed from my recollections."

I had recalled the name of a former friend, one Wilson, who, sore given to liquor, had drifted to Arizona many years before and disappeared. Suggesting "Wilson" to the Old Cattleman, I asked if he had met with such a name and character in his Wolfville rambles.

As often chanced, however, the question bore fruit in a story. It frequently needed but a slight blow from the rod of casual inquiry, and the fountains of my old friend's reminiscences gushed forth.

"No, I never crosses up with him," observed the old Cattleman; "but speakin' of Wilson puts in my mind a gent by the name of Wilkins, who it's some likely is as disrepootable as your old pard Wilson."

"What about Wilkins?" I asked.

"Nothin' thrillin', "answered the old gentleman; "nothin' you'd stay up nights to hear, I don't reckon. It's Wilkins's daughter who is the only redeemin' thing about the old Cimmaron; an' it's a heap likely right now it's her I remembers about instead of him.

"Not at all," he continued, "I don't mind onfoldin' as to Wilkins, nor yet of an' concernin' his daughter. You see this

Wilkins is herdin' 'round Wolfville when I first trails in. I never does know where he hails from. I don't reckon' though, he ever grades no ways high, an' at the crisis I'm mentionin' his speshul play is gettin' drunk mostly; an' not allowin' to hurt himse'f none with work.

"'Workin' with your fins,' says this Wilkins, 'is low an' onendoorin' to a gent with pride to wound. It ain't no use neither. I knows folks as works, an' folks as don't, an' you can't tell one from which. They gets along entirely sim'lar.

"'But how you goin' to live?' says Dave Tutt, when he makes this remark, an' who is fussin' with Wilkins for bein' so reedic'lous an' shiftless.

"'That's all right about my livin',' says Wilkins; 'don't you-all pass no restless nights on my account. Go read your Scriptures; read that bluff about feedin' the young ravens an' sparrers. Well, that's me this trip. I'm goin' to rap for a show-down on them promises an' see what's in 'em.'

"'This camp ain't strong on Holy Writ, nohow,' says Dave Tutt,   'an'
I'm partic'lar puny that a-way. It's your game though, an' your
American jedgement goes soopreme as to how you plays it.'

"This Wilkins lives in a wickeyup out on the aige of the town, an' a girl, which she's his daughter, about 19 years old, keeps camp for him. No one knows her well. She stays on her reservation mighty close, an' never seems visible much. I notices her in the New York Store once, buyin' some salt hoss, an'she ain't no dream of loveliness neither as to looks.

"Her face makes you feel she's good people though, with her big soft eyes. They has a tired, broke-down look, like somehow she's been packed more'n she can carry, an' has two or three notions about layin' down with the load.

"It's mebby two weeks after Dave Tutt's talk with Wilkins, when we're all in the Red Light takin' our forty drops, an' Sam Enright brings up this yere Wilkins.

"'It has been a question with me,' he says, 'how this old shorthorn and his girl manages for to make out; an' while I care none whatever for Wilkins, it ain't no credit to a live camp like this to permit a young female to suffer, an' I pauses yere to add, it ain't goin' to occur no more. Yesterday, allowin' to bushwhack some trooth about 'em, I waits till old Wilkins drifts over to the corral, an' then I goes projectin' 'round for facts. I works it plenty cunnin', an' sorter happens up to the old man's tepee. I calls the girl out an' puts it up I wants to see her paw a heap on some business.

"'"I wants to see him speshul,"' I says.

"'"Well, he ain't here now,"' says the girl, "so whatever'll you do?"'

"'"I don't reckon you could prance 'round some an' find him for me, could you, Miss?"' I says.

"'So the girl,' continues Enright, 'which her name is Susan, puts on her shaker an' goes stampedin' off; an' while she's gone I injuns an' spies 'round a whole lot; an', comin' down to the turn, Wilkins an' that girl ain't got nothin' to eat. The question now is, what action does Wolfville 'naugerate at a juncture sech as this?' "'What's the matter with takin' up a

26

donation like they does for a preacher, an' saw it onto the girl?' says Dan Boggs.

"'You couldn't open your game that a-way, nohow,' says Doc Peets. 'That's accordin' to Hoyle for sky-pilots an' missionary people; but a young female a-hoidin' of herse'f high spurns your money. Thar's nothin' ketches me like a female of my species in distress, an' I recalls offerin' to stake a lady, who's lost her money somehow, back in St. Looey once. This yere female was strange to me entire, but if she'd knowed me from 'way back she couldn't a-blazed up more frightful. The minute I pulls my bankroll on her, she goes cavortin' off too hostile to talk. It takes ten minutes to get her back to the agency to hear me 'pologize, an' even then she glares an' snorts like she's liable to stampede ag'in. No; you don't want to try an' give this girl no money. What we-alls needs is to hunt up somethin' for her to work at an' pay her.'

"'The Doc's right,' says Enright, 'an' the thing is to find somethin' for this yere lady to do. Any gent with a notion on the subject can't speak too quick.'

"'No party need take my remarks as personal,' says Burns, who runs the Red Light, 'as nothin' invidjous is intended; but I rises to say that a heap of my business is on credit. A gent comes in free an' sociable, names his sozodont, an' gets it. If he pays cash, all right; if he wants credit, all right. "You names your day to drink, an' you names your day to pay," is my motto, as you-alls knows. This bein' troo, onder present exigences what for a scheme would it be for me to get an outfit of books,—day-books, week-books, ledgers, an' the rest of the layout,—an' let this yere maiden keep 'em a whole lot? I throws this out as a su'gestion.'

27

"'I ain't meanin' nothin' ag'inst Burns's su'gestion,' says Texas Thompson, 'but in my opinion this camp ain't ripe for keepin' books as yet. Things like that has to be come to by degrees. I've knowed a heap of trouble arise from keepin' books, an' as long as this yere's a peaceful camp let's keep it that a-way.'

"'That settles it,' says Burns, 'thar's enough said, an' I don't keep no books.'

"'You-alls present knows me,' says Cherokee Hall, who, as I says previous, is turnin' faro in the Red Light, 'an' most of you has met me frequent in a business way. Thar's my game goin' every night reg'lar. Thar's nothin' tin-horn about it. It ain't no skin game neither. Any gent with doubts can step over an' test my box, which he'll find all comfortable on the layout awaitin' his convenience. It ain't been usual for me to blow my own bazoo to any extent, an' I only does it now as bein' preliminary to the statement that my game ain't no deadfall, an' is one as a respectable an' virchus female person could set in on with perfect safetytood to her reputation. This yere lady in question needs light, reg'lar employment, an' I lets it fly that if she wants in on any sech deal I'll go her a blue stack a week to hold down the chair as look-out for my game.'

"'Cherokee's offer is all right,' says Enright; 'it's good talk from a squar' man. Women, however, is partic'lar, an' like hosses they shies at things thar ain't no danger in. You sees how that is; a woman don't reason nothin', she feels an' mighty likely this young person is loaded to the gyards with sech notions ag'in gamblin' as would send her flyin' at the bare mention. The fact is, I thinks of somethin' sim'lar, but has to give it up. I figgers, first dash out o' the box, that a safe, easy trail to high ground is to give her a table an' let her deal a little stud for the boys. This yere wouldn't be no resk, an' the rake is a shore thing for nine or ten dollars a night. Bein' a benev'lence, I knows the boys would set in mighty free, an' the trouble would be corraled right thar. With this yere in my mind I taps her gently about our various games when I calls for her paw; an' to put it straight, she takes it reluctant an' disgusted at the mere hint. Of course we-alls has to stand these things from woman, an' we might as well p'int up some other way an' no time lost.'

"'Don't you-alls reckon for to make a speshul rake on all poker goin', same as about that Yallerhouse gent, might be an ondefeasible way to get at the neck of this business?' says Dave Tutt. 'I merely asks it as a question.'

"'That wouldn't do,' says Doc Peets, 'but anyhow yere comes Wilkins how, an' if, as Enright says, the're out of chuck up his way, I reckons I'll lose a small bet to the old shorthorn ontil sech times as we devises some scheme all reg'lar.'

"'Howdy, Wilkins?' says Doc, mighty gay an' genial, 'how's things stackin' up?'

"'Mighty ornery,' says Wilkins.

"'Feel like makin' a little wager this A. M.?' says Doc.

"'What do you-all want to gamble at?' says Wilkins.

"'Oh,' says Doc, 'I'm feelin' a heap careless about what I do gamble at. S'pose I goes you ten dollars's worth of grub the Lordsburg buckboard don't show up none to-day?'

"'If I had ten dollars I'd about call you a lot on that,' says Wilkins, 'but I'm a pore cuss an' ain't got no ten dollars, an' what's the use? None of you-alls ain't got no Red Light whiskey- chips you ain't usin', be you? S'pose you-alls gropes about in your war-bags an' sees. I'm needin' of a drink mighty bad.'

"Old Wilkins looks some queer about the eyes, an' more'n usual shaky, so we gives him a big drink an' he sorter braces up.

"'I'll back Wilkins's end of that bet you offers, Doc,' says Tutt, 'so consider it made, will you?'

"'You was offerin' to bet grub,' says the old man, powerful peevish an' fretful. 'What for do you want to bet grub? Why don't you bet money, so I gets what I wants with it? It's my money when I wins. Mebby I don't want no grub. Mebby I wants clothes or whiskey. You ain't no sport, Doc, to tie up a play with a string like that. Gimme another drink some one, I'm most dyin' for some.'

"The old man 'pears like he's mighty sick that a-way, so thar's nothin' for it but to give him another hooker, which we does accordin'.

"'I'm feelin' like I was shot hard by somethin',' he says, 'an' I don't like for to go home till I'm better, an' scare Sue. I reckon I'll camp down on this yere monte table for an hour till I comes 'round.'

"So Wilkins curls up on the table, an' no one notices him for about twenty minutes, when along comes rattlin' up the Lordsburg mail.

"'You win, Wilkins,' says Peets; 'come over to the New York Store an' cut out your stuff.' "The old man acts like he don't hear, so Doc shakes him up some. No use, thar ain't no get up in him.

"'Looks like he's gone to sleep for good,' says Doc.

"Then he walks 'round him, shakes him, an' takes a look at his eye, a-openin' of it with his finger. Finally he stands back, sticks his thumb in his belt, an' whistles.

"'What's up?' says Cherokee Hall. 'He ain't tryin' to work us for another drink I hopes.'

"Well, this is a deal,' says Doc, 'an' no humbug neither. Gents, I'm blessed if this yere old prairie-dog ain't shorely up an' died.'

"We-alls comes up an' takes a look at him, an' Doc has called the turn. Shore enough the old man has cashed in.

"`This is a hoss on us, an' no doubt about it,' says Enright. 'I ain't worryin' for Wilkins, as he most likely is ahead on the deal; but what gets me is how to break the news to this yere maiden. It's goin' to be a hair-line play. I reckons, Doc, it's you an' me.'

"So they goes over to Wilkins's wickeyup an' calls the young Sue girl out, an' Enright begins tellin' her mighty soft as how her paw is took bad down to the Red Light. But the girl seems to get it as right as if she's scouted for it a month.

"'He's dead!' she says; an' then cripples down alongside of the door an' begins to sob.

"'Thar ain't no use denyin' it, Miss,' says Enright, 'your paw struck in on the big trail where the hoof-prints all p'ints one way. But don't take it hard, Miss, thar ain't a gent don't give you sympathy. What you do now is stay right yere, an' the camp'll tend to the funeral, an' put it up right an' jest as you says, you bein' mourner-in-chief. You can trust us for the proper play; since we buries Jack King, obsequies is our long suit.'

"The little Sue girl struggles through somehow, an' has her nerve with her. The funeral, you bet, is right. This time we ropes in a preacher belongin' to some deep-water outfit over in Tucson. He somehow is strayed, an' happens along our way, an' we gets him squar' in the door. He jumps in an' gives them ceremonies a scientific whirl as ain't possible nohow to amatures. All 'round we wouldn't have put on more dog if we'd been plantin' Enright; all of course on the little Sue girl's account. Next day the outfit goes over to find out whatever she allows to do.

"'You sees, Miss; says Enright, 'anythin' you says, goes. Not waitin' to learn its name, even, I'm directed to state as how the camp backs your play an' makes good.'

"'I'm allowin' to go to the States,' says the girl, 'an' I'm obleeged to you.'

"'We was hopin',' says Enright, 'as you'd stay yere. We-alls sorter figgers you'd teach us a school. Of course thar ain't no papooses yet, but as a forced play we arranges to borrow a small herd from Tombstone, an' can do it too easy. Then, ag'in, a night-school would hit our needs right; say one night a week. Thar's a heap of ignorance in this yere camp, an' we needs a night-school bad. It would win for fifty dollars a week, Miss; an' you thinks of it.'

"No, the pore girl couldn't think of it nohow.

"'Of course, Miss, says Enright, 'we alls ain't expectin' you to open this yere academy the first kyards off the deck. You needs time to line up your affairs, an' am likewise wrung with grief. You takes your leesure as to that; meanwhile of course your stipend goes on from now.'

"But the little Sue girl couldn't listen. Her paw is dead, an' now she's due in the States. She says things is all right thar. She has friends as her paw never likes; but who's friends of hers, an' she'll go to them.

"'Well, Miss,' says Enright, mighty regretful, 'if that's how it lays, I reckons you'll go, so thar's nothin' for us to do but settle up an' fork over some dust we owes your paw. He bein' now deceased, of course you represents.'

"The girl couldn't see how any one owes her paw, "cause he's been too sick to work,' she says.

"'We owes him all the same,' says Enright, mighty ferocious. 'We onderstands well enough how we comes to owe him, don't we, Doc?'

"'You can stack in your life we do,' says Doc, plenty prompt an' cheerful. 'We-alls owes for his nailin' them hoss-thiefs when they tries to clean out the corral.'

"'That's it,' says Enright, 'for ketchin' of some rustlers who lays for our stock. It's all right, Miss; you needn't look so doubtful. You wouldn't if you knowed this camp. It's the last outfit on earth as would go an' give money to people. It's a good straight camp, Wolfville is; but business is business, an' we ain't pirootin' 'round none, givin' nothin' away, be we, Doc?'

"'Not much,' says Doc. 'It's enough for a gent to pay debts, without stampedin' 'round makin' presents of things.'

"'That's whatever,' says Enright; 'so Miss, me an Doc'll vamos over to the Red Light an' get the dust, an' I reckons we'll be back in an hour. I s'pose we owes Mister Wilkins about 'five hundred dollars, don't we, Doc?'

"'Tain't so much,' says Doc, who's guileful that a-way. As he sees the little Sue girl archin' for another buck, he pulls out a paper an' makes a bluff. 'Yere it is,—four hundred an' ninety-three dollars an' seventy-four cents. I puts it down all accurate, 'cause I don't allow no sharp to come 'round an' beat me none.'

"We-alls throws 'round an' makes up the pot to come to Doc's figger- -which I wants to say right yere, Doc Peets is the ablest gent I ever sees—an' the little Sue girl has to take it.

"Which this money lets her out right, an' she cries an' thanks us, an' the next day she takes the stage for Tucson. We're thar to say 'good-by' an' wish the little Sue girl luck.

"'Adios,' says Peets, takin' off his hat to her; 'it ain't down on the bills none, but if you-all could manage to kiss this yere outfit once apiece, Miss, it would be regarded. You needn't be afraid. Some of 'em looks a little off, but they're all right, an' b'ar huggin' is barred.'

"So the little Sue girl begins with Enright an' kisses us all, a-sobbin' meantime some free. As the affection proceeds, Cherokee sorter shoves back an' allows he'll pass.

"'Not any pass!' says Enright. 'Any gent who throws off on that thar little Sue girl, she willin', needn't look for any luck but lynchin'.'

"'That settles it,' says Cherokee, 'I saloots this yere lady.'

"So he ups an' kisses the little Sue girl like she's a hot flat-iron, an' backs into the crowd.

"'Cherokee makes me tired,' says Peets, who's ridin' herd on the play. When it comes his turn he kisses her slow an' rapturous, an' is contemptuous of Cherokee.

"When she's in the stage a-startin', Cherokee walks up, all respectful.

"'You've been away from the States some time, Miss,' he says, 'an' it's an even break you won't find things the way you expects. Now, you remember, shore; whatever game's bein' turned back thar, if it goes ag'in you, raise the long yell for a sharp called Cherokee Hall; an' his bank's yours to go behind your play.'"

CHAPTER IV.

THE WASHWOMAN'S WAR.

It was evening. The first dark foreshadowing of the coming night clothed all in half obscurity. But I knew the way; I could have travelled the little path at midnight. There he was, the Old Cattleman, under a favorite tree, the better to avoid the heavy dew. He sat motionless and seemed to be soaking himself, as one might say, in the balmy weather of that hour.

My wisdom had ordered Jim, my black man, to attend my steps. The laconic, half-sad salutation of my old friend at once gave Black Jim a mission. He was dispatched in quest of stimulants. After certain exact and almost elaborate commands to Black Jim, and that useful African's departure, I gently probed my companion with a question.

"No, thar's nothin' the matter of me; sorter pensive, that's all," was my return.

The Old Cattleman appeared silent and out of sorts. Following the coming of Black Jim, however, who brought a lusty toddy, he yielded to a better mood.

"It simply means I'm gettin' old; my settin' 'round balky this a- way. Thar's some seventy wrinkles on my horns; nothin' young or recent about that. Which now it often happens to me, like it does to old folks general, that jest when it begins to grow night, I gets moody an' bad. Looks like my thoughts has been out on some mental feed-ground all day, an' they comes stringin' in like cattle to get bedded down for the night. Nacheral, I s'pose they sorter mills an' stands 'round oneasy like for a while before they lies down all comfortable.

Old people partic'lar gets dissatisfied. If they's single-footers like me an' ain't wedded none; campin' 'round at taverns an' findin' of 'em mockeries; they wishes they has a wife a whole lot. If they be, they wish she'd go visit her folks. Gettin' old that a-way an' lonely makes folks frequent mighty contrary.

"No, as I imparts to you yeretofore,—mebby it's a month,—I never marries nothin'. I reckons too, I'm in love one round-up an' another mighty near a dozen times. But somehow I allers lose the trail an' never does run up with none of 'em once.

"Down in the Brazos country thar was a little blue-eyed girl,—back forty years it is,—an' the way I adores her plumb tires people. I reckons I ropes at her more'n fifty times, but I never could fasten. Thar comes a time when it looks powerful like I'm goin' to run my brand onto her; but she learns that Bill Jenks marks 150 calves the last spring round-up, an' me only forty, an' that settles it; she takes Jenks.

"It's astonishin' how little I deems of this yere maiden after Bill gets her. Two months before, I'd rode my pony to death to look once in her eyes. She's like sunshine in the woods to me, an' I dotes on every word she utters like it's a roast apple. But after she gets to be Bill's wife I cools complete.

"Not that lovin' Bill's wife, with his genius for shootin' a pistol, is goin' to prove a picnic,—an' him sorter peevish an' hostile nacheral. But lettin' that go in the discard, I shore don't care nothin' about her nohow when she's Bill's.

"I recalls that prior to them nuptials with Bill I gets that locoed lovin' this girl I goes bulgin' out to make some poetry over her. I compiles one stanza; an' I'm yere to remark it's harder work than a June day in a brandin' pen. Ropin' an' flankin' calves an' standin' off an old cow with one hand while you irons up her offspring with t'other, from sun-up till dark, is sedentary compared to makin' stanzas. What was the on I makes? Well, you can bet a hoss I ain't forgot it none.

"'A beautiful woman is shorely a moon, The nights of your life to illoomine; She's all that is graceful, guileful an' soon, Is woman, lovely woman.'

"I'm plumb tangled up in my rope when I gets this far, an' I takes a lay-off. Before I gathers strength to tackle it ag'in, Jenks gets her; so bein' thar's no longer nothin' tharin I never makes a finish. I allers allowed it would have been a powerful good poem if I'd stampeded along cl'ar through.

"Yes, son; women that a-way is shorely rangy cattle an' allers on the move. Thar's a time once when two of 'em comes mighty near splittin' Wolfville wide open an' leavin' it on both sides of the trail. All that ever saves the day is the ca'm jedgement an' promptitood of Old Man Enright.

"This is how Wolfville walks into this petticoat ambush. The camp is gettin' along all peaceful an' serene an' man-fashion. Thar's the post-office for our letters; thar's the Red Light for our bug-juice; thar's the O. K. Restauraw for our grub; an' thar's the stage an' our ponies to pull our freight with when Wolfville life begins to pull on us as too pastoral, an' we thirsts for the meetropolitan gayety of Tucson.

"As I says we alls has all that heart can hunger for; that is hunger on the squar'.

"Among other things, thar's a Chink runnin' a laundry an' a-doin' of our washin'. This yere tub-trundler's name is Lung, which, however. brands no cattle yere.

"It's one afternoon when Doc Peets gets a letter from a barkeep over

in Tucson sayin': Dear Doc:

Thar's an esteemable lady due in Wolfville on to-morrer's stage. She's p'intin' out to run a laundry. Please back her play. If thar's a Chinaman in town, run him out.

And obleege, yours,

Dick.

"'Whatever do you think, Enright?' says Doc Peets after readin' us the letter.

"'That's all right,' says Enright, 'the Chink goes. It's onbecomin' as a spectacle for a Caucasian woman of full blood to be contendin' for foul shirts with a slothful Mongol. Wolfville permits no sech debasin' exhibitions, an' Lung must vamos. Jack,' he says, turnin' to Jack Moore, 'take your gun an' sa'nter over an' stampede this yere opium-slave. Tell him if he's visible to the naked eye in the scenery yere-abouts to-morrow when this lady jumps into camp, he's shore asked the price of soap the last time he ever will in this vale of tears.'

"'What's the matter of lynchin' this yere Chink?' says Dan Boggs. 'The camp's deadly dull, an' it would cheer up things a whole lot, besides bein' compliments to this young female Old Monte's bringin' in on the stage.'

"'Oh no,' says Enright, 'no need of stringin him none. On second thought, Jack, I don't reckon I'd run him out neither. It dignifies him too much. S'pose you canter up to his tub-camp an' bring him over, an' we'll reveal this upheaval in his shirt-burnin' destinies by word of mouth. If he grows reluctant jest rope him 'round the neck with his queue, an' yank him. It impresses 'em an' shows 'em they're up ag'in the law. I s'pose, Peets, I voices your sentiments in this?'

"'Shore,'" says Doc Peets—which this Peets is the finest-eddicated man I ever meets. 'This Chinaman must pull his freight. We-alls owes it not only to this Tucson lady, but to the lovely sex she represents. Woman, woman, what has she not done for man! As Johanna of Arc she frees the sensuous vine-clad hills of far-off Switzerland. As Grace Darling she smooths the fever-heated pillow of the Crimea. In reecompense she asks one little, puny boon—to fire from our midst a heathen from the Orient. Gents, thar's but one answer: We plays the return game with woman. This Chinaman must go.'

"When Jack comes back with Lung, which he does prompt, Enright starts in to deal the game.

"'It ain't no use, Lung,' says Enright, 'tryin' to explain to you-all what's up. Your weak Asiatic intellect couldn't get the drop onto it no-how. You've been brought to a show-down ag'in a woman, an' you're out-held. You've got to quit; savey? Don't let us find you yere to-morrow. By third-drink time we'll be a-scoutin' for you with somethin' besides an op'ry glass, an' if you're noticed as part of the landscape you're goin' to have a heap of bad luck. I'd advise you to p'int for Red Dog, but as to that you plays your hand yourse'f.'"

"Next day that old drunkard Monte comes swingin' in with the stage; the six hosses on the jump, same as he allers does with a woman along. Over at the post-office, where he stops, a lady gets out, an' of course we-alls bows p'lite an' hopes she's well an' frisky. She allows she is, an' heads for the O. K. House.

"It floats over pretty soon that her name's Annie, an' as none of us wants to call her jest 'Annie'—the same bein' too free a play—an' hearin' she lives a year or two at Benson, we concloods to call her Benson Annie, an' let it go at that.

"'The same bein' musical an' expressive,' says Doc Peets, as we all lines up ag'in the Red Light bar, 'I su'gests we baptize this lady "Benson Annie," an' yere's to her success.'

"So we-alls turns up our glasses, an' Benson Annie it is.

"The next day the fetid Lung is a thing of the past, an' Benson Annie has the game to herse'f. Two days later she raises the tariff to fifty cents on shirts, instead of twenty-five, as previous with the Chink. But no one renigs.

"'A gent,' says Doc Peets, 'as holds that a Caucasian woman is goin' to wash a shirt for the miserable stipend of a slave of the Orient must be plumb locoed. Wolfville pays fifty cents for shirts an' is proud tharof.'

"Things goes along for mighty like a month, an' then this yere
Benson Annie allows she'll have a visitor.

"'I'm plumb, clean sick,' she says, 'of seein' nothin' but a lot of drunken, good-for-nothin' sots a-pesterin' 'round, an' I done reckons I'll have my friend Sal come over from Tombstone an' see me a whole lot. It'll be some relaxation.'

"Mebby it's four days after when this yere Sal hops outen the stage, an' for the next week thar ain't no washin' done

41

whatever, while Benson Annie an' Sal works the wire aige offen their visit.

"`A gent as would begretch two pore, hard-workin' girls a lay-off of a week,' says Enright, 'ain't clean strain, an' I don't want to know sech a hoss-thief nohow'; an' we-alls feels likewise.

"But slap on the heels of all this yere gregar'ousness on the part of Benson Annie an' Sal, the deal begins to come queer. At the end of the week the two girls has a row, an' in the turn Sal goes to t'other end of camp an' opens a laundry. That does settle it. Benson Annie gives Sal fits, an' Sal shorely sends 'em back. Then they quits speakin', an when they meets on the street they concocts snoots at each other. This scares Enright, but he does his level best an' tries to keep the boys from takin' sides.

"'In a play like this yere,' he says, 'this camp don't take no kyards. For the first time Wolfville passes out, an' offers to make it a jack'

"But as one day an' the next trails by, the boys sorter gets lined up one way an' t'other; some for Benson Annie an' some for Sal, an' things is shorely gettin' hot. Hamilton, over at the dance-hall, ups an' names his place the 'Sal Saloon,' an' Burns takes down the sign on the Red Light an' calls it the 'Benson Annie House.' Finally things sorter culminates.

"Dan Boggs, who's a open, voylent Annie man, comes a-prancin' into the Red Light one night, an' after stampin' an' rappin' his horns 'round a whole lot, allows his shirt is cleaner than Dave Tutt's.

"Tutt says he don't care nothin' for himse'f, an' none whatever for the shirt; an' while he an' Dan's allers been friends an' crossed the plains together, still he don't allow he'll stand 'round much an' see a pore ondefended female, like Sal, maligned. So Tutt outs with his gun an' gets Boggs in the laig.

"This yere brings things down to cases. Enright is worried sick at it. But he's been thinkin' mighty arduous for quite a spell, an' when Boggs gets creased, he sees somethin' must be done, an' begins to line himse'f for a play for out.

"It's the next day after Boggs gets ag'in Tutt, an' Doc Peets has plugged up the hole, when Enright rounds up the whole passel of us in the Red Light. He looks that dignified an' what you-alls calls impressive, that the barkeep, yieldin' to the gravity of the situation, allows the drinks is on the house. We-alls gets our forty drops, an' sorter stands pat tharon in silence, waitin' for Enright to onfold his game. We shore knows if thar's a trail he'll find it.

"'I Gents,' he says at last,—an' it seems like he's sorry an' hurt that a-way,—'I'll not drift into them harrowin' differences which has rent asunder what was aforetimes the peacefullest camp in Arizona. I wants you-alls, however, to take note of my remarks, for what I says is shorely goin' to go.'

"Yere Enright pauses to take a small drink by himse'f, while we-alls tarries about, some oneasy an' anxious as to what kyards falls next. At last Enright p'ints out on the trail of his remarks ag'in.

"'It is with pain an' mortification,' he says—an' yere he fixes his eye some hard an' delib'rate on a young tenderfoot named French, who's been lost from the States somethin' like six

43

months—'it is with pain an' mortification, I says, that I notes for a week past our young friend an' townsman, Willyum French, payin' marked an' ondiscreet attentions to Benson Annie, a female person whom we all respects. At all times, day an' night, when he could escape his dooties as book-keep for the stage company, he has pitched camp in her s'ciety. Wolfville has been shocked, an' a pure lady compromised. Standin' as we-alls does in the light of a parent to this pore young female, we have determined the wrong must be made right, an' Mister French must marry the girl. I have submitted these yere views to Benson Annie, an' she concurs. I've took the trouble to bring a gospel-sharp over from Tucson to do the marryin', an' I've set the happy event for to-night, to conclood with a blow-out in the dance-hall at my expense. We will, of course, yereby lose Benson Annie in them industrial walks she now adorns, for I pauses to give Mister French a p'inter; the sentiments of this camp is ag'in a married female takin' in washin'. Not to play it too low down on Mister French, who, while performin' a private dooty, is also workin' for a public good, I heads a subscription with fifty dollars for a present for the bride. I'd say in closin' that if I was Mister French I wouldn't care to object to this union. The lady is good-lookin', the subscription is cash, an' in the present heated condition of the public mind, an' with the heart of the camp set on this weddin', I wouldn't be responsible if he does. Now, gents, who'll follow my fifty dollars with fifty more? Barkeep, do your dooty while the subscription-paper goes 'round.'

"The biddin' is mighty lively, an' in ten minutes seven hundred dollars is raised for a dowry. Then French, who has been settin' in a sort of daze, gets up:

44

"'Mister Enright an' gents,' he says, `this yere is a s'prise-party to me, but it goes. It's a hoss on me, but I stands it. I sees how it is, an' as a forced play I marries Benson Annie in the interests of peace. Which the same bein' settled, if Benson Annie is yere, whirl her up an' I'll come flutterin' from my perch like a pan of milk from a top shelf, an' put an end to this onhealthful excitement.

"We-alls applauds French an' is proud to note he's game.

"`An' to be free an' open with you, French,' says Texas Thompson, so as to make him feel he's ahead on the deal; which he shore is, for this yere Benson Annie is corn-fed, 'if it ain't for a high-sperited lady back in Laredo who relies on me, I'd be playin' your hand myse'f.'

"Well, no one delays the game. Enright brings over Benson Annie, who's blushin' some, but ain't holdin' back; an' she an' French fronts up for business. This yere preacher-sharp Enright's roped up is jest shufflin' for the deal, when, whatever do you reckon takes place? I'm a Mexican if this yere Sal don't come wanderin' in, a- cryin' an' a-mournin' powerful. She allows with sobs if her dear friend Annie's goin' to get married she wants in on the game as bridesmaid.

"'Which you-all shorely gets a hand as sech,' says Doc Peets, who's actin' lookout for the deal; an' so he stakes out Sal over by the nigh side of Benson Annie, who kisses her quite frantic, an' unites her wails to Sal's. Both of 'em weepin' that a-way shorely makes the occasion mighty sympathetic an' damp. But Peets says it's the reg'lar caper, an' you can gamble Peets knows. "'Thar,' says Enright, when the last kyard's out an' the French fam'ly is receivin' congratulations, 'I reckons that now, with only one laundry, Wolfville sees a season of peace. It's all right, but I'm yere to remark that the next lady as dazzles this camp with her deebut, an' onfurls a purpose to plunge into work, ain't goin' to keep a laundry none. Gents, the bridle's plumb off the hoss. We'll now repair to the dance-hall, if so be meets your tastes, an' take the first steps in a debauch from which, when it's over, this yere camp of Wolfville dates time.'"

CHAPTER V.

ENRIGHT'S PARD, JIM WILLIS.

"If my mem'ry's dealin' a squar' game," remarked the Old Cattleman, as he moved his chair a bit more into the shade, "it's some'ers over in the foot-hills of, the Floridas when Enright vouchsafes why he hates Mexicans."

The morning was drowsy. Conversation between us had in a sleepy way ranged a wide field. As had grown to be our habit we at last settled on Wolfville and its volatile inhabitants. I asked to be enlightened as to the sage Enright, and was informed that, aside from his courage and love of strict justice, the prominent characteristic of our Wolfville Lycurgus was his wrath against Mexicans.

"Not that Enright loathes so much as he deplores 'em, "continued the old gentleman. "However, I don't aim to be held as sayin' he indorses their existence a little bit; none whatever.

"Enright's tellin' of this tale arises outen a trivial incident which a Mexican is the marrow of. We're out on the spring round-up, an' combin' the draws an' dry ARROYAS over between the cow springs an' the Floridas, when one night a Mexican runs off a passel of our ponies. The hoss-hustler is asleep, I reckons, at the time this Mexican stacks in. He says himse'f he's lyin' along the back of his bronco gazin' at the stars when this robber jumps at the ponies an' flaps a blanket or somethin', an' away patters every hoof in the band.

"This yere Mexican don't run off with only about a handful; I takes it he can't round up no more in the dark. When you-all stampedes a bunch of ponies that a-way they don't hold together like cattle, but plunges off diffusive. It's every bronco for himse'f, disdainful of all else, an' when it's sun-up you finds 'em spattered all over the scene an' not regardin' of each other much.

"But this yere Mexican, after he stampedes 'em, huddles what he can together—as I says mebby it's a dozen—an' p'ints off into the hills.

"Of course it ain't no time after the sun shows the tracks when Enright, Jack Moore, an' myse'f is on the trail. Tutt an' Dan Boggs wants in on the play, but we can't spar' so many from the round-up.

"It's one of the stolen ponies tips this Greaser's hand. It's the second day, an' we-alls loses the trail for mebby it's fifteen minutes. We're smellin' along a canyon to find it ag'in, when from over a p'int of rocks we hears a bronco nicker. He gets the scent of an acquaintance which Moore's ridin' on, an' says 'How!' pony- fashion.

"Thar's no need goin' into wearyin' details. Followin' the nicker we comes surgin' in on our prey, an' it's over in a minute. Thar's two Mexicans,—our criminal trackin' up with a pard that mornin'. But of course we-alls knows he's thar long hours back by the tracks, so it ain't no s'prise.

"This yere second Mexican is downed on the run-in. He shows a heap of interest in our comin', an' takes to shootin' us up mighty vivid with a Winchester at the time; an' so Enright, who's close in, jumps some lead into him an' stretches him. He don't manage to do no harm, nohow, more'n he creases my hoss a little. However, as this yere hoss is amazin' low-sperited, an' as bein' burnt that a-way with a bullet sorter livens him up a heap, I don't complain none. Still Enright's all-wise enough to copper the Greaser, for thar ain't no sayin' what luck the felon has with that little old gun of his if he keeps on shootin'. Which, as I observes, Enright downs him, an' his powder-burnin' an' hoss-rustlin' stops immediate.

"As for the other Mexican, which he's the party who jumps our ponies in the first place, he throws up his hands an' allows he cashes in his chips for whatever the bank says.

"We-alls ropes out our captive; sorter hog-ties him hand an' foot, wrist an' fetlock, an' then goes into camp all comfortable, where we runs up on our game.

"Jack Moore drops the loop of his lariat over the off moccasin of the deceased Mexican, an' canters his pony down the draw with him, so's we ain't offended none by the vision of him spraddled out that a-way dead. This yere's thoughtful of Jack, an' shows he's nacherally refined an' objects to remainders lyin' 'round loose.

"'No, it ain't so much I'm refined,' says Jack, when I compliments him that he exhibits his bringin' up, an' him bein' too modest that a-way to accept; 'it ain't that I'm refined none—which my nacher is shore coarse—I jest sorter protests in my bosom ag'in havin' a corpse idlin' 'round that a-way where I'm camped. Tharfore I takes my rope an' snatches deceased off where he ain't noticeable on the scenery.'

"Jack does it that gentle an' considerate, too, that when we passes the Mexican next day on our way in, except he's some raveled an' frayed coastin' along where it's rocky, an' which can't be he'ped none, he's as excellent a corpse as when he comes off the shelf, warm as the rifle Enright throws him with.

"'Whatever be we goin' to do with this yere hoss-thief pris'ner of ours?' says Jack Moore to Enright the next day, when we're saddlin' up an' organizin' to pull our freight. 'He's shore due to bother us a lot. We're plumb sixty miles from Tutt an' the boys, an' ridin' herd on this yere saddle-colored gent, a-keepin' of him from lopin' off, is mighty likely to be a heap exhaustin'. I knows men,' Jack remarks at the close, lookin' wistful at Enright, 'as would beef him right yere an' leave him as a companion piece to that compadre of his you downs.'

"'Nachers as would execute a pris'ner in cold blood,' says Enright, 'is roode an' oncivilized. Which I don't mean they is low neither; but it's onconsiderate that a-way to go an' ca'mly kill a pris'ner, an' no co't nor committee authorizin' the same. I never knows of it bein' done but once. It's Mexicans who does it then; which is why they ain't none pop'lar with me since.'

"'It's shore what you calls a mighty indurated play,' says Jack, shakin' his head, 'to go shootin' some he'pless gent you've took; but, as I states, it's a cinch it'll be a heap fatiguin' keepin' cases on this yere Mexican till we meets up with a quorum of the committee. Still it's our dooty, an' of course we don't double-deal, nor put back kyards on what's our plain dooty.'

"'What you-all states,' says Enright,'' is to your credit, but I'll tell you. Thar ain't no harm mountin' this marauder on a slow pony that a-way; an' bein' humane s'fficient to leave his hands an' feet ontied. Of course if he takes advantage of our leniency an' goes stampedin' off to make his escape some'ers along the trail, I reckons you'll shorely have to shoot. Thar's no pass-out then but down him, an' we sadly treads tharin. An',' goes on Enright, some thoughtful, if this yere Mexican, after we-alls is that patient an' liberal with him, abuses our confidences an' escapes, we leaves it a lone-hand play to you. My eyes is gettin' some old an' off, any way; an' besides, if we three takes to bangin' away simooltaneous, in the ardor of competition some of us might shoot the pony. So if this yere captive runs—which he looks tame, an' I don't expect none he will—we leaves the detainin' of him, Jack, to you entire."

"In spite of Enright's faith it shore turns out this Mexican is ornery enough, where the trail skirts the river, to wheel sudden an' go plungin' across. But Jack gets him in midstream. As he goes over the bronco's shoulder, hat first, he swings on the bridle long enough with his dyin' hand to turn the pony so it comes out ag'in on our side.

"Which I'm glad he lives s'fficient to head that hoss our way,' says jack. "It saves splashin' across after him an' wettin' your leggins a lot."

"It's that night in camp when jack brings up what Enright says about the time the Mexicans downs a pris'ner, an' tharby fixes his views of 'em.

"'It's a long trail back,' says Enright,' an' I don't like this yarn enough to find myse'f relatin' it to any excessive degrees. It draws the cinch some tight an' painful, an' I don't teach my mind to dwell on it no more'n is necessary.

"'This is all when I'm a boy; mebby I ain't twenty years yet. It's durin' the Mexican war. I gets a stack of white chips an' stands in on the deal in a boyish way. All I saveys of the war is it's ag'in the Mexicans, which, while I ain't got no feud with 'em personal at the time, makes it plenty satisfactory to me.

"'It's down off two days to the west of Chihuahua, an' seven of us is projectin' 'round seein' whatever can we tie down an' brand, when some Mexicans gets us out on a limb. It ain't a squar' deal; still I reckons it's squar' enough, too; only bein' what you-alls calls strategic, it's offensive an' sneakin' as a play.

"'This yere lieutenant who's leadin' us 'round permiscus, looks like he's some romantic about a young Mexican female, who's called the Princess of Casa Grande. Which the repoote of this yere Princess woman is bad, an' I strikes a story several times of how she's that incensed ag'in Americans she once saws off a thimbleful of loco on a captain in some whiskey he's allowin' to drink, an' he goes plumb crazy an' dies.

"'But loco or no loco, this yere Princess person is shore that good lookin' a pinto pony don't compare tharwith; an' when she gets her black eyes on our lieutenant,

that settles it; we rounds up at her hacienda an' goes into camp. "'Besides

the lieutenant thar's six of us. One of 'em's a shorthorn who matches me for age; which his name's Willis—Jim Willis. "'Now I ain't out

to make no descriptions of the friendship which goes on between this yere Willis an' me. I sees a show one time when I'm pesterin' 'round back in St. Looey—an' I'm yere to remark I don't go that far east

53

no more—which takes on about a couple of sports who's named Damon an' Pythias. Them two people's all right, an' game. An' they shore deems high of one another. But at the time I sees this yere Damon an'

Pythias, I says to myse'f, an' ever since I makes onhesitatin' assertion

tharof, that the brotherly views them two gents entertains ain't a

marker to Jim Willis an' me. "'This yere Jim I knows since we're yearlin's. We-alls jumps outen the corral together back in Tennessee, an' goes off into this Mexican war like twins. An' bein' two boys that a-way

among a band of men, I allows thar ain't nothin' before, nor then, nor after. which I loves like Jim. "'As I observes, Jim an' me's in

the outfit when this yere lieutenant comes trackin' 'round that Princess of Casa Grande; which her love for him is a bluff an' a deadfall; an' the same gets all of us before we're through. An' it gets my Jim Willis speshul. "Mebby it's the third mornin' after we- alls meanders into this nest of Mexicans, an' the lieutenant gets lined out for that Princess of Casa Grande. We ain't been turnin' out early nohow, thar bein' nothin'

to turn out about; but this third mornin' somebody arouses us a heap vigorous, like they aims to transact some business with us. Which they shorely does; it's an outfit of Greaser guerillas, an' we-alls ain't nothin' more or less than captives. "'The ornery an' ongrateful part is that the Princess sends one of her own peonies scoutin' 'round in the hills to bring in this band of cattle-eaters onto us. "'When the lieutenant hears of the perfidy of the Princess female, he's that mortified he gets a pistol the first jump he makes an' blows off the top of his head; which if he only blows off the top of hers it would have gone a heap further with the rest of us. If he'd consulted any of us, it would have shorely been advised. But he makes an impulsive play that

a-way; an' is that sore an' chagrined he jest grabs a gun in a frenzied way an' cashes his chips abrupt. "'No, as I states,' says Enright, musin' to himse'f, 'if the lieutenant had only downed that Princess who plays us in as pris'ners so smooth an' easy, it would have been

regarded. He could have gone caperin' over the brink after her with the bridle off the next second, an' we-alls would still talk well of him. "'As it is, however, this riotous female don't last two months. Which it's also a fact that takin' us that time must have been a heap

on. lucky for them Greasers. Thar's nine of 'em, an' every last man dies in the next five months; an' never a one, nor yet the Princess, knows what they're ag'inst when they quits; or what breeze blows their light out. I knows, because me an' a party whose name is Tate- -Bill Tate—never leaves them hills till the last of that outfit's got his heap of rocks piled up, with its little pine cross stickin' outen the peak tharof, showin' he's done jumped this earthly game for good. "'This Bill Tate an' me breaks camp on them Greasers together while they're tankin' up on mescal, mebby it's two days later; an' they never gets their lariats on us no more. "'"You ain't got no dates, nor speshul engagements with nobody in the States, have you?" says Tate to me when we're safe outen them Mexican's hands. ""No,"says I,"whatever makes you ask? ""Oh, nothin',"says Tate lookin' at the sky sorter black an' ugly, "only since you-all has the leesure, what for a play would it be to make a long camp back in these hills by some water-hole some'ers,

an' stand pat ontil we downs these yere Greasers—squaws an' all— who's had us treed? It oughter be did; an' if we-ails don't do it none, it's a heap likely it's goin' to be neglected complete. It's easy as a play; every hoss-thief of 'em lives right in these yere valleys, for I hears 'em talk. All we has to do is sa'nter back in the hills, make a camp; an' by bein' slow an' shore, an' takin' time an' pains, we bushwhacks an' kills the last one." "'The way I feels about Willis makes the prospect

mighty allurin',' an' tharupon Tate an' me opens a game with them Mexicans it takes five months to deal. "'But it's plumb dealt out, an' we win. When Tate crosses the Rio Grande with the army goin' back, he shorely has the skelp of every Mexican incloosive of said Princess. "'But I wanders from Willis. Where was I at when I bogs down? As I says, this

lieutenant nabs a pistol an' goes flutterin' from his limb. But this don't do them Greasers. They puts up a claim that some Americans tracks up on one of their outfit an' kills him off, they says, five days before.

They allows that, breakin' even on the deal, one of us is due to die. Tate offers to let 'em count the lieutenant, but they shakes their heads till the little bells on their sombreros tinkles, an' declines the lieutenant emphatic. "'They p'ints out this yere lieutenant dies in his own game, on his own deal. It's no racket of theirs, an' it don't go to match the man they're shy. "'One of us six who's left has to die to count even for this Greaser who's been called in them five days ago. Tate can't move 'em; all he says is no use; so he quits,

an' as he's been talkin' Spanish—which the same is too muddy a language for the rest of us—Tate turns in an' tells us how the thing sizes up. "`"One of us is shorely elected to trail out after the lieutenant,"says Tate. "The rest they holds as pris'ners. Either way it's a hard, deep crossin', an' one's about as rough a toss as the other." "'This last

Tate stacks in to mebby win out a little comfort for the one the Mexicans cuts outen our bunch to kill. "`After a brief pow-wow the Greaser who's actin' range-boss for the outfit puts six beans in a buckskin bag. Five is white an' one's black. Them Greasers is on the gamble bigger'n wolves, an' they crowds up plenty gleeful to see us take a gambler's chance for our lives. The one of us who draws a black bean is to p'int out after the lieutenant. "`Sayin' somethin' in Spanish which most

likely means" Age before beauty,"the Mexicans makes Willis an' me stand back while the four others searches one after the other into the bag for his bean. "`Tate goes first an' wins a white bean. "`Then a shiftless, no-account party whom we-alls calls "Chicken Bill" reaches in. I shorely hopes, seein' it's bound to be somebody, that this Chicken Bill acquires the black bean. But luck's ag'in us; Chicken Bill backs off with a white bean. "`When the third gent turns out a white bean the shadow begins to fall across Jim Willis an' me. I looks at Jim; an' I gives it to you straight when I says that I ain't at that time thinkin' of myse'f so much as about Jim. To see this yere deal, black as midnight, closin' in on Jim, is what's hurtin'; it don't somehow occur to me I'm likewise up ag'in the iron my se'f. "`"Looks like this yere amiable deevice is out to run its brand onto one of us,"says Jim to me; an' I looks at him. "`An' then, as the fourth finds a white bean in the bag, an' draws a deep sigh an' stands back, Jim says: "Well, Sam, it's up to us." Then Jim looks at me keen an' steady a whole lot, an' the Mexicans, bein' rather pleased with the situation, ain't goadin' of us to hurry up none.

"`When it's to Jim an' me they selects me out as the one to pull for the next bean. Jim's still lookin' at me hard, an' I sees the water in his eye.'

"`"Let me have your draw, Sam," he says.

"`"Shore,"I replies, standin' a step off from the bag." It's yours too quick."

"` But the Mexicans don't see it that a-way. It's my turn an' my draw, an' Jim has to take what's left. So the Mexicans tells Tate to send me after my bean ag'in.

"`"Hold on a second, Sam," says Jim, an' by this time he's steady as a church. "Sam," he goes on, "thar's no use you—all gettin' the short end of this. Thar's reasons for you livin', which my case is void tharof. Now let me ask you: be you up on beans? Can you tell a black from a white bean by the feel? "

"`"No," I says, "beans is all a heap the same to me."

"""That's what I allows," goes on this Jim. "Now yere's where my sooperior knowledge gets in. If these Mexicans had let me draw for you I'd fixed it, but it looks like they has scrooples. But listen, an' you beats the deal as it is. Thar's a difference in beans same as in ponies. Black beans is rough like a cactus compared to white beans, which said last vegetable is shorely as smooth as glass. Now yere's what you—all does; jest grp[e an' scout 'round in that bag until you picks out the smooth bean. That's your bean; that's the white bean. Cinch the smooth bean an' the black one comes to me."

"When Jim says all this it seems like I'm in a daze an' sorter woozy. I never doubts him for a moment. Of course I don't take no advantage of what he says. I recalls the advice my old mother gives me; it's long enough ago now. The old lady says: "Samyool, never let me hear of you weakenin'. Be a man, or a mouse, or a long-tail rat." So when Jim lays it off about them two beans bein' smooth an' rough that a-way, an' the white bein' the smooth bean, I nacherally searches out the rough bean, allowin' she'll shore be black; which shows my intellects can't cope with Jim's none.

"'The bean I brings to the surface is white. I'm pale as a ghost. My heart wilts like water inside of me, an' I feels white as the bean where it lays in my hand. Of course I'm some young them days, an' it don't need so much to stagger me. "'I recollects like it was in a vision hearin' Jim laugh. "Sam," he says, "I reads you like so much sunshine. An' I shorely fools you up a lot. Don't you reckon I allows you'll double on the trail, p'intin' south if I says 'north' at a show like this? The white bean is allers a rough, sandy bean; allers was an' allers will be; an' never let no one fool you that a- way ag'in. An' now, Sam, ADIOS."

"'I'm standin' lookin' at the white bean. I feels Jim grip my other hand as lie says "ADIOS," an' the next is the" bang! "of the Mexicans's guns. Jim's dead then; he's out in a second; never bats an eye nor wags a y'ear.

"'Which now,' says Enright at the end, as he yanks his saddle 'round so he makes a place for his head, 'which now that you-alls is fully informed why I appears averse to Greasers, I reckons I'll slumber some. I never does see one, I don't think of that boy, Jim Willis; an' I never thinks of Jim but I wants to murder a Mexican.'

"Enright don't say no more; sorter rolls up in his blankets, drops his head on his saddle, an' lays a long time quiet, like he's asleep. Jack Moore an' me ain't sayin' nothin'; merely settin' thar peerin' into the fire an' listenin' to the coyotes. At last Enright lifts his head off the saddle.

"'Mebby it's twenty years ago when a party over on the Rio Grande allows as how Jim's aimin' to cold-deck me when he onfolds about the habits of them beans. It takes seven months, a iron constitootion, an' three medicine-sharps—an' each as good as Doc Peets,—before that Rio Grande party is regarded as outen danger.'"

CHAPTER VI.

TUCSON JENNIES HEART.

"'Whyever ain't I married?' says you." The Old Cattleman repeated the question after me as he settled himself for one of our many "pow-wows," as he described them. "Looks like you've dealt me that conundrum before. Why ain't I wedded? The answer to that, son, is a long shot an' a limb in the way.

"Now I reckons the reason why I'm allers wifeless a whole lot is mainly due to the wide pop'larity of them females I takes after. Some other gent sorter gets her first each time, an' nacherally that bars me. Bill Jenks's wife on that occasion is a spec'men case. That's one of the disapp'intments I onfolds to you. Now thar's a maiden I not only wants, but needs; jest the same, Bill gets her. An' it's allers sim'lar; I never yet holds better than ace-high when the stake's a lady.

"It's troo," he continued, reflectively puffing his pipe. "I was disp'sitioned for a wife that a-way when I'm a colt. But that's a long time ago; I ain't in line for no sech gymnastics no more; my years is 'way ag'in it.

"You've got to ketch folks young to marry 'em. After they gets to be thirty years they goes slowly to the altar. If you aims to marry a gent after he's thirty you has to blindfold him an' back him in. Females, of course, ain't so obdurate. No; I s'pose this yere bein' married is a heap habit, same as tobacco an' jig-juice. If a gent takes a hand early, it's a good game, I makes no sort of doubt. But let him get to millin' 'round in the thirties or later, an' him not begun none as yet; you bet he don't marry nothin'.

"Bar an onexplainable difference with the girl's old man," he went on with an air of thought, "I s'pose I'd be all married right now. I was twenty, them times. It's 'way back in Tennessee. Her folks lives about 'leven miles from me out on the Pine Knot Pike, an' once in two weeks I saddles up an' sorter sidles over. Thar's jest her old pap an' her mother an' her in the fam'ly, an' it's that far I allers made to stay all night. Thar's only two beds, an' so I'm put to camp along of the old man the times I stays.

"Them days I'm 'way bashful an' behind on all social plays, an' am plenty awe-struck about the old foiks. I never feels happy a minute where they be. The old lady does her best to make me easy an' free, too. Comes out when I rides up, an' lets down the bars for my hoss, an' asks me to rest my hat the second I'm in the door.

"Which matters goes on good enough ontil mebby it's the eighth time I'm thar. I remembers the night all perfect. Me an' the girl sets up awhile, an' then I quits her an' turns in. I gets to sleep a-layin' along the aige of the bed, aimin' to keep 'way from the old man, who's snorln' an' thrashin' 'round an' takin' on over in the middle.

"I don't recall much of nothin' ontil I comes to, a-holdin' to the old man's y'ear with one hand an' a-hammerin' of his features with t'other. I don't know yet, why. I s'pose I'm locoed an' dreamin', an allows he's a b'ar or somethin' in my sleep that a-way, an' tries to kill him. "Son, it's 'way back a long time, but I shudders yet when I reflects on that old man's language. I jumps up when I realizes things, grabs my raiment, an', gettin' my hoss outen the corral, goes p'intin' down the pike more'n a mile 'fore I even stops to dress. The last I sees of the old man lie's buckin' an' pitchin' an' tossin', an' the females a-holdin' of him, an' he reachin' to get a Hawkins's rifle as hangs over the door. I never goes back no more, 'cause he's mighty tindictive about it. He tries to make it a grandjury matter next co't-time.

"Speakin' of nuptials, however, you can't tell much about women. Thar's a girl who shorely s'prises us once in a way out in Wolfville. Missis Rucker, who runs the O. K. Restauraw, gets this female from Tucson to fry flap-jacks an' salt hoss, an' he'p her deal her little gastronomic game. This yere girl's name is Jennie- Tucson Jennie. She looks like she's a nice, good girl, too; one of them which it's easy to love, an' in less'n two weeks thar's half the camp gets smitten. "It affects business, it's that bad. Cherokee Hall tells me thar ain't half the money gets changed in at faro as usual, an' the New York Store reports gents goin' broke ag'in biled shirts, an' sim'lar deadfalls daily. Of course this yere first frenzy subsides a whole lot after a month. "All this time Jennie ain't sayin' a word. She jest shoves them foolish yooths their enchiladas an' ckile con carne, an' ignores all winks an' looks complete.

"Thar's a party named Jim Baxter in camp, an' he sets in to win Jennie hard. Jim tries to crowd the game an' get action. It looks like he's due to make the trip too. Missis Rucker is backin' his play, an' Jennie herse'f sorter lets him set 'round in the kitchen an' watch her work; which this yore is license an' riot itse'f compared with how she treats others. Occasionally some of us sorter tries to stack up for Jim an' figger out where he stands with the the game.

"'How's it goin', Baxter?' Enright asks one day.

"'It's too many for me,' says Jim. 'Some-times I thinks I corrals her, an' then ag'in it looks like I ain't in it. Jest now I'm feelin' some dejected.'

"'Somethin' oughter be schemed to settle this yere,' says Enright.
'It keeps the camp in a fever, an' mebby gets serious an' spreads.'

"'If somebody would only prance in,' says Doc Peets, 'an' shoot Jim up some, you'd have her easy. Females is like a rabbit in a bush- pile; you has to shake things up a lot to make 'em come out. Now, if Jim is dyin' an' she cares for him, she's shorely goin' to show her hand.'

"I wants to pause right yere to observe that Doc Peets is the best- eddicated sharp I ever encounters in my life. An' what he don't know about squaws is valueless as information. But to go on with the deal.

"'That's right,' says Cherokee Hall, 'but of course it ain't goin' to do to shoot Jim up none.'

"'I don't know,' says Jim; 'I stands quite a racket if I'm shore it fetches her.'

"'What for a game,' says Cherokee, 'would it be to play like Jim's shot? Wouldn't that make her come a-runnin' same as if it's shore 'nough?'

"'I don't see why not,' says Enright.

"Well, the idee gains ground like an antelope, an' at last gets to be quite a conspir'cy. It's settled we plays it, with Dave Tutt to do the shootin'.

"'An' we makes the game complete,' says Jack Moore, 'by grabbin' Dave immediate an' bringin' of him before the committee, which convenes all reg'lar an' deecorous in the Red Light for said purpose. We-alls must line out like we're goin' to hang Dave for the killin'; otherwise it don't look nacheral nohow, an' the lady detects it's a bluff.'

"We gets things all ready, an' in the middle of the afternoon, when Jennie is draggin' her lariat 'round loose an' nothin' much to do— 'cause we ain't aimin' to disturb her none in her dooties touchin' them flapjacks an' salt hoss—we-alls assembles over in the New York Store. As a preliminary step we lays Jim on some boxes, with a wagon-cover over him, like he's deceased.

"'Cl'ar things out of the way along by Jim's head,' says Jack Moore, who is takin' a big interest. 'We wants to fix things so Jen can swarm in at him easy. You hear me! she's goin' to come stampedin' in yere like wild cattle when she gets the news.'

"When everythin's ready, Tutt an' Jack, who concloods it's well to have a good deal of shootin', bangs away with their guns about four times apiece.

"'Jest shootin' once or twice,' says Jack, 'might arouse her s'picions. It would be a heap too brief for the real thing.'

"The minute the shootin' is ceased we-alls takes Tutt an' surges over to the Red Light to try him; a-pendin' of which Dan Boggs sa'nters across to the O. K. Restauraw an' remarks, all casooal an' careless like:

"'Dave Tutt downs Jim Baxter a minute back; good clean gun-play as ever I sees, too. Mighty big credit to both boys this yere is. No shootin' up the scenery an' the bystanders; no sech slobberin' work; but everythin' carries straight to centers.'

"'Where is he?' says Jennie, lookin' breathless an' sick.

"'Jim's remainder is in the New York Store,' says Dan.

"'Is he hurt?' she gasps.

"'I don't reckon he hurts none now,' says Dan, "cause he's done cashed in his stack. Why! girl, he's dead; eighteen bullets, caliber forty-five, plumb through him.'

"'No, but Dave! Is Dave shot?' Tucson Jennie says, a-wringin' of her small paws.

"'Now don't you go to feelin' discouraged none,' says Dan, beginnin' to feel sorry for her. 'We fixes the wretch so his murderin' sperit won't be an hour behind Jim's gettin' in. The Stranglers has him in the Red Light, makin' plans to stretch him right now.'

"We-alls has consoomed drinks all 'round, an' Enright is in the chair, an' we're busy settin' up a big front about hearin' the case, when Tucson Jennie, with a scream as scares up surroundin' things to sech a limit that five ponies hops out of the corral an' flies, comes chargin' into the Red Light, an' the next instant she drifts 'round Tutt's neck like so much snow.

"'What for a game do you call this, anyhow?' says Jack Moore, who's a heap scand'lized. 'Is this yere maiden playin' anythin' on this camp?'

67

"'She's plumb locoed with grief,' says Dan Boggs, who follers her in, 'an' she's done got 'em mixed in her mind. She thinks Dave is Baxter.'

"'That's it,' says Cherokee. 'Her mind's stampeded with the shock. Me an' Jack takes her over to Jim's corpse, an' that's shore to revive her.' An' with that Cherokee an' Jack goes up to lead her away.

"'Save him, Mister Enright; save him!' she pleads, still clingin' to Tutt's neck like the loop of a lariat. 'Don't let 'em hang him! Save him for my sake!'

"'Hold on, Jack,' says Enright, who by now is lookin' some thoughtful. 'Jest everybody stand their hands yere till I counts the pot an' notes who's shy. It looks like we're cinchin' the hull onto the wrong bronco. Let me ask this female a question. Young woman,' he says to Tucson Jennie, 'be you fully informed as to whose neck you're hangin' to?'

"'It's Dave's, ain't it?' she says, lookin' all tearful in his face to make shore.

"Enright an' the rest of us don't say nothin', but gazes at each other. Tutt flushes up an' shows pleased both at once. But all the same he puts his arms 'round her like the dead-game gent he is.

"'What'll you-alls have, gents?" Enright says at last, quiet an' thoughtful. 'The drinks is on me, barkeep.'

"'Excuse me,' says Doc Peets, 'but as the author of this yere plot,
I takes it the p'ison is on me. Barkeep, set out all your bottles.'

"'Gents,' says Jack Moore, 'I'm as peaceful a person as ever jingled a spur or pulled a gun in Wolfville; but as I reflects on the active part I takes in these yere ceremonies, I won't be responsible for results if any citizen comes between me an' payin' for the drinks. Barkeep, I'm doin' this myse'f.'

"Well, it's hard enoomeratin' how many drinks we do have. Jim Baxter throws away the wagon cover an' comes over from the New York Store an' stands in with us. It gets to be a orgy.

"'Of course it's all right,' says Enright, 'the camp wins with Tutt instead of Baxter; that's all. It 'lustrates one of them beautiful characteristics of the gentler sex, too. Yere's Baxter, to say nothin' of twenty others, as besieges an' beleaguers this yere female for six weeks, an' she scorns 'em. Yere's Tutt, who ain't makin' a move, an' she grabs him. It is sech oncertainties, gents, as makes

the love of woman valuable.' "'You-alls should have asked me,' says Faro Nell, who comes in right then an' rounds up close to Cherokee. 'I could tell you two weeks ago Jennie's in love with Tutt. Anybody could see it. Why! she's been feedin' of him twice as good grub as she does anybody else.'"

CHAPTER VII.

TUCSON JENNIE'S JEALOUSY.

"No; Dave an' his wife prospers along all right. That is, they prospers all but once; that's when Jennie gets jealous."

The Old Cattleman was responding to my question. I was full of an idle interest and disposed to go further into the affairs of Tutt and Tucson Jennie.

"Doc Peets," continued the old gentleman, "allers tells me on the side thar's nothin' in Dave's conduct onbecomin' a fam'ly man that a-way, an' that Jen's simply barkin' at a knot. But, however that is, Dave don't seem to gain no comfort of it at the time. I can see myse'f she gets Dave plumb treed an' out on a limb by them accusations when she makes 'em. He shorely looks guilty; an' yet, while I stands over the play from the first, I can't see where Dave does wrong.

"However, I don't put myse'f for'ard as no good jedge in domestic affairs. Bein' single myse'f that a-way, females is ondoubted what Doc Peets calls a 'theery' with me. But nevertheless, in an onpresoomin', lowly way, I gives it as my meager jedgement, an' I gives it cold, as how a jealous woman is worse than t'rant'lers. She's plumb locoed for one thing; an' thar's no sech thing as organizin' to meet her game. For myse'f, I don't want no transactions with 'em; none whatever.

"This yere domestic uprisin' of Dave's wife breaks on Wolfville as onexpected as a fifth ace in a poker deck; it leaves the camp all spraddled out. Tucson Jennie an' Dave's been wedded goin' on six months. The camp, as I relates, attends the nuptials in a body, an', followin' of the festivities, Tucson Jennie an' Dave tumbles into housekeepin' peaceful as two pups in a basket.

"Wolfville's proud of 'em, an'every time some ign'rant bein' asks about Wolfville an' the social features of the camp, we allers mentions Tutt an' his wife, an' tells how they keeps house, sorter upholsterin' our bluff.

"That's how the deal stands, when one day up jumps this Tucson Jennie, puts on her sunbunnit, an' goes stampedin' down to the U. K. House, an' allows to Missis Rucker that she's done lived with Dave all she aims to, an' has shore pulled her picket pin for good. She puts it up Dave is a base, deceitful sharp that a-way, an' informs Missis Rucker, all mixed up with tears, as how she now desires to go back in the kitchen an' cook, same as when Dave rounds her up for his wife.

"Yere's the whole story, an' while I nurses certain views tharon, I leaves it to you entire to say how much Tucson Jennie is jestified. I knows all about it, for I'm obleeged to be in on the deal from soda to hock.

"It's mighty likely a month before the time Tucson Jennie breaks through Dave's lines this a-way. Dave an' me's due to go over towards the Tres Hermanas about some cattle. Likewise thar's an English outfit allowin' they'll go along some, to see where they've been stackin' in heavy on some ranch lands. They was eager for Dave an' me to trail along with 'em, an' sorter ride herd on' em, an' keep 'em from gettin' mixed up with the scenery—which the same is shorely complicated in the foot-hills of the Tres Hermanas—an' losin' themse'fs a heap.

"'Which you'd better do it, boys,' says Enright. 'S'pose them folks be some trouble. It's a mighty sight better than havin' 'em go p'intin' off alone that a-way. They would shore miss the way if they does; an' the first we-alls knows, these yere Britons would be runnin' cimmaron in the hills, scarin' up things a lot, an' a- stampedin' the cattle plumb off the range. It's easier to go along careful with 'em an' bring'em back.'

"It comes, then, that one mornin' Dave an' me an' these yere aliens lines out for the hills. They've got ponies, an' wagons, an' camp- outfit to that extent a casooal onlooker might think they aims to be away for years.

"As we p'ints out from the O.K. House, where them Britons has been wrastlin' their chuck pendin' the start, Tucson Jennie is thar sayin' 'goodby' to Dave. I notes then she ain't tickled to death none about somethin', but don't deem nothin' speshul of it.

"The Britons is made up of two gents, mebby as old as Enright— brothers is what they be—an' a female who's the daughter of one of 'em. Which thar's nothin' recent about this yere lady, though; an' I reckons she's mighty likely forty years old. I learns later, however, it's this female which Tucson Jennie resents when she says "adios" to Dave.

"It shore strikes me now, when years is passed, as some marv'lous how a han'some, corn-fed female like Tucson Jennie manages to found a fight with Dave over this yere towerist woman. I'm nacherally slow to go decidin' bets ag'in a lady's looks, but whatever Tucson Jennie sees in the appearance of this person which is likely to inviggle Dave is too many for me. I softens the statement a heap when I says she's uglier than a Mexican sheep.

72

"However, that don't seem to occur to Tucson Jennie; an' Doc Peets— who's the wisest sharp in Arizona—allows to me afterwards as how Tucson Jennie is cuttin' the kyards with herse'f desp'rate to see whether she declar's war at the very time we makes our start. If she does, she turns the low kyard, for she don't say nothin', an' we gets away, an' all is profound peace.

"Four days later we're in camp by a water-hole in the frill of the foot-hills. The Britons has got up a wall tent an' is shorely havin' a high an' lavish time. Dave an' me ain't payin' no attention to 'em speshul, as we don't see how none is needed. Besides, we has some hard ridin' to do lookin' up places for a line of sign camps.

"It's the second day when we notices an outfit of Injuns camped down the valley from us. They's all serene an' peaceful enough; with squaws, papooses, an' dogs; an' ain't thinkin' no more of bein' hostile than we be.

"Of course, no sooner does these yere Britons of ours behold this band of savages than they has to go projectin' round 'em. That's the worst thing about a towerist; he's that loaded with cur'osity, an' that gregar'ous an' amiable, he has to go foolin' 'round every stranger lie tracks up with. In their ign'rance they even gets that roode an' insultin' at times, that I knows 'em who's that regardless an' imp'lite as to up an' ask a rank stranger that a-way to pass 'em his gun to look at.

"An' so, as I says, no sooner does them Injuns get near us, than them three blessed foreigners is over after 'em; ropin' at em' with questions an' invadin' of 'em, an' examinin' of 'em like the whole tribe's for sale an' they aims to acquire 'em if figgers is reasonable.

73

"I never does know what the female towerist says or does to that partic'lar aborigine-nothin' most likely; but it ain't a day when one of them Injuns settles it with himse'f he wants to wed her. The towerists is in ign'rance of the views of this savage, who goes about dealin' his game Injun fashion.

"It's this a-way: Dave an' me trails in one evenin' some weary an' played; it's been a hard ride that day. Which the first thing we lays eyes on at the camp shorely livens us up a lot. Thar, tied to the wagon-wheels, is nine ponies, which the same belongs to the Injuns.

"'Whatever be these y ere broncos doin' yere?' says Dave, for we allows, the first dash outen the box, mebby the Britons makes a purchase.

"One of the towerists tells a long an' delighted story about the gen'rosity of the Injuns.

"'Actooally,' says this towerist,"them gen'rous savages leads up these yere nine ponies an' donates 'em.'

"Dave an' me asks questions; and all thar is to the deal—which it's shore enough to bust Dave's fam'ly before it's over—them Injuns brings up the nine ponies all respectful, an' leaves 'em hobbled out, mebby it's a hundred yards from the Britons, an' rides away. The Britons, deemin' this bluff as in the line of gifts, capers over an' possesses themse'fs of the ponies an' leads 'em in. That's the outside of the store.

"'Well, stranger,' says Dave in reply, takin' of the towerist one side, 'I ain't aimin' to discourage you none, but you-alls has gone an' got all tangled up in your lariat.'

"'What for an ontanglement is it?' asks the towerist.

"'Nothin',' says Dave, sorter breakin' it to him easy, 'nothin', only you've done married your daughter to one of them Injuns.'

"When Dave announces this yere trooth it shore looks like the Briton's goin' to need whiskey to uphold himse'f. But he reorganizes, an' Dave explains that the Injuns, when they trails in with the ponies, is simply shufflin' for a weddin'; they's offerin' what they-alls calls a 'price' for the woman.

"'An' when you-alls leads in the ponies,' says Dave,'that settles it. You agrees to deal right thar. To-morrow, now, this yere buck, whoever he is, will come surgin' in with his relations plumb down to third cousins; an' he expects you'll be dead ready to feed 'em, an' wind up the orgy by passin' over the bride.'

"You can bet them reecitals of Dave's is plenty horrible to the towerist. He allows we must keep it from his daughter; an' then he puts hip whole outfit in Dave's hands, to get 'em safe onto high grounds.

"'Can't we pull our freight in the night?'says the towerist, an' he's shorely anxious.

"'Too much moon,' says Dave; 'an' then, ag'in, the whole Injun outfit's below us in the draw, an' we never gets by once in a thousand times. No,' goes on Dave, 'one shore thing we can't back out nor crawl off. We-alls has to play the hand plumb through:

"Then Dave tells the towerist him an' me talks over this yere weddin' which he done goes into so inadvert; an' if thar's a chance to save him from becomin' a father-in-law abrupt, we'll play it to win.

75

"'This yere is the only wagon-track out; says Dave to me, after we pow-wows an hour. 'You go down to them Injuns, an' find the right buck that a-way, an' tell him the squaw's got a buck now. Tell him he's barred. Which at this p'int in your revelations he's due to offer a fight, an' of course you takes him. Tell him at first-drink time to-morrow mornin' he finds me ready to fight for the squaw.'

"'This whole business makes metired, though,' says Dave, a heap disgustad. ' If these eediots had let them Injuns alone-, or even if they disdains the ponies when they was brought up, this yere could be fixed easy. But now it's fight or give up the woman, so you go down, as I says, an' arrange for the dance.'

"Of course thar's no explainin' nothin' to Injuns. You might as well waste time expoundin' to coyotes an' jack-rabbits. All that's left for me to do is trail out after my savage, as Dave says, an' notify him that this weddin' he pro. poses is postponed an' all bets is off.

"I finds him easy enough, an' saws it off on him in Spanish how the game stacks up. But he ain't cheerful about it, an' displays a mighty baleful sperit. Jest as Tutt allows he's out to shoot for the squaw in a minute, an' as thar's no gettin' away from it, I tells him to paint himse'f for war an' come a-runnin'.

"I has to carry a hard face; for we're shorely in for it. Yere we be four days from Wolfville, an' the Injuns—an' I reckons thar's twenty bucks in the outfit-is camped in between us an' he'p.

"This Injun who's after the woman is named Black Dog. The next mornin' Tutt saddles up an' rides off to one side of our camp, mebby it's a quarter of a mile, an' then gets offen his pony an' stands thar. We-alls don't onfold to the towerists the details of the deal, not even to the Injun's father-in-law. The towerist female is that ign'rant of what's going' on, she's pesterin' 'round all onconscious, makin' bakin'-powder biscuit at the time. I looks at her close, an' I wonders even yet what that Black Dog's thinkin' of. But I don't get much time to be disgusted over this Black Dog's taste before he comes p'intin' out from among his people.

"The sun's jest gettin' over the hills to the east, an', as it strikes him, he's shore a fash'nable lookin' Injun. He ain't got nothin' on but a war-bunnit an' a coat of paint. The rest of his trousseau he confines to his Winchester an' belt. He's on his war- pony, an' the bronco's stripped as bare as this Black Dog is; not a strap from muzzle to tail. This bridegroom Injun's tied its mane full of ribbons, an' throws a red blanket across his pony's withers for general effects. Take it all over, he's a nifty-lookin' savage.

"So far as the dooel goes, Dave ain't runnin' no resk. He stands thar on the ground an' keeps his hoss between him an' this yere Black Dog. It's a play which forces the bridegroom's hand, too. He's due, bein' Injun, to go cirelin' Dave an' do his shootin' on the canter.

"An' that's what this weak-minded savage does. He breaks into a lope an' goes sailin' 'round Dave like a hawk. Durin' them exercises he lays over on the shoulder of his hoss an' bangs away from onder its neck with one hand, permiscus.

"This is mere frivolity. Thar ain't no white gent who could shoot none onder sech conditions; an' Injuns can't shoot nohow. They don't savey a hind sight. An', as I remarks, if Dave's hit any, it's goin' to shorely be an accident, an' accidents don't happen none in Arizona; leastwise not with guns.

'Mebby this Black Dog's banged away three times, when Dave, who's been followin' of him, through the sights for thirty seconds, onhooks his rifle, an' the deal comes to a full stop. Dave's shootin' a Sharp's, with a hundred an' twenty grains of powder, an' the way he sends a bullet plumb through that war-pony an' this yere Black Dog, who's hangin' on its off side, don't bother him a bit. The pony an' the Black Dog goes over on their heads.

"Dave rides in, an' brings the blanket an' war-bunnit. Even then, the female towerist, which is the object of the meetin', don't seem informed none of the course of events. The fact is, she never does acquire the rights of it till we-alls is two days back on the return trail.

"Thar's no more bother. Injuns is partic'lar people, that a-way, about etiquette as they saveys it, an' followin' Dave's downin' this Black Dog they ain't makin' a moan or a move. They takes it plenty solemn an' mute, an' goes to layin' out the Black Dog's obsequies without no more notice of us. It's a squar deal; they sees that; an' they ain't filin' no objections. As for our end of the game, we moves out for Wolfville, makin' no idle delays whatever.

"Goin' in, Dave, after thinkin' some, su'gests to me that it's likely to be a heap good story not to tell Tucson Jennie.

"'Females is illogical, that a-way,' says Dave, 'an' I ain't goin' to have time to eddicate Jennie to a proper view of this yere. So I reckons it's goin' to be a crafty play not to tell her.'

"The Britons has been gone two weeks when Tucson Jennie learns the story. Them towerists is plumb weary of Arizona when we trails into Wolfville, an' don't seem to tarry a second before they lines out for Tucson.

"'They jest hits a high place or two,' says Jack Moore, after he hears of them designs of the Black Dog, 'an' they'll be 'way yonder out of the country. I don't reckon none of 'em'll ever come back soon, neither.'

"But it's the towerist woman makes the trouble from start to finish. It's a letter from her which she writes back to Dave, allowin' she'll thank him some more as her preserver, that brings the news to Jennie. Tucson Jennie gets this missive, an' ups an' rifles an' reads it to herse'f a whole lot. It's then Tucson Jennie gives it out cold, Dave is breakin' her heart, an' tharupon prances 'round for her shaker an' goes over to Missis Rucker's.

"The whole camp knows the story in an hour, an' while we-alls
sympathizes with Dave of course, no one's blamin' Tucson Jennie.
She's a female, an' onresponsible, for one thing; an' then, ag'in
Dave's a heap onlikely to stand any condemnations of his wife.

"'She's as good a woman as ever wears a moccasin,' says Dave, while he's recoverin' of his sperits at the Red Light bar.

"An' we-alls allows she shorely is; an' then everybody looks pensive an' sincere that a-way, so's not to harrow Dave none an' make his burdens more.

"'But whatever can I do to fetch her back to camp?' asks Dave, appealin' to Enright mighty wretched. 'I goes plumb locoed if this yere keeps on.'

"'My notion is, we-alls better put Missis Rucker in to play the hand,' says Enright. 'Missis Rucker's a female, an' is shorely due to know what kyards to draw. But this oughter be a lesson to you, Dave, not to go romancin' 'round with strange women no more.'

"'It's a forced play, I tells you,' says Dave. 'Them Injuns has us treed. It's a case of fight or give up that she-towerist, so what was I to do?'

"`Well,' says Enright, some severe,' you might at least have consulted with this yere towerist woman some. But you don't. You simply gets a gun an' goes trackin' 'round in her destinies, an' shootin' up her prospects like you has a personal interest. You don't know but she deplores the deal complete. Peets, an' me, an' Boggs, an' all the rest of us is your friends, an' nacherally partial on your side. We-alls figgers you means well. But what I says is this: It ain't no s'prisin' thing when Tucson Jennie, a- hearin' of them pronounced attentions which you pays this towerist lady, is filled with grief. This shootin' up an Injun, cause he's plannin' to wed this female some, is what I shorely calls pronounced attentions. What do you think yourse'f, Peets?'

"'Why! I readily concedes what Dave says,' remarks Peets. 'Ondoubtedly he acts for the best as he sees it. But jest as you puts it: s'pose Dave ain't hungerin' none for this towerist woman himse'f, the headlong way he goes after this yere Black Dog, settin' of the war-jig the next sun-up, an' all without even sayin' "Let me look at your hand," to this female, jestifies them inferences of yours. Of course I don't say—an' I don't reckon none—Dave thinks of this old-maid maverick once; but, he sees himse'f, ht shore goes to war a heap precipitate an' onconsiderate, an' Tucson Jennie has ondoubted grounds to buck.

"'Which, when you-alls puts it so cl'ar, I thinks so too,' says Dave, who's listenin' to Enright an' Peets a mighty sight dejected. I But I ain't been wedded long—ain't more'n what you might call an amature husband. What you-alls oughter do now is he'p me to round her up. If Tucson Jennie's a bunch of cattle, or a band of ponies as has stampeded, you'd be in the saddle too quick.'

"Missis Rucker shore does all she knows to soften Tucson Jennie. She reminds her how in the old times, when Dave gets his chile con carne at the O. K. House, and the party from the States takes to reprovin' of Missis Rucker about thar bein' nothin' but coffee an' beans to eat, Dave onlimbers his six-shooter an' goes to the front.

"'The grub's dealt down,' says Dave, explainin' to this obnoxious tenderfoot, 'till thar's nothin' left in the box but beans, coffee, an' beans. It's a cat-hop, but it can't be he'ped none.'

"'Cat-hop or no cat-hop,' says this tenderfoot, 'I'm dead ag'in beans; an' you can gamble I ain't out to devour no sech low veg'tables; none whatever.'

"'You jest thinks you don't like beans,' says Dave, an' with that he sorter dictates at the tenderfoot with his gun, an' the tenderfoot thar-upon lays for his frijoles like he's actooally honin' tharfor.

"'Which it all shows Dave's got a good heart,' says Missis Rucker   to Tucson Jennie.

"'That's nothin' to do with his makin' love to the British woman,' says Tucson Jennie, grittin' her teeth like she could eat the sights offen a six-shooter.

"'He never makes no love to this yere woman,' says Missis Rucker.

"'When he ketches her flirtin' with that Injun,' demands Tucson Jennie, 'don't Dave shoot him up a lot? What do you-all call makin' love? He never downs no Injuns for me, an' I'm his lawful wife.' An' yere Missis Rucker allows, when she reports to Enright an' Dave an' the rest of the outfit in the Red Light, Tucson Jennie weeps like her heart is shorely broke.

"'Which the pore girl's to be pitied,' says Enright. 'Dave,' he goes on, turnin' to Tutt some fierce, 'you don't deserve no sech devotion as this.'

"'That's whatever,' says Dan Boggs, lookin' red an' truculent, 'this yere Tucson Jennie's a angel.'

"But thar we be, up ag'inst it, an' not a man knows a thing to do to squar' the deal with Dave's wife. We-alls, calls for drinks all 'round, an' sets about an' delib'rates. At last Dave speaks up in a low-sperited way.

"'I reckons she done jumps the game for good,' he says. 'But if she's goin', I wants her to have a layout. If you-alls cares to go over to the New York Store, I allows I'll play in a blue stack or two an' win her out some duds. I wants her to quit the deal ahead.'

"So Dave sets out for the New York Store, an' the rest of us sorter straggles along. Thar's nothin' gay about us. Dave gets a shawl an' a dress; nothin' gaudy; it's a plain red an' yaller. Missis Rucker packs 'em over to Tucson Jennie an' gets that wrapped up in the deal she forgets utter to rustle us our grub.

"Which, it's the onexpeeted as happens in Wolfville same as everywhere else. The minute Tucson Jennie sees the raiment, an' realizes how Dave loves her, that settles it. Her heart melts right thar. She ain't sayin' nothin'; jest ropes onto the dry-goods an' starts sobbin' out for the 'doby where she an' Dave lives at.

"Dave, when he observes this yere from 'cross the street, shakes hands all 'round, but don't trust himse'f with no remarks. He gives our paws a squeeze like he knows he can rely on our friendship an' hunts his way across to Tucson Jennie without a word.

"'It's all right about bein' yoothful an' light, that a-way,' says Enright, after Dave pulls his freight, 'but Tutt oughter remember yereafter, before he goes mixin' himse'f up with sech vain things as towerists an' Injuns an' British, that he's a married man.'"

CHAPTER VIII.

THE MAN FROM RED DOG.

"Let me try one of them thar seegyars."

It was the pleasant after-dinner hour, and I was on the veranda for a quiet smoke. The Old Cattleman had just thrown down his paper; the half-light of the waning sun was a bit too dim for his eyes of seventy years.

"Whenever I beholds a seegyar," said the old fellow, as he puffed voluminously at the principe I passed over, "I thinks of what that witness says in the murder trial at Socorro.

"'What was you-all doin' in camp yourse'f,' asks the jedge of this yere witness, 'the day of the killin'?'

"'Which,' says the witness, oncrossin' his laigs an' lettin' on he ain't made bashful an' oneasy by so much attentions bein' shown hire, 'which I was a-eatin' of a few sardines, a-drinkin' of a few drinks of whiskey, a-smokin' of a few seegyars, an' a-romancin' 'round.'"

After this abrupt, not to say ambiguous reminiscence, the Old
Cattleman puffed contentedly a moment.

"What murder trial was this you speak of?" I asked. "Who had been killed?"

"Now I don't reckon I ever does know who it is gets downed," he replied. "This yere murder trial itse'f is news to me complete. They was waggin' along with it when I trails into Socorro that time, an' I merely sa'nters over to the co't that a-way to hear what's goin' on. The jedge is sorter gettin' in on the play while I'm listenin'.

"'What was the last words of this yere gent who's killed?' asks the jedge of this witness.

"'As nearly as I keeps tabs, jedge,' says the witness, `the dyin' statement of this person is: "Four aces to beat."'

"'Which if deceased had knowed Socorro like I does,' says the jedge, like he's commentin' to himse'f, 'he'd shorely realized that sech remarks is simply sooicidal.'"

Again the Old Cattleman relapsed into silence and the smoke of the principe.

"How did the trial come out?" I queried. "Was the accused found guilty?"

"Which the trial itse'f," he replied, "don't come out. Thar's a passel of the boys who's come into town to see that jestice is done, an' bein' the round-up is goin' for'ard at the time, they nacherally feels hurried an' pressed for leesure. Theyalls oughter be back on the range with their cattle. So the fifth day, when things is loiterin' along at the trial till it looks like the law has hobbles on, an' the word goes round it's goin' to be a week yet before the jury gets action on this miscreant who's bein' tried, the boys becomes plumb aggravated an' wearied out that a-way; an', kickin' in the door of the calaboose, they searches out the felon, swings him to a cottonwood not otherwise engaged, an' the right prevails. Nacherally the trial bogs down right thar."

After another season of silence and smoke, the Old Cattleman struck in again.

"Speakn' of killin's, while I'm the last gent to go fosterin' idees of bloodshed, I'm some discouraged jest now by what I've been readin' in that paper about a dooel between some Eytalians, an' it shorely tries me the way them aliens plays hoss. It's obvious as stars on a cl'ar night, they never means fight a little bit. I abhors dooels, an' cowers from the mere idee. But, after all, business is business, an' when folks fights 'em the objects of the meetin' oughter be blood. But the way these yere European shorthorns fixes it, a gent shorely runs a heap more resk of becomin' a angel abrupt, attendin' of a Texas cake-walk in a purely social way.

"Do they ever fight dooels in the West? Why, yes—some. My mem'ry comes a-canterin' up right now with the details of an encounter I once beholds in Wolfville. Thar ain't no time much throwed away with a dooel in the Southwest. The people's mighty extemporaneous, an' don't go browsin' 'round none sendin' challenges in writin', an' that sort of flapdoodle. When a gent notices the signs a-gettin' about right for him to go on the war-path, he picks out his meat, surges up, an' declar's himse'f. The victim, who is most likely a mighty serious an' experienced person, don't copper the play by makin' vain remarks, but brings his gatlin' into play surprisin'. Next it's bang! bang! bang! mixed up with flashes an' white smoke, an' the dooel is over complete. The gent who still adorns our midst takes a drink on the house, while St. Peter onbars things a lot an' arranges gate an' seat checks with the other in the realms of light. That's all thar is to it. The tide of life ag'in flows onward to the eternal sea, an' nary ripple.

"Oh, this yere Wolfville dooel! `Well, it's this a-way. The day is blazin' hot, an' business layin' prone an' dead—jest blistered to death. A passel of us is sorter pervadin' 'round the dance-hall, it bein' the biggest an' coolest store in camp. A monte game is strugglin' for breath in a feeble, fitful way in the corner, an' some of us is a-watchin'; an' some a-settin' 'round loose a- thinkin'; but all keepin' mum an' still, 'cause it's so hot.

"Jest then some gent on a hoss goes whoopin' up the street a-yellin' an' a-whirlin' the loop of his rope, an' allowin' generally he's havin' a mighty good time.

"'Who's this yere toomultuous man on the hoss?' says Enright, a- regardin' of him in a displeased way from the door.

"'I meets him up the street a minute back,' says Dan Boggs, 'an' he allows he's called "The Man from Red Dog." He says he's took a day off to visit us, an' aims to lay waste the camp some before he goes back.'

"About then the Red Dog man notes old Santa Rosa, who keeps the Mexican baile hall, an' his old woman, Marie, a-fussin' with each other in front of the New York Store. They's locked horns over a drink or somethin', an' is pow-wowin' mighty onamiable.

"'Whatever does this yere Mexican fam'ly mean,' says the Red Dog man, a-surveyin' of 'em plenty scornful, 'a-draggin' of their domestic brawls out yere to offend a sufferin' public for? Whyever don't they stay in their wickeyup an' fight, an' not take to puttin' it all over the American race which ain't in the play none an' don't thirst tharfor? However, I unites an' reeconciles this divided household easy.'

"With this the Red Dog man drops the loop of his lariat 'round the two contestants an' jumps his bronco up the street like it's come outen a gun. Of course Santa Rosa an' Marie goes along on their heads permiscus.

"They goes coastin' along ontil they gets pulled into a mesquite- bush, an' the rope slips offen the saddle, an' thar they be. We-alls goes over from the dance-hall, extricatin' of 'em, an' final they rounds up mighty hapless an' weak, an' can only walk. They shorely lose enough hide to make a pair of leggin's.

"'Which I brings 'em together like twins,' says the Red Dog man, ridin' back for his rope. 'I offers two to one, no limit, they don't fight none whatever for a month.'

"Which, as it shorely looks like he's right, no one takes him. So the Red Dog man leaves his bluff a-hangin' an' goes into the dance- hall, a-givin' of it out cold an' clammy he meditates libatin'.

"'All promenade to the bar,' yells the Red Dog man as he goes in. 'I'm a wolf, an' it's my night to howl. Don't 'rouse me, barkeep, with the sight of merely one bottle; set 'em all up. I'm some fastidious about my fire-water an' likes a chance to select.'

"Well, we-alls takes our inspiration, an' the Red Dog man tucks his onder his belt an' then turns round to Enright.

"'I takes it you're the old he-coon of this yere outfit?' says the Red Dog man, soopercillious-like.

"'Which, if I ain't,' says Enright, 'it's plenty safe as a play to let your wisdom flow this a-way till the he-coon gets yere.'

"'If thar's anythin',' says the Red Dog man, 'I turns from sick, it's voylence an' deevastation. But I hears sech complaints constant of this yere camp of Wolfville, I takes my first idle day to ride over an' line things up. Now yere I be, an' while I regrets it, I finds you-alls is a lawless, onregenerate set, a heap sight worse than roomer. I now takes the notion—for I sees no other trail—that by next drink time I climbs into the saddle, throws my rope 'round this den of sin, an' removes it from the map.'

"'Nacherally,' says Enright, some sarcastic, 'in makin' them schemes you ain't lookin' for no trouble whatever with a band of tarrapins like us.'

"'None whatever,' says the Red Dog man, mighty confident. 'In thirty minutes I distributes this yere hamlet 'round in the landscape same as them Greasers; which feat becomin' hist'ry, I then canters back to Red Dog.'

"'Well,' says Enright, 'it's plenty p'lite to let us know what's comin' this a-way.'

"'Oh! I ain't tellin' you none,' says the Red Dog man, 'I simply lets fly this hint, so any of you-alls as has got bric-a-brac he values speshul, he takes warnin' some an' packs it off all safe.'

"It's about then when Cherokee Hall, who's lookin' on, shoulders in between Enright an' the Red Dog man, mighty positive. Cherokee is a heap sot in his idees, an' I sees right off he's took a notion ag'in the Red Dog man.

"'As you've got a lot of work cut out,' says Cherokee, eyein' the
Red Dog man malignant, 's'pose we tips the canteen ag'in.'

"'I shorely goes you,' says the Red Dog man. 'I drinks with friend, an' I drinks with foe; with the pard of my bosom an' the shudderin' victim of my wrath all sim'lar.'

"Cherokee turns out a big drink an' stands a-holdin' of it in his hand. I wants to say right yere, this Cherokee's plenty guileful.

"'You was namin',' says Cherokee, 'some public improvements you aims to make; sech as movin' this yere camp 'round some, I believes?'

"'That's whatever,' says the Red Dog man, 'an' the holycaust I 'nitiates is due to start in fifteen minutes.'

"'I've been figgerin' on you,' says Cherokee, 'an' I gives you the result in strict confidence without holdin' out a kyard. When you- all talks of tearin' up Wolfville, you're a liar an' a hoss-thief, an' you ain't goin' to tear up nothin'.'

"'What's this I hears!' yells the frenzied Red Dog man, reachin' for his gun.

"But he never gets it, for the same second Cherokee spills the glass of whiskey straight in his eyes, an' the next he's anguished an' blind as a mole.

"'I'll fool this yere human simoon up a lot,' says Cherokee, a-hurlin' of the Red Dog man to the floor, face down, while his nine- inch bowie shines in his hand like the sting of a wasp. 'I shore fixes him so he can't get a job clerkin' in a store,' an' grabbin' the Red Dog man's ha'r, which is long as the mane of a pony, he slashes it off close in one motion.

"'Thar's a fringe for your leggin's, Nell,' remarks Cherokee, a- turnin' of the crop over to Faro Nell. 'Now, Doc,' Cherokee goes on to Doc Peets, 'take this yere Red Dog stranger over to the Red Light, fix his eyes all right, an' then tell him, if he thinks he needs blood in this, to take his Winchester an' go north in the middle of the street. In twenty minutes by the watch I steps outen the dance-hall door a-lookin' for him. P'int him to the door all fair an' squar'. I don't aim to play nothin' low on this yere gent. He gets a chance for his ante.'

"Doc Peets sorter accoomilates the Red Dog man, who is cussin' an' carryin' on scand'lous, an' leads him over to the Red Light. In a minute word comes to Cherokee as his eyes is roundin' up all proper, an' that he's makin' war-medicine an' is growin' more hostile constant, an' to heel himse'f. At that Cherokee, mighty ca'm, sends out for Jack Moore's Winchester, which is an 'eight-squar',' latest model.

"'Oh, Cherokee!' says Faro Nell, beginnin' to cry, an' curlin' her arms 'round his neck. 'I'm 'fraid he's goin' to down you. Ain't thar no way to fix it? Can't Dan yere settle with this Red Dog man?'

"'Cert,' says Dan Boggs, 'an' I makes the trip too gleeful. Jest to spar' Nell's feelin's, Cherokee, an' not to interfere with no gent's little game, I takes your hand an' plays it.'

"'Not none,' says Cherokee; 'this is my deal. Don't cry, Nellie,' he adds, smoothin' down her yaller ha'r. 'Folks in my business has to hold themse'fs ready to face any game on the word, an' they never weakens or lays down. An' another thing, little girl; I gets this Red Dog sharp, shore. I'm in the middle of a run of luck; I holds fours twice last night, with a flush an' a full hand out ag'in 'em.'

"Nell at last lets go of Cherokee's neck, an', bein' a female an' timid that a-way, allows she'll go, an' won't stop to see the shootin' none. We applauds the idee, thinkin' she might shake Cherokee some if she stays; an' of course a gent out shootin' for his life needs his nerve.

"Well, the twenty minutes is up; the Red Dog man gets his rifle offen his saddle an' goes down the middle of the street. Turnin' up his big sombrero, he squar's 'round, cocks his gun, an' waits. Then Enright goes out with Cherokee an' stands him in the street about a hundred yards from the Red Dog man. After Cherokee's placed he holds up his hand for attention an' says:

"'When all is ready I stands to one side an' drops my hat. You-alls fires at will.'

"Enright goes over to the side of the street, counts 'one,' 'two,' 'three,' an' drops his hat. Bangety! Bang! Bang! goes the rifles like the roll of a drum. Cherokee can work a Winchester like one of these yere Yankee 'larm-clocks, an' that Red Dog hold-up don't seem none behind.

"About the fifth fire the Red Dog man sorter steps for'ard an' drops his gun; an' after standin' onsteady for a second, he starts to cripplin' down at his knees. At last he comes ahead on his face like a landslide. Thar's two bullets plumb through his lungs, an' when we gets to him the red froth is comin' outen his mouth some plenteous.

"We packs him back into the Red Light an' lays him onto a monte- table. Bimeby he comes to a little an' Peets asks him whatever he thinks he wants.

"'I wants you-alls to take off my moccasins an' pack me into the street,' says the Red Dog man. 'I ain't allowin' for my old mother in Missoury to be told as how I dies in no gin-mill, which she shorely 'bominates of 'em. An' I don't die with no boots on, neither.'

"We-alls packs him back into the street ag'in, an' pulls away at his boots. About the time we gets 'em off he sags back convulsive, an' thar he is as dead as Santa Anna.

"'What sort of a game is this, anyhow?' says Dan Boggs, who, while we stands thar, has been pawin' over the Red Dog man's rifle. 'Looks like this vivacious party's plumb locoed. Yere's his hind-sights wedged up for a thousand yards, an' he's been a-shootin' of cartridges with a hundred an' twenty grains of powder into 'em. Between the sights an' the jump of the powder, he's shootin' plumb over Cherokee an' aimin' straight at him.'

"'Nellie,' says Enright, lookin' remorseful at the girl, who colors up an' begins to cry ag'in, 'did you cold-deck this yere Red Dog sport this a-way?'

"'I'm 'fraid,' sobs Nell, 'he gets Cherokee; so I slides over when you-alls is waitin' an' fixes his gun some.'

"'Which I should shorely concede you did,' says Enright. 'The way that Red Dog gent manip'lates his weepon shows he knows his game; an' except for you a-settin' things up on him, I'm powerful afraid he'd spoiled Cherokee a whole lot.'

"'Well, gents,' goes on Enright, after thinkin' a while, 'I reckons we-alls might as well drink on it. Hist'ry never shows a game yet, an' a woman in it, which is on the squar', an' we meekly b'ars our burdens with the rest.'"

CHAPTER IX.

CHEROKEE HALL.

"An' you can't schedoole too much good about him," remarked the Old Cattleman. Here he threw away the remnant of the principe, and, securing his pipe, beat the ashes there-out and carefully reloaded with cut plug. Inevitably the old gentleman must smoke. His tone and air as he made the remark quoted were those of a man whose convictions touching the one discussed were not to be shaken. "No, sir," he continued; "when I looks back'ard down the trail of life, if thar's one gent who aforetime holds forth in Wolfville on whom I reflects with satisfaction, it's this yere Cherokee Hall."

"To judge from his conduct," I said, "in the hard case of the Wilkins girl, as well as his remark as she left on the stage, I should hold him to be a person of sensibilities as well as benevolent impulse."

It was my purpose to coax the old gentleman to further reminiscence.

"Benev'lent!" retorted the old man. "Which I should shore admit it! What he does for this yere young Wilkins female ain't a marker. Thar's the Red Dog man he lets out. Thar's the Stingin' Lizard's nephy; he stakes said yooth from infancy. 'Benev'lent!' says you. This party Cherokee is that benev'lent he'd give away a poker hand. I've done set an' see him give away his hand in a jack-pot for two hundred dollars to some gent 'cross the table who's organizin' to go ag'in him an' can't afford to lose. An' you can onderscore it; a winnin' poker hand, an' him holdin' it, is the last thing a thoroughbred kyard-sharp'll give away. But as I says, I sees this Cherokee do it when the opp'sition is settin' in hard luck an' couldn't stand to lose.

"How would he give his hand away? Throw it in the diskyard an' not play it none; jest nacherally let the gent who's needy that a-way rake in the chips on the low hand. Cherokee mebby does it this fashion so's he don't wound the feelin's of this yere victim of his gen'rosity. Thar's folks who turns sens'tive an' ain't out to take alms none, who's feelin's he spar's that a-way by losin' to 'em at poker what they declines with scorn direct. "'Benev'lent,' is the way you puts it! Son, 'benev'lent' ain't the word. This sport Cherokee Hall ain't nothin' short of char'table.

"Speakin' wide flung an' onrestrained, Cherokee, as I mentions to you before, is the modestest, decentest longhorn as ever shakes his antlers in Arizona. He is slim an' light, an' a ondoubted kyard- sharp from his moccasins up. An' I never knows him to have a peso he don't gamble for. Nothin' common, though; I sees him one night when he sets ca'mly into some four-handed poker, five thousand dollars table stake, an' he's sanguine an' hopeful about landin' on his feet as a Cimmaron sheep. Of course times is plenty flush in them days, an' five thousand don't seem no sech mammoth sum. Trade is eager an' values high; aces-up frequent callin' for five hundred dollars before the draw. Still we ain't none of us makin' cigarettes of no sech roll as five thousand. The days ain't quite so halcyon as all that neither.

"But what I likes speshul in Cherokee Hall is his jedgement. He's every time right. He ain't talkin' much, an' he ain't needin' advice neither, more'n a steer needs a saddle-blanket.

But when he concloodes to do things, you can gamble he's got it plenty right.

"One time this Cherokee an' Texas Thompson is comin' in from Tucson on the stage. Besides Cherokee an' Texas, along comes a female, close-herdin' of two young-ones; which them infants might have been t'rant'lers an' every one a heap happier. Sorter as range-boss of the whole out. fit is a lean gent in a black coat. Well, they hops in, an' Cherokee gives 'em the two back seats on account of the female an' the yearlin's.

"'My name is Jones,' says the gent in the black coat, when he gets settled back an' the stage is goin', I an' I'm an exhortin' evangelist. I plucks brands from the burnin'.'

"'I'm powerful glad to know it,' says Texas, who likes talk. 'Them games of chance which has vogue in this yere clime is some various, an' I did think I shorely tests 'em all; but if ever the device you names is open in Wolfville I overlooks the same complete.'

"'Pore, sinkin' soul!' says the black-coat gent to the female; 'he's a-flounderin' in the mire of sin. Don't you know,' he goes on to Texas, 'my perishin' friend, you are bein' swept downward in the river of your own sinful life till your soul will be drowned in the abyss?"

"'Well, no,' says Texas, 'I don't. I allows I'm makin' a mighty dry ford of it.'

"'Lost! lost! lost!' says the black-coat gent, a-leanin' back like he's plumb dejected that a-way an' hopeless. 'It is a stiff-necked gen'ration an' sorely perverse a lot.'

96

"The stage jolts along two or three miles, an' nothin' more bein' said. The black-coat gent he groans occasionally, which worries Texas; an' the two infants, gettin' restless, comes tumblin' over onto Cherokee an' is searchin' of his pockets for mementoes. Which this is about as refreshin' to Cherokee as bein' burned at the stake. But the mother she leans back an' smiles, an' of course he's plumb he'pless. Finally the black. coat gent p'ints in for another talk.

"'What is your name, my pore worm?' says the black-coat gent, addressin' of Texas; 'an' whatever avocation has you an' your lost companion?'

"I Why,' says Texas, 'this yere's Hall—Cherokee Hall. He turns faro in the Red Light; an',' continues Texas, a-lowerin' of his voice, 'he's as squar' a gent as ever counted a deck. Actooally, pard, you might not think it, but all that gent knows about settin' up kyards, or dealin' double, or anv sech sinful scheme, is mere tradition.' "'Brother,' says the female, bristlin' up an' tacklin' the black- coat gent, 'don't talk to them persons no more. Them's gamblers, an' mighty awful men;' an' with that she snatches away the yearlin's like they's contam'nated.

'This is relief to Cherokee, but the young-ones howls like coyotes, an' wants to come back an' finish pillagin' him. But the mother she spanks 'em, an' when Texas is goin' to give 'em some cartridges outen his belt to amoose 'em, she sasses him scand'lous, an' allows she ain't needin' no attentions from him. Then she snorts at Texas an' Cherokee contemptuous. The young-ones keeps on yellin' in a mighty onmelodious way, an' while Cherokee is ca'm an' don't seem like he minds it much, Texas gets some nervous. At last

Texas lugs out a bottle, aimin' to compose his feelins', which they's some harrowed by now.

"`Well, I never!' shouts the woman; 'I shorely sees inebriates ere now, but at least they has the decency not to pull a bottle that a- way

before a lady.' "This stampedes Texas complete, an' he throws the whiskey

outen the stage an' don't get no drink. "It's along late in the mornin' when the stage strikes the upper end of Apache Canyon. This yere canyon

is lately reckoned some bad. Nothin' ever happens on the line, but

them is the days when Cochise is cavortin' 'round plenty loose, an' it's mighty possible to stir up Apaches any time a-layin' in the hills

along the trail to Tucson. If they ever gets a notion to stand up the stage, they's shore due to be in this canyon; wherefore Cherokee an' Texas an' Old Monte who's drivin' regards it s'picious. "'Send 'em through on the jump, Monte,' says Cherokee, stickin' out his head. "The six hosses lines out at a ten-mile gait, which rattles things, an' makes the black-coat gent sigh, while the young-ones pours forth some appallin' shrieks. The female gets speshul mad at this, allowin'

they's playin' it low down on her fam'ly. But she takes it out in cuffin' the yearlin's now an' then, jest to keep 'em yellin', an' don't say nothin'. "Which the stage is about half through the canyon, when up on both sides a select assortment of Winchesters begins to bang an' jump permiscus; the same goin' hand-in-hand with whoops of onusual merit. With the first shot Old Monte pours the leather into the team, an' them hosses surges into the collars like cyclones. "It's lucky aborigines ain't no shots. They never yet gets the phelosophy of a

hind sight none, an' generally you can't reach their bullets with a ten-foot pole, they's that high above your head. The only thing as

gets hit this time is Texas. About the beginnin', a little cloud of dust flies outen the shoulder of his coat, his face turns pale, an' Cherokee knows he's creased. "'Did they get you, Old Man?' says Cherokee, some anxious. "'No,' says Texas, tryin' to brace himse'f. 'I'll be

on velvet ag'in in a second. I now longs, however, for that whiskey I hurls overboard so graceful.' "The Apaches comes tumblin' down onto the trail an' gives chase, a-shootin' an' a-yellin' a heap zealous. As they's on foot, an' as Old Monte is makin' fifteen miles an hour by now, they merely manages to hold their own in the race, about forty yards to the r'ar.

"This don't go on long when Cherokee, after thinkin', says to Texas, 'This yere is the way I figgers it, If we-alls keeps on, them Injuns is that fervent they runs in on us at the ford. With half luck they's due to down either a hoss or Monte—mebby both; in which event the stage shorely stops, an' it's a fight. This bein' troo, an' as I'm 'lected for war anyhow, I'm goin' to caper out right yere, an' pull on the baile myse'f. This'll stop the chase, an' between us, pard, it's about the last chance in the box this pore female an' her offsprings has. An' I plays it for 'em, win or lose.'

"'Them's my motives; says Texas, tryin' to pull himse'f together. 'Shall we take this he-shorthorn along?' An' he p'ints where them four tenderfoots is mixed up together in the back of the stage.

"'He wouldn't be worth a white chip,' says Cherokee, 'an' you-all is too hard hit to go, Texas, yourse'f. So take my regards to Enright an' the boys, an' smooth this all you know for Faro Nell. I makes the trip alone.'

"'Not much,' says Texas. 'My stack goes to the center, too.'

"But it don't, though, 'cause Texas has bled more'n he thinks. The first move he makes he tips over in a faint.

"Cherokee picks up his Winchester, an', openin' the door of the stage, jumps plumb free, an' they leaves him thar on the trail.

"'It's mebby an hour later when the stage comes into Wolfville on the lope. Texas is still in a fog, speakin' mental, an' about bled to death; while them exhortin' people is outen their minds entire.

"In no time thar's a dozen of us lined out for Cherokee. Do we locate him? Which I should say we shorely discovers him. Thar's a bullet through his laig, an' thar he is with his back ag'in a rock wall, his Winchester to the front, his eyes glitterin', a-holdin' the canyon. Thar never is no Injun gets by him. Of course they stampedes prompt when they hears us a-comin', so we don't get no fight.

"'I hopes you nails one, Cherokee,' says Enright; 'playin' even on this yere laig they shoots.'

"'I win once, I reckons', says Cherokee, 'over behind that big rock to the left.'

"'Shore enough he's got one Injun spread out; an', comin' along a little, Jack Moore turns up a second.

"'Yere's another,' says Jack, 'which breaks even on the bullet in
Texas.'

"'That's right,' says Cherokee, 'I remembers now than is two. The kyards is comin' some Tast, an' I overlooks a bet.'

"We-alls gets Cherokee in all right, an' next day 'round comes the female tenderfoot to see him.

"'I wants to thank my defender,' she says.

"'You ain't onder no obligations, whatever, ma'am', says Cherokee, risin' up a little, while Faro Nell puts another goose-h'ar piller onder him. 'I simply prefers to do my fightin' in the canyon to doin' it at the ford; that's all. It's only a matter of straight business; nothin' more'n a preference I has. Another thing, ma'am; you-all forgives it, seein' I'm a gent onused to childish ways: but when I makes the play you names, I simply seizes on them savages that a-way as an excuse to get loose from them blessed children of your'n a whole lot.'"

CHAPTER X.

TEXAS THOMPSON'S "ELECTION."

"An' between us," remarked the Old Cattle man, the observation being relevant to the subject of our conversation on the occasion of one of our many confabs, "between you an' me, I ain't none shore about the merits of what you-all calls law an' order. Now a pains-takin' an' discreet vig'lance committee is my notion of a bulwark. Let any outfit take a bale of rope an' a week off, an' if their camp ain't weeded down to right principles an' a quiet life at the end tharof, then I've passed my days as vain as any coyote which ever yelps.

"Of course thar dawns a time when Wolfville has to come to it, same as others. They takes to diggin' for copper; an' they builds the Bird Cage Op'ry House, an' puts in improvements general. We even culminates in a paper, which Doc Peets assures us is the flower of our progress. Nacherally on the heels of all them outbursts we gives up our simple schemes, organizes, an' pulls off an 'lection. But as Old Man Enright is made alcalde tharby, with Jack Moore marshal, the jolt is not severe nor the change so full of notice.

"It's not long prior to these yere stampedes into a higher moonicipal life, however, when quite a b'ilin' of us is in the Red Light discussin' some sech future. Our rival, Red Dog, is allowin' it's goin' to have a mayor or somethin', an' we sorter feels like our hands is forced.

"'For myse'f,' says Old Man Enright, when the topic is circ'latin', with the whiskey followin' suit, an' each gent is airin' his idees an' paintin' his nose accordin' to his taste, 'for myse'f, I can see it comin'. Thar's to be law yere an' 'lections;

an' while at first it's mighty likely both is goin' to turn out disturbin' elements, still I looks on their approach without fear. Wolfville is too strong, an' Wolfville intelligence is too well founded, to let any law loco it or set it to millin'.'

"'Still,' says Dan Boggs, 'I must remark I prefers a dooly authorized band of Stranglers. A vig'lance committee gets my game right along. They's more honest than any of these yere lawsharps who's 'lected to be a jedge; an' they's a heap more zealous, which last is important.'

"'Boggs is right,' replies Enright. 'It may not become me, who is head of the local body of that sort, to make boasts of the excellence of a vig'lance committee; but I ain't bluffin' on a four- flush when I challenges any gent to put his tongue to an event where a vig'lance committee stretches a party who ain't in need tharof; or which goes wastin' its lariats on the desert air. I puts it to you- alls without heat or pride, gents; Jedge Lynch is right every time.'

"'Put me down,' says Doc Peets, at the same time makin' signs for the barkeep to remember his mission on earth, 'put me down as coincidin' in them sentiments. An' I says further, that any party who's lookin' for the place where the bad man is scarce, an' a law- abidin' gent has the fullest liberty, pegged out to the shorest safetytood, let him locate where he finds the most lynchin's, an' where a vig'lance committee is steadily engaged discriminatin' 'round through the community.

Which a camp thus provided is a model of heavenly peace.'

"'You can gamble, if anybody's plumb aware of these yore trooths, it's me,' says Texas Thompson.

'When I'm down in the South Paloduro country, workin' a passel of Bar-K-7 cattle, I aids in an effort to 'lect a jedge an' institoot reg'lar shore-'nough law; an' the same comes mighty near leavin' the entire hamlet a howlin' waste. It deciminates a heap of our best citizens.

"'This yere misguided bluff comes to pass peculiar; an' I allers allows if it ain't for the onforeseen way wherein things stacks up, an' the muddle we-alls gets into tryin' to find a trail, the Plaza Paloduro would have been a scene of bleatin' peace that day, instead of a stric'ly corpse-an'-cartridge occasion. The death rate rises to that degree in fact that the next roundup is shy on men; an' thar ain't enough cartridges in camp, when the smoke blows away, to be seed for a second crop. On the squar', gents, that 'lection day on the South Paloduro was what you-alls might term a massacre, an' get it right every time.'

"'Well, what of this yere toomultuous 'lection?' demands Dave Tutt, who gets impatient while Texas refreshes himse'f in his glass. 'You- all reminds me a mighty sight, Texas, of the Tucson preacher who pulls his freight the other day. They puts it to him, the Tucson folks do, that he talks an' he talks, but he don't p'int out; an' he argufies an' he argufies, but he never shows wherein. A party who's goin' to make a pulpit-play, or shine in Arizona as a racontoor, has done got to cult'vate a direct, incisive style.'

"'That's all c'rect,' remarks Texas, some savage, as he recovers his nose outen his glass; 'never you fret me none about my style not bein' incisive. Thar be other plays where any gent who comes puttin' it all over me with roode an' intemp'rate remarks will find me plenty incisive; not to say some soon:

"'Yere!' interrupts Enright, quick an' sharp. 'This is plumb outside the line. Texas ain't got no call to wake up so malignant over what's most likely nothin' worse than humor on Tutt's part; an', Tutt, it ain't up to you none neither, to go spurrin' Texas in the shoulder in the midst of what I'm yere to maintain is a mighty thrillin' narration.'

"'Texas is good people,' says Dave, 'an' the last gent with which I thirsts to dig up the war-axe. Which I'm proud to be his friend; an' I means no offense when I su'gests that he whirl a smaller loop when he onbosoms himse'f of a tale. I yere tenders Texas my hand, assurin' of him that I means my language an' ain't holdin' out nothin'. Shake!' An' at this Dave reaches his pistol-hand to Texas Thompson, an' the same is seized prompt an' friendly.

"'This yere is my fault,' says Texas. 'I reckons now my wife recoverin' that Laredo divorce I'm mentionin' to you-alls, sorter leaves me a heap petulant, that a-way. But to go back to this war- jig I was relatin' about down at Plaza Paloduro.

"'It's this a-way: No, Nellie; thar's no female in it. This yere grows from a business transaction; an' the effort tharfrom to improve on present conditions, institoot a reign of law, an' lect a jedge.

"'Which the comin' of a miscreant named Cimmaron Pete, from some'ers over near the 'Doby Walls, is the beginnin' of the deal. This Cimmaron Pete comes trailin' in one day; an' a shorthorn called Glidden, who runs a store at the ford, comes ropin' at Cimmaron Pete to race ponies. ""What for stakes do you-all aim to race for?" demands this Cimmaron Pete.

"""I'll run you for hoss an' saddle," says Glidden.

"'"Say hoss ag'in hoss," says Cimmaron Pete, "an' I'm liable to go you. Saddles is hard to get, an' I won't resk mine. Ponies, however, is easy. I can get 'em every moonlight night."

"'When them sports is racin',—which the run is to be a quarter of a mile, only they never finishes,—jest as Cimmaron begins to pull ahead, his pony bein' a shade suddener than Glidden's, whatever does the latter do but rope this Cimmaron Pete's pony by the feet an' down him.

"'It's shore fine work with a lariat, but it comes high for Glidden. For, as he stampedes by, this Cimmaron turns loose his six-shooter from where he's tangled up with his bronco on the ground; an' as the first bullet gets Glidden in the back of his head, his light goes out like a candle.

"'When the committee looks into the play they jestifies this Cimmaron. "While on the surface," they says, "the deal seems a little florid; still, when a gent armed with nothin' but a cold sense of jestice comes to pirootin' plumb through the affair with a lantern, he's due to emerge a lot with the conviction that Glidden's wrong." So Cimmaron is free in a minute.

"'But thar's Glidden's store! Thar's nobody to claim it; thar bein' no fam'ly to Glidden nohow; not even a hired man.

"'"Which, as it seems to be a case open to doubt," observes this yere Cimmaron, "I nacherally takes this Glidden party's store an' deals his game myse'f."

"'It ain't much of a store; an' bein' as the rest of us is havin' all we-alls can ride herd on for ourse'fs, no gent makes objections, an' Cimmaron turns himse'f loose in Glidden's store, an' begins to sell things a whole lot. He's shorely doin' well, I reckons, when mebby it's a week later he comes chargin' over to a passel of us an' allows he wants the committee to settle some trouble which has cut his trail.

""It's about the debts of this yere Glidden, deceased," says Cimmaron. "I succeeds to the business of course; which it's little enough for departed ropin' my pony that time. But you-alls can gamble I ain't goin' 'way back on this yere dead person's trail, an' settle all his gray an' hoary indebtnesses. Would it be right, gents? I puts it to you-alls on the squar'; do I immerse myse'f, I'd like for to be told, in deceased's liabilities merely for resentin' of his wrongs ag'in me with my gun? If a gent can go blindly shootin' himse'f into bankruptcy that a-way, the American gov'ment is a rank loser, an' the State of Texas is plumb played out."

When we-alls proceeds to ferret into this yere myst'ry, we finds thar's a sharp come up from Dallas who claims that Cimmaron's got to pay him what Glidden owes. This yere Dallas party puts said indebtednesses at five stacks of blues.

"'An' this yere longhorn's got 'em to make good, "says the Dallas sharp, p'intin' at Cimmaron, "'cause he inherits the store."

"'Now, whatever do you-alls think of that?" says Cimmaron, appealin' to us. "Yere I've told this perverse sport that Glidden's done cashed in an' quit; an' now he lays for me with them indebtednesses. It shorely wearies me."

"'It don't take the vig'lance committee no time to agree it ain't got nothin' to say in the case.

"'" It's only on killin's, an' hoss-rustlin's, an' sim'lar breaks." explains Old Monroe, who's chief of the Paloduro Stranglers, "where we-alls gets kyards. We ain't in on what's a mere open-an'-shet case of debt."

"'But this Dallas sharp stays right with Cimmaron. He gives it out cold he's goin' to c'lect. He puts it up he'll shore sue Cimmaron a lot.

"'You-alls don't mean to say thar ain't no jedge yere?" remarks the Dallas sharp, when Old Monroe explains we ain't organized none for sech games as law cases. "Well, this yere Plaza Paloduro is for certain the locodest camp of which I ever cuts the trail! You-alls better get a hustle on right now an' 'lect a jedge. If I goes back to Dallas an' tells this story of how you-alls ain't got no jedge nor no law yere, they won't let this Plaza Paloduro get close enough to 'em in business to hand 'em a ripe peach. If thar's enough sense in this camp to make bakin'-powder biscuit, you-alls will have a jedge 'lected ready for me to have law cases with by second-drink time to-morrow mornin'."

"'After hangin' up this bluff the Dallas sharp, puttin' on a heap of hawtoor an' dog, walks over to the tavern ag'in, an' leaves us to size up the play at our lcesure.

"'What this obdurate party from Dallas says," finally remarks Old Monroe, "is not with. out what the Comanches calls tum-tum. Thar's savey an' jestice in them observations. It's my idee, that thar bein' no jedge yere, that a-way, to make a money round-up for a gent when his debtor don't make good, is mighty likely a palin' offen our fence. I shorely thinks we better rectify them omissions an' 'lect a jedge at once."

"'Which I'm opposed to these proceedin's," interrupts Cimmaron. "I'm plumb adverse to co'ts. Them law-wolves gets into 'em, an' when they can't find no gate to come at you, they ups an' pushes down a panel of fence, an' lays for you, cross-lots. I'm dead ag'in these proceedin's."

"'See yere," says Old Monroe, turnin' on this Cimmaron," you-all is becomin' too apparent in this camp; what I might describe as a heap too obvious. Now if you gets your stack in ag'in when it ain't your turn; or picks up anybody's hand but your own, I'll find a short way of knockin' your horns off. You don't seem gifted enough to realize that you're lucky to be alive right now."

"'Bar Cimmaron, who lapses into silence after Old Monroe gives him notice, the entire camp lines up fav'rable on the idee to 'lect a jedge. They sends over to the corral an' gets a nose-bag for to deposit the votes; an' it's decided that Old Monroe an' a Cross-Z party named Randall has got to do the runnin'. Randall is plenty p'lite, an' allows he don't want to be jedge none nohow, an' says, give it to Old Monroe; but the latter gent, who is organizin' the play, insists that it wouldn't be legal.

"'"Thar's got to be two gents to do the runnin'," so Old Monroe says, "or it don't go. The 'lection ain't legal that a-way onless thar's two candidates."

"'They puts Bronco Charlie an' a sport named Ormsby in to be 'lection supervisors. They was to hold the nose-bag; an' as votes is dropped in, they's to count 'em out accordin' to Hoyle, so we-alls can tell where the play's headin'. Bronco Charlie is jedge for Randall, an' Ormsby fronts up all sim'lar for Old Monroe. The 'lection we-alls decides to hold in the Lone Star Saloon, so's to be conducted with comfort.

"""Make your game, now, gents," says Old Monroe, when everythin' is shorely ready. "Get in your votes. These yere polls is open for one hour."

"""One for Randall," says Bronco Charlie as Old Monroe votes.

"""An' one for Old Monroe," remarks Ormsby when Randall votes next.

"'This gives the deal tone to have Randall an' Old Monroe p'int out by votin' for each other that a-way, and thar ain't one of us who don't feel more respectable by it.

"'It's the opinion of level-headed gents even yet, that the Plaza Paloduro could have pulled off this 'lection an' got plumb away, an' never had no friction, if it ain't for a Greaser from San Antonio who tries to ring in on us. Thar's twenty-one of us has voted, an' it stands nine for Randall an' twelve for Old Monroe; when up lopes this yere Mexican an' allows he's locoed to vote. "'Who do you-all think you're goin' to vote for?" asks Ormsby.

"""Senior Monroe," says the Mexican, p'intin' at Old Monroe.

"'Stop this deal," yells Bronco Charlie, "'I challenges that vote.
Mexicans is barred."

"'Which Mexicans is not barred," replies Ormsby. "An' the vote of this yere enlightened maverick from south of the Rio Grande goes. Thirteen for Old Monroe."

"'Twelve for Old Monroe," remonstrates Bronco Charlie, feelin' for his gun.

"'Thirteen for Old Monroe," retorts Ormsby, as his Colt's comes into action an' he busts Bronco's arm at the elbow.

"'As his obstinacy has destroyed the further efficiency of my colleague," goes on Ormsby, as he shakes down the ballots in the nose-bag, "I'll now conduct these yere polls alone. Gents who haven't voted will please come a-runnin'. As I states a moment ago, she stands thirteen for Old Monroe."

"'An' I says she's twelve for Old Monroe," shouts Red River Tom, crowdin' for'ard. "'You-all can't ring in Mexicans an' snake no play on us. This yere 'lection's goin' to be on the squar', or it's goin' to come off in the smoke."

"'With this, Red River, who's been sorter domineerin' at Ormsby with his six-shooter while he's freein' his mind, slams her loose. Red River over-shoots, an' Ormsby downs him with a bullet in his laig.

"'Thirteen for Old Monroe," says Ormsby.

"'But that's where the 'lection ends. Followin' the subsidence of
Red River Tom, the air is as full of lead as a bag of bullets. Through the smoke, an' the flashes, an' the noise, you can hear
Ormsby whoopin'

"'Thirteen for Old Monroe."

"'You can gamble Ormsby's as squar' a 'lection jedge as any gent could ask. You gets a play for your money with Ormsby; but he dies the next day, so he never is 'lection jedge no more. Five gents gets downed, an' a whole corralfull

111

is hurt. I, myse'f, reaps some lead in the shoulder; an' even at that I never goes nearer than the suburbs of the fight.

"'No; Cimmaron Pete claws off all sound, an' no new holes in him. But as the Dallas party, who comes caperin' over with the first shot, is layin' at the windup outside the Lone Star door, plumb defunct, thar's an end to the root of the disorder.

"'The 'lection itse'f is looked on as a draw. Old Monroe allows that, all things considered, he don't regard himse'f as 'lected none; and Randall, who a doctor is feelin' 'round in for a bullet at the time, sends over word that he indorses Old Monroe's p'sition; an' that as long as the Dallas sharp hits the trail after Glidden, an' is tharby able to look after his debts himse'f, he, Randall, holds it's no use disturbin' of a returned sereenity, an' to let everythin' go as it lays.

"'An' that,' concloods Texas Thompson, as he reaches for his licker, 'is what comes of an effort at law an' order in Plaza Paloduro. I ain't over-statin' it, gents, when I says, that that 'lection leaves me plumb gun-shy for over a year.'"

CHAPTER XL.

A WOLFVILLE FOUNDLING.

"Does Jack Moore have sand? Son, is this yere query meant for humor by you? Which for mere sand the Mohave desert is a fool to Jack."

The Old Cattleman's face was full of an earnest, fine sincerity. It was plain, too, that my question nettled the old fellow a bit; as might a doubt cast at an idol. But the sharpness had passed from his tone when he resumed

"Not only is Jack long on sand that a-way, but he's plumb loaded with what you-alls calls 'nitiative. Leastwise that's what one of these yere fernologists allows, who straggles into camp an' goes to thumbin' our bumps one day.

"'Which this young person,' says the bumpsharp, while his fingers is caperin' about on Jack's head, I is remarkable for his 'nitiative. He's the sort of gent who builds his fire before he gets his wood; an' issues more invites to drink than he receives. Which his weakness, speakin' general, is he overplays.'

"Which this yere bump party might have gone wrong in his wagers a heap of times; but he shorely calls the turn on Jack when he says he's some strong on 'nitiative.

"An' it's this yere proneness for the prematoor, an' nacheral willin'ness to open any pot that a-way, that makes Jack sech a slam- up offishul. Bein' full of 'nitiative, like this fernologist states, Jack don't idle along ontil somethin's happened. Not much; he abates it in the bud.

"Once when most of the outfit's over in Tucson, an' Jack is sorter holdin' down the camp alone, a band of rustlers comes trackin' in, allowin' they'll run Wolfville some. Which, that's where Jack's 'nitiative shows up big. He goes after 'em readily, like they's antelope. Them hold-ups is a long majority over Jack, an' heeled; but that Jack stands thar— right up ag'in the iron—an' he tells 'em what he thinks an' why he thinks it for; makes his minority report onto 'em all free, like he outnumbers 'em two to one; an' winds up by backin' the game with his gun in a way that commands confidence.

"'You-alls hears my remarks,' he says at the close, briefly flashin' his six-shooters on the outfit; 'thar ain't no band of bad men in Arizona can tree this town an' me informed. Now go slow, or I'll jest stretch a few of you for luck. It's sech consoomin' toil, a- diggin' of sepulchers in this yere rock-ribbed landscape, or I'd do it anyhow.'

"An' tharupon them rustlers, notin' Jack's got the drop on 'em, kicks up a dense cloud of dust an is seen no more.

"But bein' replete with sand an' 'nitiative, that a-way, don't state all thar is good of Jack. Let any pore, he'pless party cut Jack's trail, an' he's plumb tender. On sech times Jack's a dove; leastwise he's a dove a whole lot.

"One hot afternoon, Enright an' Doc Peets is away about some cattle I reckons. Which the rest of us is noomerous enough; an' we're sorter revolvin' 'round the post-office, a-waitin' for Old Monte an' the stage. Yere she comes, final, a-rattlin' an' a-creakin'; that old drunkard Monte a-poppin' of his whip, the six hosses on the canter, an' the whole sheebang puttin' on more dog than a Mexican officer of revenoo. When the stage draws up, Old Monte throws off the mailbags an' the Wells-Fargo box, an' gets down an' opens the door. But nobody emerges out.

"'Well, I'm a coyote! ' says Monte, a heap disgusted, `wherever is the female?'

"Then we-alls peers into the stage an' thar's only a baby, with mebby a ten-months' start down this vale of tears, inside; an' no mother nor nothin' along. Jack Moore, jest as I says when I begins, reaches in an' gets him. The baby ain't sayin' nothin', an' sorter takes it out in smilin' on Jack; which last pleases him excessive.

"'He knows me for a hundred dollars!' says Jack. 'I'm an Apache if he ain't allowin' he knows me! Wherever did you get him, Monte?'

"'Give me a drink,' says Monte, p'intin' along into the Red Light.
'This yere makes me sick.'

"After Old Monte gets about four fingers of carnation onder his belt, he turns in an' explains as how the mother starts along in the stage all right enough from Tucson. The last time he sees her, so he puts it up, is at the last station back some twenty miles in the hills; an' he s'poses all the time later, she's inside ridin' herd on her progeny, ontil now.

"'I don't reckon,' says Old Monte, lookin' gloomy-like at the infant, 'that lady is aimin' to saw this yore young-one onto the stage company none?'

"'Don't upset your whiskey frettin' about the company,' says Jack, a-plantin' of the infant on the bar, while we-alls crowds in for a look at him. `The camp'll play this hand; an' the company ain't goin' to be in it a little bit.'

"'I wish Enright an' Peets was yere,' says Cherokee Hall, 'to be heard hereon; which I shore deems this a grave occasion. Yere we- alls finds ourse'fs possessed of an onexpected child of tender years; an' the question nacheral enough is, whatever'll we do with it?'

"'Let's maverick it,' says Dan Boggs, who's a mighty good man, but onthinkful that a-way.

"'No,' says Cherokee; 'its mother'll come hoppin' along to-morrow, a-yellin'. This yere sot Monte has jest done drove off an' left her some'ers up the trail; she'll come romancin' along in time.'

"'Meanwhile,' says Jack, 'the infant's got to be took care of, to which dooty I volunteers. Thar's a tenderfoot a-sleepin' in the room back of the dance-hall, an' he's that 'feminate an' effeet, he's got a shore-'nough bed an' some goose-ha'r pillers; which the same I do yereby confiscate to public use to take care of this yearlin'. Is the sentiment pleasin'?'

"'Jack's scheme is right,' says Boggs; 'an' I'm present to announce he's allers right. Let the shorthorn go sleep onder a mesquite-bush; it'll do him good a whole lot.'

"'I'm some doobersome of this play,' says Cherokee. 'Small infants is mighty myster'ous people, an' no livin' gent is ever onto their game an' able to foresee their needs. Do you-all reckon now you can take care of this yere young-one, Jack? Be you equal to it?'

"'Take care of a small baby like this' says Jack, plenty scornful; 'which the same ain't weighin' twenty pounds? Well, it'll be some funny if I can't. I could break even with him if he's four times as big. All I asks is for you-alls to stand by in crisises an' back the play; an', that settled, you can go make side bets we-alls comes out winners on the deal.'

'I ain't absolootly shore,' says Dave Tutt, 'bein' some shy of practice with infants myse'f, but jedgin' by his lookin' smooth an' silky, I offers fifty dollars even he ain't weaned none yet.'

"'I won't bet none on his bein' weaned complete; says Jack, 'but
I'll hang up fifty he drinks outen a bottle as easy as Old Monte!

"'I'll go you once,' says Tutt; 'it's fifty dollars even he grows contemptuous at a bottle, an' disdains it.'

"Which we-alls talks it over an' decides that Jack's to nurse said infant; after which a passel of us proceed's to make a procession for the tenderfoot's bed, which he shorely resigns without a struggle. We packs it back to Jack; an' Cherokee Hall an' Boggs then goes over to the corral an' lays for a goat to milk her. This yere goat is mighty reluctant, an' refuses to enter into the sperit of the thing; but they swings an' rastles with her, makes their p'int right along, an' after a frightful time comes back with'most a dipper-full.

"'That's all right,' says Jack, who's done camped in a room back of the Red Light, 'now hop out an' tell the barkeep to give you a pint bottle. We-alls has this yere game payin' div'dends in two minutes.'

"Jack gets his bottle an' fills her up with goat's milk; an' makes a stopper outen cotton cloth an' molasses for the infant to draw it through. Which it's about this time the infant puts up a yell, an' refuses peace ag'in till Jack gives him his six-shooter to play with.

"'Which shows my confidence in him,' says Jack. 'Thar's only a few folks left I'll pass my gun to.'

"Jack gets along with him first-rate, a-feedin' of him the goat's milk, which he goes for with avidity; tharby nettin' Jack that fifty from Dave Tutt. Boggs builds a fire so Jack keeps the milk warm. Jack turns loose that earnest he don't even go for no grub; jest nacherally has 'em pack it to him.

"'We-alls'll have to stand night gyards on this yere foundlin' to- night, I reckons?" asks Boggs of Jack, when he's bringin' Jack things.

"'I s'pose most likely we'll have to make a play that a-way,' says
Jack.

"'All right,' says Boggs, tappin' his shirt with his pistol-finger; 'you-all knows me an' Cherokee. We're in on this yere any time you says.'

"So a band of us sorter camps along with Jack an' the infant ontil mebby it's second-drink time at night. The infant don't raise the war-yell once; jest takes it out in goat's milk; an' in laughin', an' playin' with Jack's gun.

"'Excuse me, gents,' finally says Jack, mighty dignified, 'but I've been figgerin' this thing, an' I allows it's time to bed this yere young-one down for the night. If you-alls will withdraw some, I'll see how near I comes to makin' runnin' of it. Stay within whoopin' distance, though; so if he tries to stampede or takes to millin' I can get he'p.'

"We-alls lines out an' leaves Jack an' the infant, an' turns in on faro an' poker an' sim'lar devices which is bein' waged in the Red Light. Mebby it's an hour when Jack comes in.

"'Boggs,' he says; 's'pose you-all sets in an' plays my hand a minute with that infant child, while I goes over an' adjourns them frivolities in the dance-hall. It looks like this yere camp is speshul toomultuous to-night.'

"Boggs goes in with the infant, an' Jack proceeds to the baile house an' states the case.

"'I don't want to onsettle the reg'lar programme,' says Jack, 'but this yere young-one I'm responsible for, gets that engaged in the sounds of these yere revels, it don't look like he's goin' to sleep none. So if you-alls will call the last waltz, an' wind her up for to-night, it'll shorely be a he'p. The kid's mother'll be yere by sun-up; which her advent that a-way alters the play all 'round, an' matters then goes back to old lines.'

"'Enough said,' says Jim Hamilton, who runs the dance-hall. 'You can gamble this temple of mirth ain't layin' down on what's right, an' tonight's shindig closes right yere. All promenade to the bar. We takes a drink on the house, quits, an' calls it a day.'

"Then Jack comes back, a heap grave with his cares, an' relieves
Boggs; who's on watch, straddled of a chair, a-eyein' of the infant,

who, a-settin' up ag'in a goose-ha'r piller, is likewise a-eyein' of
Boggs.

"'He's a 'way up good infant, Jack,' says Boggs, givin' up his seat.

"'You can bet your life he's a good infant,' says Jack; 'but it shore looks like he don't aim to turn in an' slumber none. Mebby the goat's milk is too invigeratin' for 'him, an' keeps him awake that a-way.'

"About another hour goes by, an' out comes Jack into the Red Light ag'in.

"'I ain't aimin' to disturb you-alls none,' he says, 'but, gents, if you-alls could close these games yere, an' shet up the store, I'll take it as a personal favor. He can hear the click of the chips, an' it's too many for him. Don't go away; jest close up an' sorter camp 'round quiet.'

"Which we-alls does as Jack says; closes the games, an' then sets 'round in our chairs an' keeps quiet, a-waitin' for the infant to turn in. A half-hour later Jack appears ag'in.

"'It ain't no use, gents,' he says, goin' back of the bar an' gettin' a big drink; 'that child is onto us. He won't have it. You can gamble, he's fixed it up with himse'f that he ain't goin' to sleep none to-night. I allows it's 'cause he's among rank strangers, an' he figgers it's a good safe play to lookout his game for himse'f.'

"'I wonder couldn't we sing him to sleep,' says Cherokee Hall.

"'Nothin' ag'in a try,' says Jack, some desp'rate, wipin' his lips after the drink.

"'S'pose we-alls gives him "The Dyin' Ranger" an' "Sandy Land" for an hour or so, an' see,' says Boggs.

"In we trails. Cherokee lines up on one side of the infant, an' Jack on t'other; an' the rest of us takes chairs an' camps 'round, We starts in an' shore sings him all we knows; an' we keeps it up for hours. All the time, that child is a-settin' thar, a-battin' his eyes an' a-starin', sleepless as owls. The last I remembers is Boggs's voice on 'Sandy Land'

"'Great   big   taters   on   sandy   land,
Get thar, Eli, if you can.'

"The next thing I'm aware of, thar's a whoop an' a yell outside. We- alls wakes up—all except the infant, who's wide awake all along— an' yere it is; four o'clock in the mornin', an' the mother has come. Comes over on a speshul buckboard from the station where that old inebriate, Monte, drove off an' left her. Well, son, everybody's plumb willin' an' glad to see her. An' for that matter, splittin' even, so's the infant."

CHAPTER XII.

THE MAN FROM YELLOWHOUSE.

"That's straight, son; you shorely should have seen Jack Moore," continued the Old Cattleman, after a brief pause, as he hitched his chair into a comfortable position; "not seein' Jack is what any gent might call deeprivation.

"Back in the old days," he went on, "Jack Moore, as I relates, is kettle-tender an' does the rope work of the Stranglers. Whatever is the Stranglers? Which you asks Borne late. I mentions this assembly a heap frequent yeretofore. Well, some folks calls 'em the 'vig'lance committee'; but that's long for a name, so in Wolfville we allers allooded to 'em as `Stranglers.' This yere is brief, an' likewise sheds some light.

"This Jack Moore—which I'm proud to say he's my friend— I reckons is the most pro bono publico gent in the Southwest. He's out to do anythin' from fight to fiddle at a dance, so's it's a public play.

"An' then his idees about his dooties is wide. He jest scouts far an' near, an' don't pay no more heed to distance an' fatigue than a steer does to cobwebs.

"'A offishul," says Jack, 'who don't diffuse himse'f 'round none, an' confines his endeavors to his own bailiwick, is reestricted an' oneffectooal, an' couldn't keep down crime in a village of prairie- dogs.' An' then he'd cinch on his saddle, an' mebby go curvin' off as far north as the Flint Hills, or east to the Turkey-track.

"That's right; when it comes to bein' active, Jack is what you might call an all-round seelection. An' clean strain? Game as hornets. Never knowed him to quit anythin' in his life—not even whiskey. I says to him myse'f one time: 'Jack; whyever don't you renig on whiskey? Looks like it's sorter gettin' behind you some, ain't it? Some day mebby it outholds you when you can't stand to lose.'

"'Sometimes I thinks I'll pass it up, myse'f,' says Jack, 'but don't you know, I can't do it. I'm too sperited, that a-way, an' chivalrous. That's whatever! I'm too chivalrous.' An' I shore reckons he was.

"But as for doin' his dooty! Which the same is simply relaxation to Jack Moore. I recalls one instance speshul. One day thar comes trailin' along into Wolfville a party from down 'round Yallerhouse some'ers. This yere Yallerhouse gent looks disperited an' off color as to health. But of course we-alls don't refer none to it; for whether this stranger's sick or well is his business, not ours; leastwise in its first stages. This yere's before Doc Peets inhabits Wolfville or he'd informed us touchin' this party's that a-way.

"Which the Yallerhouse gent tracks along into the Red Light, an' tells the barkeep to set out the nose-paint. He drinks alone, not invitin' of the pop'lace, whereby we knows for shore he's offen his feed.

"Well, after he corrals his forty drops, this invalid camps down in one corner of the stage station, an' next mornin' he wakes up outen his head an' plumb locoed.

"'This yere Yallerhouse man,' says Dan Boggs, comin' along into the Red Light about first-drink time the same mornin', an' speakin' general, 'is what conserv'tive opinion might call "some sick." I stops a minute ago an' asks him how he's stackin' up like, but it ain't no use. He's plumb off his mental reservation, an' crazy as a woman's watch.'

"'Whatever do you allow is the matter of him, Boggs?' asks Old   Man Enright.

"'Smallpox,' says Boggs, mighty confident.

"'Smallpox!' repeats Enright; 'be you shore?'

"'That's what I says,' answers Boggs; 'an' you can gamble my long suit is pickin' out smallpox every time. I knows the signal smoke like my own campfire.'

"'Well, see yere,' says Dave Tutt, who's come in, 'I jest now rounds up them symptoms of this Yallerhouse gent; an' talkin' of smallpox, I offers a hundred dollars even he ain't got no smallpox. Bein' out solely for legit'mate sport,' continues Tutt, 'an' not aimin' to offend Boggs none, I willin'ly calls it fifty to one hundred he ain't got nothin'.'

"'Which I takes both bets,' says Boggs, 'an' deems 'em easy. Which both is like robbin' a bird's-nest. Yere's the circ'latin' medium. Thar; cover it an' file it away with the barkeep to wait results.' So Tutt an' Boggs makes their bets mighty eager, an' the barkeep holds the stakes.

"As soon as it gets blown through Wolfville this Yallerhouse party has smallpox, everybody comes canterin' over to the Red Light, gets a drink, an' wants to hold a mass meetin' over it. By partic'lar request Enright takes the chair an' calls 'em to order.

"'This yere meetin',' says Enright, meanwhile beatin' with the butt of his six-shooter on the poker-table, 'is some sudden an' permiscus; but the objects is easy an' plain. We-alls convenes ourse'fs to consider the physical condition of this party from Yallerhouse, which report says is locoed an' can't talk none for himself. To make this inquiry a success, we-alls oughter see this Yallerhouse gent; an' as thar is fewer of him than of us, I app'ints Jack Moore, Dan Boggs, an' Short Creek Dave, a committee, of three, to bring him before us in a body. Pendin' the return of the committee the meetin' will take a drink with the chair.'

"In about no time back comes the outfit, packin' the Yallerhouse man all easy enough in a blanket, an' spreads him out on the floor. He looks sorter red 'round in spots, like somethin's been stingin' of him, but it's evident, as Boggs says, he's locoed. He lays thar, rollin' his eyes an' carryin' on to himse'f, but he don't address the chair or offer to take no part in the meetin'. Enright quaffs his drink all slow an' dignified, an' gazes at the Yallerhouse man on the floor.

"'Well, gents,' says Enright at last, settin' down his glass, an' givin' the poker-table a little tap with his gun, 'yere's the party, an' the question is now: "What's he got?" Do I hear any remarks?'

"'Bein' in the lines, Mister Pres'dent,' says Boggs, 'of previous assertion, an' for the purpose of bringin' the question squar' before this house, I now moves you this yere Yallerhouse party has the smallpox. I ain't aimin' herein at playin' it low on Tutt, an' su'gests that the chair, in puttin' the question, also informs the meetin' as to them wagers; which the money tharof is now in the war- bags of the barkeep. I believes in givin' every gent all necessary light wherein to make up his mind; an', as I says, to open the game all logical, I ag'in moves this Yallerhouse man has the smallpox.'

"'Yo tambien,' yells a Mexican over near the door.

"'Put that Greaser out!' shouts Enright, at the same time bangin' the table. 'This ain't no international incident at all, an' nothin' but the clean-strain American wolf is eligible to howl.'

"The Greaser goes out on his saddle-colored head, an' Enright   puts Boggs's motion.

"'Every gent,' says Enright, 'in favor of this Yallerhouse man havin' the smallpox, say "Aye"; contrary "No."'

"Everybody shouts 'Aye!'

"'Which the "Ayes" has it unanimous,' says Enright. 'The Yallerhouse party has the smallpox, an' the next chicken on the parliamentary roost is the question: "Whatever is to be done to make this yere malady a success?" Is thar any su'gestions?'

"'Mister Pres'dent,' says Texas Thompson, risin' in his place, 'I've done took no hand in these proceedin's so far, through ignorance of the purposes of this yere convocation. Said purposes bein' now for the first time lined out all right in my mind, an' the question bein', "What's to be done with our captive?" I asks your indulgence. My first idee is that our dooty an' our path is plain; the same bein' simply to take a lariat an' hang this Yallerhouse person to the dance-hall windmill; but this course, on second thought, seems prematoor an' the offsprings of nacheral impulse. Still, somethin' must be done; an' while my mind is by no means cl'ar, I su'gests we turn the gent over to Jack Moore, which is the marshal hereof, to ride herd on him till further orders; an' I makes a motion to that effect.'

"'Seconds the motion!' says Short Creek Dave.

"'You don't have to put that motion, Mister Pres'dent,' says Jack; 'I've been cirelin' the idee some myse'f, an' I reckons it's my dooty to take charge of this Yallerhouse gent. You can bet anythin' which gets sawed onto me as my dooty goes, an' don't make no doubt about it. Yere's how I trails out on this: If it ain't my dooty to take care of this person, whose dooty is it? 'Tain't nobody's. Tharfore I plays the hand.'

"'Which the same bein' eminent satisfactory,' says Dave Tutt, risin', as if he thinks of somethin' speshul, 'I now inquires whether this yere is held decisive of them bets I makes with Boggs. I holdin', meanwhile, contrary views emphatic.'

"'This bein' a question of priv'lege,' says Enright, 'the chair will answer it. These proceedin's decides your bets with Boggs, an' the barkeep pays Boggs the dinero. This is a gov'ment of the people, for the people, by the people, an' founded on a vox populi bluff. The voice of the majority goes. You tharfore lose your bets to Boggs; drinks on Boggs, of course. Thar is another matter,' continues Enright, 'a bet we overlooks. Takin' care of this Yallerhouse gent will cost a stack or two, an' means must be provided. I tharfore makes as an order that yereafter thar's to be a rake on tens-up or better, showed, to make a fund to back this play; said rake to go ontil Mister Moore reports said Yallerhouse gent as safe or ceased to be.'

"Jack takes this Yallerhouse party over to the calaboose an' lays him away on some blankets. The calaboose is dry, an' what you-alls might call, commodious. It's a slam-up camp; yes indeed! Never has but Steve Stevenson in it. Puts Steve in one night when he's dead- drunk. The calaboose is new then, an' we-alls is that proud an' anxious to try it an' put it to some use, we couldn't resist, so in Steve goes.

"About four hours later Steve comes back up to the Red Light, hotter'n a burnt boot. Seems like he comes to, an' is that outraged an' indignant about bein' corralled that a-way, he busts the corner outen the calaboose an' issues forth a whole lot to find who does it.

"When he comes into the Red Light he revives himse'f with a drink, an' then inquires whether it's humorous, or do we mean it? Seein' how speshul low Steve takes it, we-alls allows it's a joke; an' Steve, while he evident feels some fretted, concloods to let it go at that.

"But on account of the hole through which Steve emerges, an' which he makes liberal an' big, the calaboose is a mighty commodious place. So Jack beds down the Yallerhouse man all right an' starts in to bringin' him through. The rest of us don't crowd 'round none to watch the play, don't hover over it that a-way, 'cause we ain't aimin' to acquire nothin' ourse'fs.

"Jack has a heap of trouble an' worry. Never sees no smallpox do you? Folks locoed most usual,—clean off up in the air an' pitchin' on their ropes. Of course the Yallerhouse gent has all he needs. That rake on tens-up them days would have took care of a fam'ly. But he keeps Jack herdin' him all the time. Otherwise, not bein' watched, an' crazy that a-way, he's liable to come stampedin' over to the Red Light, or some'ers else, any time, an' skeer us up some.

"'He's a world-beater,' says Jack one day, when he comes over for a drink. 'He's shorely four kings an' an ace. You can't ride him with buckin'-straps an' a Spanish bit. It's got so now—his disease bein' at a crisis like—that I simply has to be with this Yallerhouse party day an' night. He'd shorely lay waste this camp if I didn't.'

"At last the Yallerhouse party an' Jack somehow beats the smallpox, but Yallerhouse comes out shy an eye. The smallpox gouges it out one of them times when Jack ain't lookin' out his game sharp. It's his pistol eye, too; which makes him feel the loss more keen, an' creates general sympathy. The Yallerhouse man gets some morose over it, which ain't, after all, onnacheral. A gent ain't got so many eyes he can afford to go short one on every little game he plays. So he finds fault with Jack a lot, an' allows if he has him back in the States he'd sue him for neglect of dooty.

"'Which, I shorely likes that!' says Jack to the Yallerhouse party, gettin' peevish over his fault-findin'. 'Don't you know it's merely owin' to the mercy of hell an' my watchful care, you-all ain't bustin' your harp-strings an' raisin' all round discord among the heavenly hosts on high right now, instead of bein' safe an' well yere in Wolfville? You don't act like a gent who saveys when he makes a winnin'. S'pose you be an eye out; you're still lookin' at things terrestrial with the other. You talks of gross neglect of dooty! Now let me inform you of somethin': You come pesterin' 'round me some more an' I'll bend a gun over your head.'

"'Which if it ain't my six-shooter eye which's out,' says the Yallerhouse party, mighty ugly, 'do you know what I'd do?

131

Well, this yere would be the basis of a first-class gun-play. You can gamble thar wouldn't be no jim-crow marshal go pirootin' 'round, losin' no eye of mine an' gettin' away with it, an' then talk of bendin' guns on me; none whatever.'

"But it all preys on Jack. An' a-seein' of this Yallerhouse gent 'round camp a-lookin' at him in a fault-findin' way outen his one eye sorter aggravates Jack like it's a nightmare.

"'I wouldn't mind it so much,' says Jack to me, confidential, 'if this Yallerhouse gent quits a laig or an arm behind, 'cause in which event we pieces him out with wood, easy. But about eyes, it's different. An eye out is an eye out; an' that settles it.'

"One day Jack can't b'ar it no longer, an', resolvin' to end it, he walks up to the Yallerhouse party in the Red Light, all brisk an' brief.

"'It's a rough deal on a one-eyed gent,' says Jack, 'an' I shore asks pardon an' states regrets in advance. But things has got to a show-down. I'm slowly becomin' onfit for public dooty. Now yere's an offer, an' you can have either end. You-all can get a hoss an' a hundred dollars of me, an' pull your freight; or you can fix yourse'f with a gun an' have a mighty stirrin' an' eventful time with me right yere. As an outcome of the last, the public will have one of us to plant, an' mebby a vacancy to fill in the post of kettle-tender. Which is it, an' what do you say?'

"'What for a hoss is she?' asked the Yallerhouse party.

"'Which she's a pinto,' says Jack; 'as excellent a paint pony as ever is roped.'

"'Does this yere threat you-all makes incloode a saddle an' spurs?' asks the Yallerhouse party.

"'It shorely does,' replies Jack. 'Is it a go?'

"'Well,' says the Yallerhouse man, after ponderin' it up one way an' down the other, 'this idee of settlin' for eyes for a hoss an' a hundred dollars is far from bein' usual with me. If I has my eye ag'in, I'd shorely stay an' shoot it out, an' admire to be present. But now sech thoughts is vanity. So round up your money an' your pony at the Red Light in fifteen minutes by the watch, an' as soon as I gets a bottle filled I'm ready to go. I shorely should not regret leavin' an' outfit which puts folks in jail for bein' sick, an' connives by reckless an' criminal neglect of dooty at their bein' blinded for life.'"

CHAPTER XIII.

JACKS UP ON EIGHTS.

"No; you can hazard your wealth a lot, thar's no sooperstition lurkin' 'round in me or my environs; none whatever. I attaches no importance to what you-all calls omens."

Somebody had undertaken a disquisition on dreams, and attempted to cite instances where the future had been indicated in these hazy visions of our sleep. This had served to turn the Old Cattleman's train of thought upon the weird.

"Thar's signs, of course, to which I'd shorely bow, not to say pay absorbin' heed. If some gent with whom I chooses to differ touchin' some matter that's a heap relevant at the time, ups an' reaches for his gun abrupt, it fills me full of preemonitions that the near future is mighty liable to become loaded with lead an' interest for me. Now thar's an omen I don't discount. But after all I ain't consentin' to call them apprehensions of mine the froot of no sooperstition, neither. I'm merely chary; that's all.

"It's Cherokee Hall who is what I onhesitatin'ly describes as sooperstitious. Cherokee is afflicted by more signs an' omens in carryin' on his business than an almanac. It's a way kyardsharps gets into, I reckons; sorter grows outen their trade. Leastwise I never creeps up on one yet who ain't bein' guided by all sorts of miracles an' warnin's that a-way. An' sometimes it does look like they acquires a p'inter that comes to 'em on straight lines. As 'llustratin' this yere last, it returns to me some vivid how Cherokee an' Boggs gets to prophesyin' one day, an' how they calls off the play between 'em so plumb c'rrect that a-way, it's more than amazin'; it's sinister.

"It's a hot August day, this occasion I has in mind, an' while not possessin' one of them heat-gauges to say ackerate, I'm allowin' it's ridin' hard on sech weather as this. A band of us is at the post-office a-wrastlin' our letters, when in trails Cherokee Hall lookin' some moody, an' sets himse'f down on a box.

"'Which you-all no doubt allows you'll take some missives yourse'f this mornin',' says Doc Peets, a-noticin' of his gloom, an' aimin' to p'int his idees up some other trail. Doc, himse'f, is feelin' some gala. 'Pass over them documents for Cherokee Hall, an' don't hold out nothin' onto us. We-alls is 'way too peevish to stand any offishul gaieties to-day.'

"'Thar's no one weak-minded 'nough to write to me none,' says Cherokee. `Which I remarks this yere phenomenon with pleasure. Mail- bags packs more grief than joy, an' I ain't honin' for no hand in the game whatever. It's fifteen years since I buys a stamp or gets a letter, an' all thirst tharfor is assuaged complete.'

"'Fifteen years is shore a long time,' says Enright, sorter to himse'f, an' then we-alls hops into our letters ag'in. Finally Cherokee breaks in once more.

"` I ain't aimin' to invest Wolfville in no sooperstitious fears,' says Cherokee, 'an' I merely chronicles as a current event how I was settin' into a little poker last night, an' three times straight I picks up "the hand the dead man held," jacks up on eights, an' it wins every time.'

"`Who lose to it?' asks Dan Boggs.

"'Why,' says Cherokee, 'it's every time that old longhorn as comes in from Tucson back some two weeks ago.'

"'That settles it,' says Boggs, mighty decided. 'You can bet your saddle an' throw the pony in, Death is fixin' his sights for him right now. It's shorely a warnin', an' I'm plumb glad it ain't none of the boys; that's all.'

"You see this yere stranger who Cherokee alloods at comes over from Tucson a little while before. He has long white ha'r an' beard, an', jedgin' from the rings on his horns, he's mebby a-comin' sixty. He seems like he's plenty of money, an' we takes it he's all right. His leavin' Tucson shows he has sense, so we cashes him in at his figger. Of course we-alls never asks his name none, as askin' names an' lookin' at the brands on a pony is speshul roode in the West, an' shows your bringin' up; but he allows he's called 'Old Bill Gentry ' to the boys, an' he an' Faro Nell's partic'lar friendly.

"'Talkin' to him,' says Nell, ' is like layin' in the shade. He knows everythin', too; all about books an' things all over the world. He was a-tellin' me, too, as how he had a daughter like me that died 'way back some'ers about when I was a yearlin'. He feels a heap bad about it yet, an' I gets so sorry for him; so old an' white-ha'red.'

"'An' you can gamble,' says Dave Tutt, 'if Nell likes him, he's all right.'

"'If Nell likes him, that makes him all right,' says Cherokee.

"We-alls is still talkin' an' readin over our mail in the post-office, when all at once we hears Jack Moore outside.

"'What's this yere literatoor as affronts my eyes, pasted onto the outside of Uncle Sam's wickeyup?' says Jack, mighty truculent. We. alls goes out, an' thar, shore-'nough, is a notice offerin' fifteen hundred dollars reward for some sharp who's been a-standin' up the stage over towards Prescott.

"'Whoever tacks this up? I wonder,' says Enright. `It never is yere ten minutes ago.'

"'Well, jest you-all hover 'round an' watch the glory of its comin' down,' says Jack, a-cuttin' of it loose with his bowie, an' tearin' it up. 'I yerewith furnishes the information cold, this camp of Wolfville knows its business an' don't have to be notified of nothin'. This yere outfit has a vig'lance committee all reg'lar, which I'm kettle-tender tharfor, an' when it comes nacheral to announce some notice to the public, you-alls will perceive me a- pervadin' of the scenery on a hoss an' promulgatin' of said notice viver voce. Am I right, Enright?'

"'Right as preachin', Jack,' says Enright. 'You speaks trooth like a runnin' brook.'

"'But whoever sticks that notice?—that's the information I pants for,' says Boggs, pickin' up an' readin' of the piece. "'I reckons I posts that notice some myse'f,' says a big, squar'-built gent we- alls don't know, an' who comes in the other mornin' with Old Monte on the stage. As he says this he's sa'nterin' about the suburbs of the crowd, listenin' to the talk.

"'Well, don't do it no more, partner,' says Jack, mighty grave. 'As a commoonity Wolfville's no doubt 'way wrong, but we-alls has our prides an' our own pecooliar little notions, that a-way, about what looks good; so, after now, don't alter the landscape none 'round yere till you c'lects our views.'

"'I'm offerin' even money, postin' notices don't hurt this yere camp a little bit,' says the stranger.

"'Comin' right to cases,' says Enright, 'it don't hurt none, but it grates a whole lot. The idee of a mere stranger a-strollin' in an' a-pastin' up of notices, like he's standin' a pat hand on what he knows an' we not in it, is a heap onpleasant. So don't do it no more.'

"'Which I don't aim to do it no more,' says the squar'-built gent, 'but I still clings to my idee that notices ain't no set-back to this camp.'

"'The same bein' a mere theery,' says Doc Peets, 'personal to yourse'f, I holds it would be onp'lite to discuss it; so let's all wheel onder cover for a drink.'

"At this we-alls lines up on the Red Light bar an' nacherally drinks ends the talk, as they allers ought.

"Along towards sundown we-alls gets some cooler, an' by second-drink time in the evenin' every one is movin' about, an', as it happens, quite a band is in the Red Light; some drinkin' an' exchangin' of views, an' some buckin' the various games which is goin' wide open all 'round. Cherokee's settin' behind his box, an' Faro Nell is up at his shoulder on the lookout stool. The game's goin' plenty lively when along comes Old Gentry. Cherokee takes a glance at him an' seems worried a little, reflectin', no doubt, of them 'hands the dead man held,' but he goes on dealin' without a word.

"'Where's you-all done been all day?' says Nell to the old man. 'I ain't seen you none whatever since yesterday.'

"'Why, I gets tired an' done up a lot, settin ag'inst Cherokee last night,' says the old man, 'an' so I prowls down in my blankets an' sleeps some till about an hour ago.'

"The old man buys a stack of blues an' sets 'em on the ten. It's jest then in comes the squar'-built gent, who's been postin' of the notice former, an' p'ints a six-shooter at Gentry an' says

"'Put your hands up! put 'em up quick or I'll drill you! Old as you be, I don't take no chances.'

"'At the first word Nell comes off her stool like a small landslide, while Cherokee brings a gun into play on the instant. The old man's up even with the proceedin's, too; an' stands thar, his gun in his hand, his eyes a-glitterin' an' his white beard a-curlin' like a cat's. He's clean strain.

"'Let me get a word in, gents,' says Cherokee, plenty ca'm, 'an' don't no one set in his stack on. less he's got a hand. I does business yere my way, an' I'm due to down the first hold-up who shoots across any layout of mine. Don't make no mistake, or the next census'll be shy, shore.'

"'What be you-alls aimin' to cel'brate anyhow?' says Jack Moore, gettin' the squar'-built gent's gun while Boggs corrals Gentry's. ' Who's Wolfville entertainin' yere, I'd like for to know?'

"'I'm a Wells-Fargo detective,' says the squar'-built gent, 'an' this yere,' p'intin' to Old Gentry, 'is Jim Yates, the biggest hold- up an' stage-robber between hell an' 'Frisco. That old tarrapin'll stop a stage like a young-one would a clock, merely to see what's into it. He's the party I'm pastin' up the notice for this mornin."

"'He's a liar!' says the old man, a-gettin' uglier every minute. `Give us our six-shooters an throw us loose, an' if I don't lance the roof of his lyin' mouth with the front sight of my gun, I'll cash in for a hold-up or whatever else you-alls says.'

"'What do you say, Enright?' says Jack. 'Let's give 'em their jewelry an' let 'em lope. I've got money as says the Wells-Fargo bill-paster can't take this old' Cimmaron a little bit.'

"'Which I trails in,' says Boggs, 'with a few chips on the same kyard.'

"'No,' says Enright, 'if this yere party's rustlin' the mails, we-alls can't call his hand too quick. Wolfville's a straight camp an' don't back no crim'nal plays; none whatever.'

"Enright tharupon calls a meetin' of the Stranglers, an' we-alls lines out for the New York Store to talk it over. Before we done pow-wows two minutes up comes Old Monte, with the stage, all dust an' cuss-words, an' allows he's been stood up out by the cow springs six hours before, an' is behind the mail-bag an' the Adams Company's box on the deal. We-alls looks at Old Man Gentry, an' he shorely seems to cripple down. "'Gentry,' says Peets, after Old Monte tells his adventures, 'I hears you tell Nell you was sleepin' all day. S'pose you takes this yere committee to your budwer an' exhibits to us how it looks some.'

"'The turn's ag'in me,' says the old man, 'an' I lose. I'll cut it short for you-alls. I holds up that stage this afternoon myse'f.'

"'This yere's straight goods, I takes it,' says Enright, 'an' our dooty is plain. Go over to the corral an' get a lariat, Jack.'

"'Don't let Enright hang the old man, Cherokee,' says Nell, beginnin' to weep a whole lot. 'Please don't let 'em hang him.'

"'This holdin' a gun on your friends ain't no picnic,' whispers Cherokee to Nell, an' flushin' up an' then turnin' pale, 'but your word goes with me, Nell.' Then Cherokee thinks a minute. 'Now, this yere is the way we does,' he says at last. 'I'll make 'em a long talk. You-all run over to the corral an' bring the best hoss you sees saddled. I'll be talkin' when you comes back, an' you creep up an' whisper to the old man to make a jump for the pony while I covers the deal with my six-shooter. It's playin' it low on Enright an' Doc Peets an' the rest, but I'll do it for you, Nell. It all comes from them jacks up on eights.'

"With this, Cherokee tells Nell 'good-by,' an' squar's himse'f. He begins to talk, an' Nell makes a quiet little break for the corral.

"But no hoss is ever needed. Cherokee don't talk a minute when Old Gentry comes buckin' offen his chair in a 'pleptic fit. A 'pleptic fit is permiscus an' tryin', an' when Old Gentry gets through an' comes to himse'f, he's camped jest this side of the dead line. He can only whisper.

"'Come yere,' says he, motionin' to Cherokee. 'Thar's a stack of blues where I sets 'em on the ten open, which you ain't turned for none yet: Take all I has besides an' put with it. If it lose, it's yours; if it win, give it to the little girl.'

"This is all Old Gentry says, an' he cashes in the very next second on the list.

"Enright goes through'em, an' thar's over two thousand dollars in his war-bags; an', obeyin' them last behests, we-alls goes over to the Red Light an' puts it on the ten along of the stack of blues. It's over the limit, but Cherokee proceeds with the deal, an' when it comes I'm blessed if the ten ain't loser an' Cherokee gets it all.

"'But I won't win none ag'in a dead man; says Cherokee. An' he gives it to Nell, who ain't sooperstitious.

"'Do you-alls b'ar in mind,' says Boggs, as we takes a drink later, 'how I foresees this yere racket the minute I hears Cherokee a- tellin' about his "Jacks up on eights"—the "hand the dead man holds?"'"

CHAPTER XIV.

THE RIVAL DANCE-HALLS.

It was sweet and cool after the rain, and the Old Cattleman and I, moved by an admiration for the open air which was mutual, found ourselves together on the porch.

As in part recompense for his reminiscences of the several days before, I regaled my old friend with the history of a bank-failure, the details as well as the causes of which were just then forcing themselves upon me in the guise of business.

"The fact is," I said, as I came to the end of my story, "the fact is, the true cause of this bank's downfall was a rivalry—what one might call a business feud—which grew into being between it and a similar institution which had opened as its neighbor. In the competition which fell out they fairly cut each other's throat. They both failed."

"An' I takes it," remarked the Old Cattleman in comment, "one of these yere trade dooels that a-way goes on vindictive an' remorseless, same as if it's a personal fight between cow-folks over cattle."

"Quite right," I said. "Money is often more cruel than men; and a business vendetta is frequently mere murder without the incident of blood. I don't suppose the life of your Arizona town would show these trade wars. It would take Eastern—that is, older—conditions, to provoke and carry one on."

"No," replied the old gentleman, with an air of retrospection, "I don't recall nothin' of the sort in Wolfville. We're too much

144

in a huddle, anyway; thar ain't room for no sech fracas, no how. Now the nearest we-alls comes to anythin' of the kind is when the new dance- hall starts that time.

"Which I reckons," continued the Old Cattle. man, as he began arranging a smoke, "which I now reckons this yere is the only catyclism in trade Wolfville suffers; the only time it comes to what you-all Eastern sports would call a showdown in commerce. Of course thar's the laundry war, but that's between females an' don't count. Females—while it's no sorter doubt they's the noblest an' most exhilaratin' work of their Redeemer—is nervous that a-way, an' due any time to let their ha'r down their backs, emit a screech, an' claw an' lay for each other for luck. An', as I says, if you confines the festivities to them females engaged, an' prevents the men standin' in on the play, it's shore to wind up in sobs an' forgiveness, an' tharfore it don't go.

"As I says, what I now relates is the only industrial trouble I recalls in Wolfville. I allers remembers it, 'cause, bein' as how I knows the party who's the aggravatin' cause tharof, it mortifies me the way he jumps into camp an' carries on.

"When I sees him first is ages before, when I freights with eight mules over the Old Fort Bascome trail from Vegas to the Panhandle. This sharp—which he's a tenderfoot at the time, but plumb wolf by nacher-trails up to me in the Early Rose Saloon in Vegas one day, an' allows he'd like to make a deal an' go projectin' over into the Panhandle country with me for a trip. "Freightin' that a-way three weeks alone on the trail is some harrowin' to the sperits of a gent who loves company like me, so I agrees, an' no delay to it.

"Which I'm yere to mention I regrets later I'm that easy I takes this person along. Not that he turns hostile, but he's allers havin' adventures, an' things keeps happenin' to him; an' final, I thinks he's shorely dead an' gone complete—the same, as I afterward learns, bein' error; an', takin' it up one trail an' down another, that trip breaks me offen foolin' with shorthorns complete, an' I don't go near 'em for years, more'n if they's stingin' lizards.

"Whatever does this yere maverick do to me? Well, nothin' much to me personal; but he keeps a-breedin' of events which pesters me.

"We're out about four days when them mishaps begins. I camps over one sun on the Concha to rest my mules. I'm loaded some heavy with six thousand pounds in the lead, an' mebby four thousand pounds in the trail wagon; an' I stops a day to give my stock a chance to roll an' breathe an' brace up. My off-wheel mule—a reg'lar shave-tail— is bad med'cine. Which he's not only eager to kick towerists an' others he takes a notion ag'inst; but he's likewise what you-alls calls a kleptomaniac, an' is out to steal an' sim'lar low-down plays.

"I warns this yere tenderfoot—his name's Smith, but I pulls on him when conversin' as 'Colonel'—I warns this shorthorn not to fuss 'round my Jerry mule, bein', as I states, a mule whose mood is ornery.

"'Don't go near him, Colonel,' says I; 'an' partic'lar don't go crowdin' 'round to get no r'ar views of him. You-all has no idee of the radius of that mule; what you might call his sweep. You never will till he's kicked you once or twice, an' the information ain't worth no sech price. So I don't reckon I'd fool with him, none whatever.

"'An' speshul, Colonel,' I goes on, for I shore aims to do my dooty by him, 'don't lay nothin' 'round loose where this yere Jerry mule can grab it off. I'm the last freighter on the Plains to go slanderin' an' detractin' of a pore he'pless mule onless it's straight; but if you-all takes to leavin' keepsakes an' mementoes layin' about casooal an' careless that a-way, Jerry'll eat 'em; an' the first you saveys your keepsakes is within Jerry's interior, an' thar you be.

"'The fact is, stranger, this Jerry mule's a thief,' I says. 'If he's a human, Jerry would be lynched. But otherwise he's a sincere, earnest mule; an up hill or at a quicksand crossin' Jerry goes into his collar like a lion; so I forgives him bein' a thief an' allows it's a peccadillo."

"'Well, you bet!' says this tenderfoot Colonel, 'this yere Jerry better not come no peccadillos on me.'

"'If you-all maintains about twenty feet,' I replies, 'between Jerry's hind-Hocks an' you; an' if you keeps your bric-a-brac in your war-bags, you an' Jerry'll get along like lambs. Now, I warns you, an' that's got to do. If Jerry an' you gets tangled up yereafter you-all ain't goin' to harbor no revenges ag'in him, nor make no ranikaboo plays to get even.'

"As I states, I'm camped on the Concha, an` the Colonel, who's allers out to try experiments an' new deals, puts it up he'll go down to the river an' take a swim. Tharupon he lines out for the water.

"Jerry's hangin' about camp—for he's sorter a pet mule—allowin' mebby I submits a ham-rind or some sech delicacy to him to chew on; an' he hears the Colonel su'gest he'll swim some. So when the Colonel p'ints for the Concha, Jerry

147

sa'nters along after, figgerin', mighty likely, as how he'll pass the hour a-watchin' the Colonel swim.

"I'm busy on flapjacks at the time—which flapjacks is shore good food—an' I don't observe nothln' of Jerry nor the Colonel neither. They's away half an hour when I overhears ejac'lations, though I can't make out no words. I don't have to get caught in no landslide to tumble to a game, an' I'm aware at once that Jerry an' the Colonel has got their destinies mixed.

"Nacherally, I goes over to the held of strife, aimin' to save Jerry, or save the Colonel, whichever has the other down. When I bursts on the scene, the Colonel starts for me, splutterin' an' makin' noises an' p'intin' at Jerry, who stands thar with an air of innocence. The Colonel's upper lip hangs down queer, like an ant- eater's, an' he can't talk. It's all mighty amazin'.

"'What's all this toomult about?' I says.

"The short of the riot is this: The Colonel goes in for a swim, an' he lays out his false teeth that a-way on a stone. When he comes for his teeth they's shorely gone, an' thar stands Jerry puttin' it on he's asleep. Them teeth is filed away in Jerry.

"Which the Colonel raves 'round frightful, an' wants to kill Jerry an' amputate him, an' scout for the teeth. But I won't have it. I'm goin' to need Jerry down further on the quicksand fords of the Canadian; an', as I explains, them teeth is a wreck by now, an' no good if he get's 'em ag'in; Jerry munchin' of his food powerful.

"After a while I rounds up the Colonel an' herds him back to camp. Jerry has shore sawed off a sore affliction on that tenderfoot when he takes in them teeth; I can see that. His lip hangs like a blacksmith's apron, an' he can't talk a little bit; jest makes signs or motions, like he's Injun or deef.

"It's mebby two weeks later when Jerry gets another shot at the Colonel. It's the evenin' after the night Jerry sneaks into camp, soft-foot as a coyote, noses open the grub-box, an' eats five bottles of whiskey; all we has. We've pitched camp, an' I've hobbled this Jerry mule an' his mate—the other wheeler—an' throwed 'em loose, an' is busy hobblin' my nigh-swing mule, when trouble begins fomentin' between my tenderfoot an' Jerry.

"The fact is it's done fomented. This Colonel, bein' some heated about that whiskey, an' plumb sore on Jerry on account of them teeth, allows to himse'f he'll take a trace-chain an' warp Jerry once for luck.

"If this yere tenderfoot had been free with me, an' invited me into his confidence touchin' his designs, I'd took a lariat an' roped an' throwed Jerry for him, an' tied the felon down, an' let the Colonel wallop him an hour or so: but the Colonel's full of variety that a- way, or mebby he thinks I'll side with Jerry. Anyhow, he selects a trace-chain, an', without sayin' a word, dances all cautious towards his prey. Which this is relaxation for Jerry.

[drawing of Jerry kicking the Colonel with caption: "That he'pless shorthorn stops both heels.]

"While that Colonel tenderfoot is a rod away, Jerry turns his tail some sudden in his direction, an' the next instant that he'pless shorthorn stops both heels some'ers about the second button of his shirt. That settles it; the Colonel's an invalid immediate. I shorely has a time with him that night.

149

"The next day he can't walk, an' he can't ride in the wagon 'cause of the jolts. It all touches my heart, an' at last I ups an' make a hammock outen a Navajo blanket, which is good an' strong, an' swings the Colonel to the reach of the trail wagon.

"It's mostly a good scheme. Where the ground's level the Colonel comes on all right; but now an' then, when a wheel slumps into a rut, the Colonel can't he'p none but smite the ground where he's the lowest, an' it all draws groans an' laments from him a heap.

"One time, when the Colonel's agony makes him groan speshul strong, I sees Jerry bat his eyes like he enjoys it; an' then Jerry mentions somethin' to his mate over the chain. We're trottin' along the trail at the time, an', bein' he's the nigh-wheeler—which is the saddle- mule of a team—I'm ridin' Jerry's compadre, an' when I notes how Jerry is that joyous about it I reaches across an' belts him some abrupt between the y'ears with the butt of a shot-filled black- snake. It rather lets the whey outen Jerry's glee, an' he don't get so much bliss from that tenderfoot's misfortunes as he did.

"It goes along all right ontil I swings down to the crossin' of the Canadian. It's about fourth-drink time in the afternoon, an' I'm allowin' to ford the Canadian that evenin' an' camp on t'other side. The river is high an' rapid from rain some'ers back on its head waters, an' it's wide an' ugly. It ain't more'n four foot deep, but the bottom is quicksand, an' that false, if I lets my wagons stop ten seconds anywhere between bank an' bank, I'm goin' to be shy wagons at the close. I'll be lucky if I win out the mules. It's shore a hard, swift crossin'.

"I swings down, as I says, to the river's aige with my mind filled up about the rush I've got to make. It's go through on the run or bog down. First I settles in my saddle, gives the outfit the word, an' then, pourin' the whip into the two leaders, I sends the whole eight into the water on the jump. The river is runnin' like a scared wolf, an' the little lead mules hardly touches bottom.

"As the trail wagon takes the water, an' the two leaders is plumb in to the y'ears, a howl develops to the r'ar. It's my pore tenderfoot in his hammock onder the trail wagon. He shrieks as the water gets to him; an' it all hits me like a bullet, for I plumb overlooks him, thinkin' of that quicksand crossin'.

"It's shore too late now; I'm in, an' I can't stop. To make things more complex, as the water cuts off the tenderfoot's yell like puffin' out a candle, a little old black mule, which is my off- p'inter, loses his feet an' goes down. I pours the leather into the team the harder, an' the others soars into their collars an' drug my black p'inter with 'em; only he's onder water. Of course I allows both the black p'inter an' the Colonel's shorely due to drown a whole lot.

"We gets across, the seven other mules an' me; an' the second he's skated out on the sand on his side, the drowned mule gets up an' sings as triumphant as I ever hears. Swimmin' onder the river don't wear on him a bit.

"Then I goes scoutin' for the Colonel, but he's vanished complete. Nacherally, I takes him for a dead-an'-gone gent; an' figgers if some eddy or counter-current don't get him, or he don't go aground on no sand-bar, his fellow-men will fish him out some'ers between me an' New Orleans, an' plant him an' hold services over him.

"Bein' as I can't be of no use where it's a clean-sweep play like this, I dismisses the Colonel from my mind. After hobblin' an' throwin' loose my team, I lugs out the grub-box all sorrowful an' goes into camp.

"Which I should allers have played the Colonel for dead, if it ain't that years later he one day comes wanderin' into Wolfville. He ain't tender now; he's as hard as moss-agates, an' as worthless.

"I renews my acquaintance with him, an' he tells how he gets outen the Canadian that day; but beyond that we consoomes a drink or two together, I rather passes him up. Thar's a heap about him I don't take to.

"The Colonel lays 'round Wolfville mebby it's a week, peerin' an' spyin' about. He says he's lookin' for an openin'. An' I reckons he is, for at the end of a week he slaps up a joint outen tent-cloth an' fence-boards, an' opens a dance-hall squar' ag'inst Jim Hamilton's which is already thar.

"This yere alone is likely to brood an' hatch trouble; but, as if takin' a straight header into Hamilton's game ain't enough, this Colonel of mine don't get no pianer; don't round-up no music of his own; but stands pat an' pulls off reels, an' quadrilles, an' green- corn dances to Hamilton's music goin' on next door.

"I'm through the Lincoln County war, an' has been romancin' about the frontier for years; but I never tracks up on no sech outrage in my life as this disgraceful Colonel openin' a hurdy-gurdy ag'in Hamilton's, an' maverickin' his music that a-way, an' dancin' tharunto.

"It's the second night, an' Hamilton concloods he'll see about it some. He comes into the Colonel's joint, ca'm an' considerate, an' gives it out thar's goin' to be trouble if the Colonel don't close his game or play in his own fiddlers.

"'Which if you-all don't close your game or hunt out your own music,' says Hamilton, 'I'm mighty likely to get my six-shooter an' close it for you.'

"'See yere,' says my Colonel—which he's shore been learnin' since I parts with him on the Canadian—'the first hold-up who comes foolin' 'round to break up a baile of mine, I'll shorely make him hard to find. What business you got fillin' up my place with your melodies? You rolls your tunes in yere like you owns the ranch; an' then you comes curvin' over an' talks of a gun-play 'cause, instead of layin' for you for that you disturbs my peace with them harmonies, I'm that good-nachered I yields the p'int an' dances to 'em. You-all pull your freight,' says the Colonel, 'or I'll fill you full of lead.'

"This argument of the Colonel's dazzles Hamilton to that degree he don't know whether he's got the high hand or not. He thinks a minute, an' then p'ints over to the Red Light for Enright an' Doc Peets. As he leaves the rival dance-hall, the Colonel, who's callin' off his dances, turns to the quadrille, which is pausin pendin' the dispoote, an' shouts:

"'You bet I knows my business! Right hand to your partner; grand right an' left!'

"When Hamilton turns away they's shore makin' things rock an' tremble; an' all to the strains of 'The Arkansaw Traveller,' which is bein' evolved next door at Hamilton's expense.

"Which somethin's goin' to pop; says Hamilton, mighty ugly to Enright an' the rest of us, as he pours a drink into his neck.

153

'I allows in the interests of peace that I canters over an' sees you- alls first. I ain't out to shake up Wolfville, nor give Red Dog a chance to criticise us none as a disorderly camp; but I asks you gents, as citizens an' members of the vig'lance committee, whether I'm to stand an' let this yere sharp round-up my music to hold his revels by, an' put it all over me nightly?'

'"I don't see no difference,' says Dan Boggs, 'between this convict a-stealin' of Hamilton's music, than if he goes an' stands up Old Monte an' the stage.'

'"The same bein' my idee exact,' says Texas Thompson. 'Yere's Hamilton caterin' to this camp with a dance-hall. It's a public good thing. If a gent's morose, an' his whiskey's slow placin' itse'f, he goes over to Hamilton's hurdy-gurdy an' finds relaxation an' relief. Now yere comes this stranger— an' I makes it fifty dollars even he's from Massachusetts— an' what does he do? Never antes nor sticks in a white chip, but purloins Hamilton's strains, an' pulls off his dances tharby. It's plumb wrong, an' what this party needs is hangin'.'

'"Oh, I don't know,' says Cherokee Hall, who's in on the talk. 'Hamilton's all right, an' a squar' man. All he wants is jestice. Now, while I deems the conduct of this stranger low an' ornery; still, comin' down to the turn, he's on his trail all right. As this sharp says: Who gives Hamilton any license to go fillin' his hurdy- gurdy full of dance-music? S'pose this gent would come caperin' over an' set in a stack ag'in Hamilton for overloadin' his joint with pianer an' fiddle noises without his consent; an' puttin' it up he's out to drag the camp if Hamilton don't cease? The only way Hamilton gets 'round that kind of complaint is, he don't own them walses an' quadrilles after they fetches loose from his fiddle; that they ain't his quadrilles no more, an' he's not responsible after they stampedes off into space.'

"'That's straight,' says Dave Tutt, 'you-alls can't run no brand on melodies. A gent can't own no music after he cuts it loose that a- way. The minute it leaves the bosoms of his fiddles, that's where he lets go. After that it belongs to any gent to dance by, cry by, set by, or fight by, as he deems meet an' pleasant at the time.'

"'What do you-alls say?' says Hamilton to Enright an' Peets. 'Does this yere piece of oppression on a leadin' citizen, perpetrated by a rank outsider, go? I shore waits for your reply with impatience, for I eetches to go back an' shoot up this new hurdy-gurdy from now till sun-up.'

"Enright takes Doc Peets down by the end of the bar—an' thar's no doubt about it, that Peets is the wisest longhorn west of the Missoury—an' they has a deep consultation. We-alls is waitin'. some interested, to see what they says. It's shore a fine p'int this Colonel's makin' to jestify an' back his game.

"'Get a move on you, Enright!' at last says Dan Boggs, who is a hasty, eager man, who likes action; 'get a move on you, you an' Peets, an' settle this. You're queerin' the kyards an' delayin' the play.'

"'Well, gents,' says Enright at last, comin' back where we-alls is by the door, 'Peets an' me sees no need decidin' on them questions about who owns a tune after said tune has been played. But thar is a subject, that a-way, which requires consideration; an' which most likely solves this dance-hall deadlock. In all trade matters in a growin' camp like Wolfville, it's better to preserve a equilibrium. It's ag'in

155

public interest to have two or three dance-halls, or two or three saloons, all in a bunch that a-way. It's better they be spraddled 'round wide apart, which is more convenient. So Peets an' me proposes as a roole for this yere camp that two hurdy-gurdies be forbid to be carried on within five hundred feet of each other. As it looks like nobody objects, we concloods it's adopted. Nacherally, the last hurdy-gurdy up has to move, which disposes of this yere trouble.'

"'Before I ends what I has to say,' goes on Enright, 'I wants to thank our townsman, Mister Hamilton, for consultin' of the Stranglers prior to a killin'. It shows he's a law-abidin' gent an' a credit to the camp. An' mighty likely he prolongs his stay on earth. If he'd pranced in an' skelped this maraudin' stranger, I don't reckon we could avoid swingin' him at the end of a lariat without makin' a dangerous preceedent. As it is, his rival will be routed an' his life made sereen as yeretofore.'

"'As to the execution of this new roole,' concloods Enright, 'we leaves that to Jack Moore. He will wait on this party an' explain the play. He must up stakes an' move his camp; an' if he calls on another shindig after he's warned, we-alls takes our ponies an' our ropes an' yanks his outfit up by the roots. A gent of his enterprise, however, will come to a dead halt; an' his persecutions of Hamilton will cease.'

"'An' you-all calls this yere a free American outfit!' says my Colonel, mighty scornful, when Jack Moore notifies him. 'If I don't line out for t'other end of camp you-alls is allowin' to rope my joint an' pull it down! Well, that lets me out; I quits you. I'd be shorely degraded to put in my time with any sech low-flung passel of sports. You-all may go back an' tell your folks that as you leaves you hears me give the call to my guests, "All promenade to the bar"; an' the dancin' is done. To-morrow I departs for Red Dog to begin life anew. Wolfville is too slow a camp for any gent with any swiftness to him.'"

CHAPTER XV.

SLIM JIM'S SISTER.

"Which thar's folks in this caravansary I don't like none," remarked the Old Cattleman, as I joined him one afternoon on the lawn. His tone was as of one half sullen, half hurt, and as he jerked his thumb toward the hotel behind us, it was a gesture full of scorn. "Thar's folks thar, takin' 'em up an' down, horns, hide, tallow, an' beef, who ain't worth heatin' a runnin'-iron to brand."

"What's the trouble?" I inquired, as I organized for comfort with my back against the elm-tree which shadowed us.

"No trouble at all," replied my old friend sourly, "leastwise nothin' poignant. It's that yoothful party in the black surtoot who comes pesterin' me a moment ago about the West bein', as he says, a roode an' irreligious outfit."

"He's a young preacher," I explained. "Possibly he was moved by an anxiety touching your soul's welfare."

"Well, if he's out to save souls," retorted the old gentleman, "he oughter whirl a bigger loop. No, no, he won't do,"he continued, shaking his head with an air of mournful yet resentful decision, "this yere gent's too narrow; which his head is built too much the shape of a quail-trap. He may do to chase jack-rabbits an' sech, but he's a size too small for game like me. Save souls, says you! Why, if that onp'lite young person was to meet a soul like mine comin' up the trail, he'd shorely omit what to do entire; he'd be that stampeded. He'd be some hard to locate, I takes it, after he meets up with a soul like mine a whole lot."

The Old Cattleman made this proclamation rather to himself than me, but I could detect an air of pride. Then he went on:

"'This yere West you emanates from,' says this young preacher-sharp to me that a-way, 'this yere West you hails from is roode, an' don't yield none to religious inflooences.'

"'Well,' I says back to him, fillin' my pipe at the same time, 'I reckons you shorely can c'llect more with a gun than a contreebution box in the West, if that's what you-all is aimin' at. But if you figgers we don't make our own little religious breaks out in Arizona, stranger, you figgers a heap wrong. You oughter have heard Short Creek Dave that time when he turns 'vangelist an' prances into the warehouse back of the New York Store, an' shows Wolfville she's shore h'ar-hung an' breeze-shaken over hell that a-way. Short Creek has the camp all spraddled out before he turns his deal-box up an' closes his game.'

"'But this yere Short Creek Dave,' he remonstrates to me, 'ain't no reg'lar licensed divine. He ain't workin' in conjunctions with no shore 'nough' sociation, I takes it. This Short Creek person is most likely one of them irrelevant exhortin' folks, an' that makes a difference. He don't belong to no reg'lar denom'nation.'

"'That's troo, too,' I says. 'Short Creek ain't workin' with no reg'lar religious round-up; he's sorter runnin' a floatin' outfit, criss-crossin' the range, prowlin' for mavericks an' strays on his own game. But what of that? He's shorely tyin' 'em down an' brandin' 'em right along.'

"'Oh, I don't dispoote none the efficacy of your friend's work that a-way,' replies the young preacher-sharp, 'but it's irreg'lar; it's plumb out of line. Now what you-alls needs in the West is real churches, same as we-alls has in the East.'

"'I ain't none shore of that.' I says, 'an' I'm gettin' a little warm onder the collar some with them frills he puts on; 'I ain't none shore. The East needn't deem itse'f the only king in the deck; none whatever. The West can afford the usual rooles an' let all bets go as they lays, an' still get up winner on the deal. I takes it you-alls never notes the West sendin' East for he'p?'

"'But that ain't the idee,' he urges. 'Churches that a-way is the right thing. They molds a commoonity, churches does. You b'ars witness yourse'f that where churches exists the commoonity is the most orderly an' fuller of quietood an' peace.'

"'Not necessarily I don't,' I replies back, for I'm goin' to play my hand out if it gets my last chip, 'not necessarily. What I b'ars witness to is that where the commoonity is the most orderly that a- way an' fuller of quietood an' peace, the churches exists.'

"'Which I'm shorely some afraid,' he says,—an' his looks shows he's gettin' a horror of me,—'you belongs to a perverse generation. You- all is vain of your own evil-doin'. Look at them murders that reddens the West, an' then sit yere an' tell me it don't need no inflooences.'

"'Them ain't murders,' I answers; them's killin's. An' as for inflooenccs, if you-all don't reckon the presence of a vig'lance committee in a camp don't cause a gent to pause an' ponder none before he pulls his gun, you dwells in ignorance. However, I'm yere to admit, I don't discern no sech sin-encrusted play in a killin' when the parties breaks even at the start, an' both gents is workin' to the same end unanimous. It does some folks a heap of good to kill 'em a lot.'

"It's at this p'int the young preacher-sharp pulls his freight, an' I observes, by the way he stacks me up with his eyes that a-way, he allows mebby I'm locoed."

The Old Cattleman said no more for a moment, but puffed at his cob pipe in thought and silence. I had no notion of involving myself in any combat of morals or theology, so I did not invade his mood. At last I suggested in a half-tone of inoffensive sympathy that the West was no doubt much misunderstood.

"Life there," I remarked, "amid new and rough conditions must be full of hardship and tragedy."

This vague arrow in the air had the effect of sending the old fellow off at a tangent. His bent was evidently discursive, and all thoughts of his late religious controversy seemed to pass from his mind.

"Full of hardship an' tragedy is your remark," he retorted, "an' I joins you tharin. Take them disasters that pounces on Slim Jim. What happens in the case of this yere Slim Jim tenderfoot," the old fellow continued as a damp gleam of sympathy shone in his eye, "is both hardship an' tragedy. Which of course thar's a mighty sight of difference. A hardship a gent lives through; but it's a tragedy when his light's put out. An' as Slim Jim don't live through this none, it's nacherally a tragedy that a-way.

"I frequent sees bad luck to other folks, as well as comin' to me personal, in the years I inhabits the grass country, but this was shorely the toughest. It even overplays anythin'

161

Rainbow Sam ever is ag'inst; an' the hard luck of Rainbow Sam is a proverb of Arizona.

"'Which I reckons I was foaled with a copper on me,' says this Rainbow Sam to Enright one day. 'In all my born days I never makes a killin'—never gets up winner once. I was foaled a loser, an' I'll keep a-losin' ontil this yere malady—which it's consumption-which has me in charge delivers me to the angels an' gets its receipt.'

"It's a mockery what transpires touchin' this Rainbow Sam. Jest as he states, the consumption's got him treed an' out on a limb. Doc Peets says, himse'f, nothin' can he'p him; an' when Peets quits a little thing like consumption an' shoves his chair back, you-alls can gamble a gent's health, that a-way, is on a dead kyard.

"I recalls how Rainbow Sam dies; which he rides out into eternity easy an' painless. We-alls is into a poker-game nne night-that is, five of us—when Doc Peets is called away.

"'See yere, Rainbow,' says Peets to Rainbow Sam, who's penniless an' tharfore lookin' on; 'you never has a morsel of luck in your life. Now, yere: You play my hand an' chips awhile. I'm on velvet for three hundred an' fifty, an' I'd as soon you'd lose it into the game as any sport I knows. An' to rouse your moral nacher I wants to tell you, whatever you rakes in you keeps. Now thar's luck at the jump; you can't lose an' you may win, so set in yere. Napoleon never has half the show.'

"Peets goes away for an hour about somethin', an' Rainbow Sam takes his seat; an', merely to show how one gent outlucks another, while Peets has had the luck of dogs it's that profuse an' good, it looks like the best Rainbow can get

162

is an even break. For half an hour he wins an' he loses about equal; an' he's shore tryin' hard to win, too.

"'If I takes in a couple of hundred or so,' says this Rainbow to me, 'I allows I'll visit my folks in the States once for luck.'

"But he never visits them folks he adverts to. It's on Boggs's deal, an' he's throwin' the kyards 'round when Rainbow's took bad. His consumption sorter mutinies onto him all at once. He's got the seat on the left of Boggs, too,—got the age.

"'Play my hand,' he says to Hamilton, who's stepped in from the dance-hall; 'play my hand, Jim, till I feels a little better. I'll be all right in a moment. Barkeep, deal me some whiskey.'

"So Rainbow walks over to the bar, an' Hamilton picks up his kyards. I notes that Rainbow steps off that time some tottersome; but he's so plumb weak that a-way, cats is robust to him; an' so I deems nothin' tharof. I'm skinnin' my kyards a bit interested anyhow, bein' in the hole myse'f.

"Everybody comes in this deal, an' when the chips is in the center— this yere's before the draw—Hamilton, speakin' up for Rainbow, says:

"'These yere's Doc Peets's chips anyhow?'

"'Which they shorely be,' says Boggs, 'so play 'em merciless, 'cause Peets is rich.'

163

"'That's what I asks for,' says Hamilton, 'for I don't aim to make no mistakes with pore Rainbow's money.'

"'That's all right,' says Boggs, 'dump 'em in. If you-all lose, it's
Peets's; if you win, it's Rainbow's.'

"'Play 'em game an' liberal, Old Man,' says Rainbow over by the bar,—an' it strikes me at the time his tones is weak an' queer; but bein' as I jest then notes a third queen in my hand, I don't have no chance to dwell on the fact. 'Play 'em game an' free,' says Rainbow ag'in. 'Free as the waters of life. Win or lose, she's all the same a hundred year from now.'

"Hamilton takes another look an' then raises the ante a hundred dollars. This yere is table stakes; this game was; an' the stakes is five hundred.

"'Which I plays this,' says Hamilton, as he comes up with the hundred raise, 'the same as I would for myse'f, which the same means plenteous an' free as a king.'

"Thar's three of us who stays, one of the same bein' me. I allers recalls it easy, 'cause it frost-bites my three queens for over three hundred dollars before the excitement dies away. Boggs, who's so vociferous recent about Hamilton playin' wide open, stays out; not havin' as good as nine-high.

"On the draw Hamilton allows Rainbow's hand needs one kyard, an' he gets it. I takes one also; the same bein' futile, so far as he'pin' my hand goes; an' the others takes kyards various.

"Thar's only one raise, an' that's when it gets to Hamilton. He sets in a little over two hundred dollars, bein' the balance of the stake; an' two of us is feeble-minded enough to call. What does he have? Well, it's ample for our ondoin' that a-way. It's a straight flush of diamonds; jack at the head of the class. It shorely carries off the pot like it's a whirlwind. As near as I can measure, Hamilton claws off with about six hundred dollars for Rainbow on that one hand.

"'Yere you be, Rainbow!' shouts Boggs. 'Come a-runnin'! It's now you visits them relations; you makes a killin' at last.'

"It turns out some late for Rainbow though. Thar's no reply to Boggs's talk, an' when we-alls goes over to him where he's set down by the end of the bar thar, with his arm on a monte-table, an' his chin on his shirt, Rainbow Sam is dead.

"'Which I regrets,' says Doc Peets when he returns, 'that Rainbow don't stay long enough to onderstand how luck sets his way at last. It most likely comforts him an' makes his goin' out more cheerful.'

"'It's a good sign, though,' says Cherokee Hall, 'that straight flush is. Which it shows Rainbow strikes a streak of luck; an' mebby it lasts long enough to get him by the gates above all right. That's all I asks when my time comes; that I dies when I'm commencin' a run of luck.'

"Oh! about this Slim Jim tenderfoot an' his tragedy! Do you know I plumb overlooks him. I gets trailed off that a-way after pore old Rainbow Sam, an' Slim Jim escapes my mem'ry complete.

"Which the story of this gent, even the little we-alls knows, is a heap onusual. No one, onless he's the postmaster, ever does hear his name. He sorter ha'nts about Red Dog an' Wolfville indiscriminate for mighty nigh a year; an' they calls him 'Slim Jim' with us, an' 'The Tenderfoot' in Red Dog; but, as I says, what's his real name never does poke up its head.

"Whatever brings this yere Slim Jim into the cow country is too boggy a crossin' for me. Thar ain't a thing he can do or learn to. We-alls has him on one round-up, an' it's cl'ar from the jump he ain't meant by Providence for the cattle business. The meekest bronco in the bunch bucks him off; an' actooally he's that timid he's plumb afraid of ponies an' cattle both.

"We-alls fixes Slim Jim's saddle with buckin'-straps; an' even fastens a roll of blankets across the saddle-horn; but it ain't enough. Nothin' bar tyin' Slim Jim into the saddle, like the hoss- back Injuns does to papooses, could save him.

"An' aside from nacheral awk'ardness an' a light an' fitful seat in a saddle, it looks like this Slim Jim has baleful effects on a bronco. To show you: One mornin' we ropes up for him a pony which has renown for its low sperits. It acts, this yere pony does, like it's suffered some disapp'intment which blights it an' breaks its heart; an' no amount of tightenin' of the back cinch; not even spurrin' of it in the shoulder an' neck like playful people who's out for a circus does, is ever known to evolve a buck-jump outen him, he's that sad. Which this is so well known, the pony's name is 'Remorse.'

"As I says, merely to show the malignant spell this yere Slim Jim casts over a bronco, we-alls throws him onto this Remorse pony one mornin'.

"'Which if you can't get along with that cayouse,' remarks Jack Moore at the time, 'I reckons it's foreordained you-all has to go afoot.'

166

"An' that's how it turns out. No sooner is Slim Jim in the saddle than that Remorse pony arches his back like a hoop, sticks his nose between his knees, an' gives way to sech a fit of real old worm- fence buckin' as lands Slim Jim on his sombrero, an' makes expert ponies simply stand an' admire.

"That's the last round-up Slim Jim attempts; workin' cattle he says himse'f is too deep a game for him, an' he never does try no more. So he hangs about Wolfville an' Red Dog alternate, turnin' little jim-crow tricks for the express company, or he'pin' over to the stage company's corrals, an' sorter manages to live.

"Now an' then some party who's busy drinkin', an' tharfore hasn't time for faro, an' yet is desirous the same be played, stakes Slim Jim ag'inst the game; an' it happens at times he makes a small pick- up that a-way. But his means of livelihood is shorely what you-alls would call precar'ous.

"An' yet, as I sends my mind back over the trail, I never knows of nothin' bad this yere Slim Jim does. You needn't go inferrin' none, from his havin' a terror of steers an' broncos that a-way, that he's timid plumb through. Thar's reason to deem him game when he's up ag'inst mere man.

"Once, so they tells the story, Curly Bill rounds up this Slim Jim in a Red Dog hurdy-gurdy an' concloods to have some entertainment with him.

"'Dance, you shorthorn!' says this yere Curly Bill, yankin' out his six-shooter an' p'intin' it mighty sudden at Slim Jim's foot; 'shuffle somethin' right peart now, or you-all emerges shy a toe.'

"Does this Slim Jim dance? Never cavorts a step. At the first move he swarms all over this Curly Bill like a wild-cat, makes him drop his gun, an' sends him out of the hurdy-gurdy on a canter. That's straight; that's the painful fact in the case of Curly Bill, who makes overgay with the wrong gent.

"Later, mebby an hour, so the party says who relates it to me, Curly Bill sends back word into the hurdy-gurdy, tellin' the barkeep, if his credit's good after sech vicissitoodes, to treat the house. He allows the drinks is on him, an' that a committee can find him settin' on the post office steps sorter goin' over himse'f for fractures, if it's held necessary for him to be present when the drinks is took.

"Which of course any gent's credit is good at the bar that a-way; an' so a small delegation of three ropes up this yere Curly Bill an' brings him back to the hurdy-gurdy, where he gets his gun ag'in, an' Slim Jim an' him makes up.

"'Which I renounces all idee of ever seein' you dance some,' says Curly Bill, when he an' Jim shakes; 'an' I yereby marks your moccasins plumb off my list of targets.'

"Everybody's pleased at this; an' the barkeep is delighted speshul, as one of them reeconciliations that a-way is mighty condoosive to the sale of nose-paint. I'm yere to remark, if thar ain't no more reeconciliations on earth, an' everybody stands pat on them hatreds an' enmities of his, whiskey-drinkin' falls off half.

"I only su'gest this turn-up with Curly Bill to 'lustrate that it's about as I says, an' that while Slim Jim's reluctant an' hesitatin' in the presence of wild steers, an' can't adhere to a pony much, this yere girlishness don't extend to men none; which last he faces prompt an' willin' as a lion.

"Thar's times when I shorely ponders the case of this Slim Jim a mighty sight, 'cause he keeps strikin' me as a good gent gone bad, an' as bein' the right gent in the wrong place.

"'This pore maverick is plumb Eastern, that's all,' says Enright one day, while he's discussin' of this Slim Jim. 'He ain't to blame, but he ain't never goin' to do, none whatever, out yere. He can't no more get used to Arizona than one of the Disciples, an' he might camp 'round for years.'

"It's mebby hard onto a year when along comes the beginnin' of the end as far as this Slim Jim's concerned, only we-alls don't know it. The postmaster says afterward he gets a letter; an' by what's found on the remainder it looks like the postmaster's right, an' this letter sets him goin' wrong. I allers allows, after he gets this missive, that he sees the need of money that a-way an' plenty of it; an' that it's got to come quick.

"Most likely he's been bluffin' some parties in the East about how rich he is an' how lucrative he's doin',—sech bluffs bein' common in the West,—an' now along comes events an' folks he's fooled, an' his bluff is called.

"When it arrives, none of us knows of this yere letter the postmaster mentions, an' which is later read by all; but it's about that time Slim Jim acts queer an' locoed. He's flustered an' stampeded about somethin', we-alls notes that; an' Dave Tutt even forgets himse'f as a gent so far as to ask Slim Jim what's up.

"'Which you looks oneasy these autumn days,' says Tutt to Slim Jim. 'What's wrong?'

"'Nothin',' says Slim Jim, lookin' a bit woozy, 'nothin' wrong. A friend of mine is likely to show up yere; that's all.'

"'Which he has the air of a fugitive from jestice when he says it,' observes Tutt, when he speaks of it after all's over; 'though jedgin' by the party who's on his trail that time I don't reckon he's done nothin' neither.'

"It's shorely the need of money drives this Slim Jim to turnin' route-agent an' go holdin' up the stage, for the evenin' he quits camp he says to Cherokee Hall: 'S'pose I asks you-all to lend me money, quite a bundle, say, would you do it?'

"'I turns faro for my money,' says Cherokee; 'which I merely mentions it to show I comes honestly by my roll. As to borrowin' of me, you-all or any gent in hard lines can get my money by showin' he needs it worse than I do; an' to encourage you I might say I don't need money much. So, go on an' tell me the news about yourse'f, an' if it's as bad as the way you looks, I reckons I'll have to stake you, even if it takes half my pile.' Tharupon Cherokee urges Slim Jim to onfold his story.

"But Slim Jim gets shy an' won't talk or tell Cherokee what's pesterin' him, or how much money he needs.

"'No,' he says, after thinkin' a little, 'I never begs a stake yet, an' I never will. Anyhow I sees another way which is better.'

"Countin' noses afterwards, it's probably this talk with Cherokee is the last Slim Jim has before he breaks over into the hills on the hunt for money. He goes afoot, too; for he don't own no pony, an' he couldn't, as I explains previous, stay on him if he does.

"But he fixes himse'f with a Winchester which he gets from the stage-company people themse'fs on a talk he makes about takin' some reecreation with the coyotes, an' p'ints straight over into Rawhide Canyon,—mebby it's six miles from camp. When the stage gets along an hour later, this Slim Jim's made himse'f a mask with a handkerchief, an' is a full-fledged hold-up which any express company could be proud to down. Old Monte relates what happens in the canyon, 'cause from where he's stuck up on the box he gets a better view.

"'Yere's how this happens,' says Old Monte, while renooin' his yooth with Red Light licker after he's got in. 'It's a little hazy in the canyon, comin' evenin' that a-way, an' my eyes is watery with the shootin' goin' on, an' I tharfore don't say I notes things none minoote; but as near as I can, you gets the story.

"'Thar's only one passenger, an' she's a woman. Which for that matter she's a beautiful girl, with eyes like a buck antelope's; but bein' she's layin' over to the stage station defunct right now, along with this yere Slim Jim, I don't dwell none on how she looks.'

"'When I pulls out from Tucson I has this yere young female inside; an' the company puts two Wells-Fargo gyards on top of the coach, the same bein' the first time in months. These Wells-Fargo parties ain't along for hold-ups, but jest 'cause they has business over yere, an' so comes by stage same as other gents.

"'It all goes smooth ontil I'm rattlin' along in Rawhide Canyon not half-a-dozen miles from where we-alls is now drinkin' all free an' amiable, like life's nothin' but sunshine.

"'The first p'inter I has that I'm up ag'inst it, bang! goes a Winchester, an' throws my off leader dead ag'inst the trail. Thar's no goin' 'round the dead hoss, an' bar the nacheral rarin' an' pitchin' of the other five on beholdin' of the ontimely end of their companion that a-way, the whole business comes to a dead stop.

"'"Hold up your hands!" says a voice up the rocks on one side.

"'My hands is already up, for I'm an old stage-driver, gents, an' you-alls can gamble I knows my trade. I'm hired to drive. It ain't no part of my game to fight hold-ups an' stand off route-agents that a-way, an' get shot dead for it by their pards the next trip; so, as I says, the moment that Winchester goes off, I clamps my fingers back of my head an' sets thar. Of course I talks back at this hold- up a heap profane, for I don't aim to have the name of allowin' any gent to rustle my stage an' me not cuss him out. "'But these yere Wells-Fargo sharps, they never holds up their hands. That's nacheral enough, for them gents is hired to fight, an' this partic'lar trip thar's full six thousand dollars to go to war over.

"With the first shot the Wells-Fargo gents—they was game as goats both of 'em—slides offen the coach an' takes to shootin'. The guns is makin' a high old rattle of it, an' I'm hopin' the hold-up won't get to over-shootin' an' drill me, when the first casooalty occurs. One of the Wells-Fargo sports gets a bullet plumb through his frame, an' is dead an' out in the crack of a whip.

"'It looks like the hold-up sees him tumble, for it's then he cuts loose a whoop, jumps down onto the trail an' charges. He comes a- shootin', too, an' the way the lead an' fire fetches forth from that Winchester he's managin' shore reminds me of them Roman candles last July.

"'All this yere don't take ten seconds. An' it don't last ten seconds more. As my hold-up comes chargin' an' shootin' towards the stage, I overhears a scream inside, an' the next moment that young female passenger opens the door an' comes scamperin' out.

"'If she tries she couldn't have selected no worse epoch. She hits the ground, an' the second she does—for I'm lookin' over at her at the time—she stops one of that hold-up's bullets an' goes down with a great cry.

"'It's on me, gents, at this p'int to take all resks an' go down an' look-out the play for the girl. But I never gets a chance, an' it's as well I don't; for towards the last the shootin' of the remainin' Wells-Fargo person is reckless an' inordinate. It's plumb reedundant; that shootin' is. But as I remarks, I never has no occasion to go to the girl; for as I feels the impulse I hears the hold-up shout:

"'"God! it's Mary! It's my sister!"

"'Thar's a letter on him we finds later, which shows this statement about my passenger bein' his sister is troo; an' that she's p'intin' out when downed, now they's orphans—which the letter states their father's jest cashed in—to come an' keep house for him. As the hold-up makes this yere exclamation about the girl bein' his relative that a-way, his Winchester goes a-rattlin' onto the trail an' he gathers her in his arms. However, he don't last longer than a drink of whiskey now. He don't no more'n lift her up, before even he kisses her, the remainin' Wells-Fargo gent downs him, an' the riot's over complete.

"'Three killed an' none wounded is how results stacks up; an' after me an' the live Wells-Fargo gent cl'ars the dead leader outen the trail, we-alls lays out the remainders inside all peaceful, an' comes a-curvin' on to Wolfville. It's then, as we puts 'em in the coach, I sees that my hold-up's that onfortunate felon, Slim Jim. Which I was shorely astonished. I says to the Wells-Fargo gent, as we looks at Slim Jim:

"""Pard, the drinks is due from me on this. If I has a week to guess in, I'd never said 'Slim Jim.'"

CHAPTER XVI.

JAYBIRD BOB'S JOKE.

"Whatever makes this yere jaybird Bob believe he's a humorist," said the Old Cattleman one afternoon as we slowly returned from a walk, "whatever it is misleads him to so deem himself is shorely too many for me. Doc Peets tells him himse'f one day he's plumb wrong.

"'You-all's nacherally a somber, morose party,' says Doc Peets this time, 'an' nothin' jocose or jocund about you. Your disp'sition, Jaybird, don't no more run to jokes than a prairie-dog's.'

"'Which I would admire to know why not?' says Jaybird Bob.

"'Well,' goes on Doc Peets, 'you thinks too slow—too much like a cow in a swamp. Your mind moves sluggish that a-way, an' sorter sinks to the hocks each step. If you was born to be funny your intellects would be limber an' frivolous.'

"'Bein' all this is personal to me,' says Jaybird Bob, 'I takes leave to regard you as wrong. My jokes is good, high-grade jokes; an' when you-all talks of me bein' morose, it's a mere case of bluff.' An' so Jaybird goes on a-holdin of himse'f funny ontil we- alls has him to bury.

"No; Jaybird ain't his shore-'nough name; it's jest a handle to his 'dentity, so we-alls picks it up handy and easy. Jaybird's real name is Graingerford,—Poindexter Graingerford. But the same is cumbersom an' onwieldy a whole lot; so when he first trails into Wolfville we- alls considers among ourse'fs an' settles it's a short cut to call him 'Jaybird Bob,' that a-way. An' we does.

"It's on the spring round-up this yere Jaybird first develops that he regards himse'f witty. It's in the morning as we-alls has saddled up an' lines out to comb the range roundabout for cattle. Thar's a tenderfoot along whose name is Todd, an', as he's canterin' off, Jaybird comes a-curvin' up on his bronco an' reaches over an' tails this shorthorn's pony.

"What's tailin' a pony? It's ridin' up from the r'ar an' takin' a half-hitch on your saddle. horn with the tail of another gent's pony, an' then spurrin' by an' swappin' ends with the whole outfit,- -gent, hoss, an' all.

"It's really too toomultuous for a joke, an' mebby breaks the pony's neck, mebby the rider's. But whether he saves his neck or no, the party whose pony is thus tailed allers emergers tharfrom deshevelled an' wrought-up, an' hotter than a wolf. So no one plays this yere joke much; not till he's ready to get shot at.

"As I says, this Jaybird watches Todd as he rides off. Bein' new on the range that a-way, Todd don't ride easy. A cow saddle ain't built like these yere Eastern hulls, nohow. The stirrup is set two inches further back for one thing, an' it's compiled a heap different other ways. Bein' onused to cow saddles, an' for that matter cow ponies, this Todd lops over for'ard an' beats with his elbows like he's a curlew or somethin' flyin', an' I reckons it's sech proceedin's makes Jaybird allow he's goin' to be funny an' tail Todd's pony.

"As I explains, he capers along after Todd an' reaches over an' gets a handful of the pony's tail; an' then, wroppin' it 'round his saddle-horn, he goes by on the jump an' spreads

Todd an' his bronco permiscus about the scene. This yere Todd goes along the grass on all fours like a jack-rabbit.

"Which Todd, I reckons, is the hostilest gent in south-east Arizona. Before ever he offers to get up, he lugs out his six-shooter an' makes some mighty sincere gestures that a-way to shoot up Jaybird. But he's slow with his weepon, bein' spraddled out on the grass, an' it gives Dave Tutt an' Enright a chance to jump in between an' stop the deal.

"We-alls picks Todd up, an' rounds up his pony,—which scrambles to its feet an' is now cavortin' about like its mind is overturned,— an' explains to him this yere is a joke. But he's surly an' relentless about it; an' it don't take no hawk to see he don't forgive Jaybird a little bit.

"'Tailin' a gent's pony,' says Todd, 'is no doubt thrillin' amoosement for folks lookin' on, but thar's nothin' of a redeemin' nature in it from the standp'int of the party whose pony's upheaved that a-way. Not to be misonderstood at this yere crisis,' goes on this Todd, 'I wants to announce that from now for'ard life will have but one purpose with me, which'll be to down the next gent whoever tails a pony of mine. The present incident goes as a witticism; but you can gamble the next won't be so regarded.'

"That sorter ends the talk, an' all of us but the cook an' the hoss- hustlers bein' in the saddle by now, we disperses ourse'fs through the scenery to work the cattle an' proceed with the round-up we-alls is on. We notes, though, that tailin' Todd's pony don't go ag'in with safety.

"It's when we-alls rides away that Doc Peets—who's out with the round-up, though he ain't got no cattle-brand himse'f—tells Jaybird he's not a humorist, like I already repeats.

"But, as I su'gests, this Jaybird Bob can't believe it none. He's mighty shore about his jokes bein' excellent good jokes; an' while it's plain Todd ain't got no confidence in him an' distrusts him complete since he tips over his bronco that mornin', it looks like Jaybird can't let him alone. An' them misdeeds of Jaybird's keeps goin' on, ontil by the merest mistake—for it's shore an accident if ever one happens in the cow country—this yere tenderfoot shoots up Jaybird an' kills him for good.

"It looks to us like it's a speshul Providence to warn folks not to go projectin' about, engaged in what you might call physical jests none. Still, this yere removal of Jaybird don't take place till mighty near the close of the round-up; an' intervenin', he's pirootin' 'round, stockin' the kyards an' settin' up hands on the pore shorthorn continuous.

"One of Jaybird's jokes—'one of his best,' Jaybird calls it— results in stampedin' the herd of cattle we-alls is bringin' along at the time—bein' all cows an' their calves—to a brandin'-pen. Which thar's two thousand, big an' little, in the bunch; an' Jaybird's humor puts 'em to flight like so many blackbirds; an' it takes two days hard ridin' for the whole outfit to bring 'em together ag'in.

"Among other weaknesses this Todd imports from the States is, he's afraid of snakes. Rattlesnakes is his abhorrence, an' if each is a disembodied sperit he can't want 'em further off. He's allers alarmed that mebby, somehow, a rattlesnake will come pokin' in onder his blankets nights, an' camp with him while he's asleep. An' this yere wretched Jaybird fosters them delusions.

"'About them serpents,' I overhears Jaybird say to him one evenin' while we-alls is settin' 'round;—all but Moore an' Tutt, who's ridin' herd; "bout them serpents; a gent can't be too partic'lar. It looks like they has but one hope, which it's to crawl into a gent's blankets an' sleep some with him. Which, if he moves or turns over, they simply emits a buzz an' grabs him I knows of forty folks who's bit that a-way by snakes, an' nary a one lives to explain the game.'

"'Be rattlesnakes thick in Arizona?' I hears Todd say to this Jaybird.

"'Be they thick?' answers Jaybird. 'Well, I shore wishes I had whiskey for all the rattlesnakes thar is yereabouts. I don't want to go overstatin' the census to a gent who is out playin' for information, an' who's learnin' fast, but I s'pose now thar ain't none less than a billion snakes in southeast Arizona alone. If I could saw off the little passel of cattle I has on this range, you can gamble I'd pull my freight to-morrow. It's all right for sech old Cimmarons as Enright, an' sech parties as that sawbones Peets, to go bluffin' about thar' bein' no rattlesnakes to speak of, an' that they couldn't p'ison you to death no how; but you bet I ain't seen forty of my nearest friends cash in of snake-bites, an' not learn nothin'. An' almost every time it's a rattlesnake as comes slidin' into bed with 'em while they's locked in dreams, an' who gets hot an' goes to chewin' of 'em, because they wants to turn out before the snake does. Rattlesnakes that a-way wants to sleep till it's fourth-drink time an' the sun's 'way up yonder. An' when a gent goes to rollin' out of his blankets say at sun-up, it makes 'em monstrous angry to be disturbed; an' the first he knows of where they be an' how they looks on early risin', their teeth's in him up to the gyard, an' before night thar's one less gent to cook for, an' an extra saddle rides along in the grub-wagon with the blankets when they next moves camp.'

"Of course all this is a heap impressive to Todd; an' while Enright an' Peets both tells him Jaybird's havin' fun with him, you can see he's mortal afraid every night when he spreads his blankets, an' he makes a cirele about where he sleeps at with a horse-ha'r lariat he's got from a Mexican, an' who tells him it'll tickle the snakes' necks when they goes to crawl across it, an' make 'em keep away.

"The way this yere Jaybird manages to stampede the bunch that time is this a-way. Jaybird comes ridin' in from the cattle about three hours before sun-up, to turn out Tutt, who is due to take his place on herd. Jaybird's got a rawhide rope that he's drugged about in the grass, which makes it damp an' cold. As Jaybird rides up to camp he sees this Todd rolled in his blankets, snorin' to beat four of a kind.

"Nacherally Jaybird's out to be joyous in a second. He rides up close to this he'pless shorthorn as he lays asleep, an' tosses a loop of his wet rawhide across his countenance where it's turned up in the moonlight. As it settles down cold an' startlin' on Todd's skin, Jaybird yells:

"Snake, Todd! Thar's a rattlesnake on you bigger'n a dog.'

"Jaybird says later as how this Todd behaves tremendous. He b'iles up into the atmosphere with a howl like a wolf; an', grabbin' a blanket in each hand, he starts out over the plains in a state of frenzy. Which the worst is he charges headlong toward the herd; an' what with them shrieks he volunteers, an' the blankets flappin' an' wavin', thar ain't a cow in the bunch who stays in her right mind a moment. Which she springs to her feet, an takin' her offspring along, goes surgin' off into the hills for good. You couldn't head or stop 'em then. It's the completest case of stampede I ever turns out to behold.

"No; this yere Todd never gathers the rights of the eepisode. He's that peevish an' voylent by nacher no one tells him it's Jaybird; an' onless, in the light of knowin' more, he has since figgered out the trooth, he allows to this day a rattlesnake as big as a roll of blankets tries to recline on his face that time.

"To keep peace in camp an' not let him go to pawin' 'round for real trouble with the festive Jaybird, Enright stands in to cap the game himse'f; an' puts it up in confab with this Todd the next day as how he sees the rattlesnake, an' that it's mighty near bein' a whopper.

"'It's shore,' says Enright, when he an' Todd is conversin' tharon, 'the most giant serpent I ever sees without the aid of licker. An' when he goes streakin' off into the gloom, bein' amazed an' rattled by your cries, he leaves, so far as I'm concerned, a trail of relief behind. You-all can gamble, I wasn't interruptin' of no sech snake, nor makin' of no pretexts for his detainment.

"'What for was his rattles like?' says Todd; an' he gets pale at the mere sound of Enright's talk.

"'As to them rattles,' says Enright, like he's mighty thoughtful tryin' to recall 'em to mind, 'as to this reptile's rattles, it's that dark that while I sees 'em I couldn't but jest. So far as I notes anythin' they looks like a belt full of car- tridges, sorter corrugated an' noomerous.

"Now this yere which I relates, while no doubt burnin' experiences to Todd, is after all harmless enough. An' to

182

people not careful about the basis of their glee it might do some to laugh at. But it all closes up on a play with nothin' gay nor merry in it; leastwise not for Jaybird Bob.

"This yere finish joke of jaybird's transpires one evenin' as the cook's startin' in to rustle some chuck. The grub-wagon's been stopped in the mouth of Peeled Pine Canyon. Every gent's in camp but this yere tenderfoot Todd. Enright, who's actin' as round-up boss for the outfit—for everybody's cattle's bein' worked together that a-way, like we allers does—has sent Todd peerin' 'round for cattle, 'way off up the valley into which the Peeled Pine Canyon opens. This yere shorthorn's due to be back any time now, 'cause it's only a question of how far up the valley does he go. He don't run no show to be lost, for nothin' less aerial than goats could climb out of the canyon he's in, an' tharfore he's bound to find camp.

"Of course, knowin' every gent's station in the day's ridin', we- alls is plenty aware that this tenderfoot Todd is some'ers above us in the valley. None of the rest of us is turnin' our minds to him probably, except Jaybird Bob. It all of a bump like a buckin' pony strikes Jaybird that he's missin' a onusual chance to be buoyant.

"'What for a play would it be,' says Jaybird, rousin' up from where he lays watchin' of the cook slice salt hoss for the fryin'-pan, 'what for a game would it be, I says, for a passel of us to lay out up the draw, an' bush-whack this yere ontaught person Todd as he comes ridin' down to camp? We- alls could hop out at him, a-whoopin' an' shoutin', an' bein' wropped up in blankets, he allows it's shore Injuns an' goes plumb locoed.'

"'You-all will keep harrowin' away at this Todd party, Jaybird,' says Enright, 'ontil you arises from the game loser. Now I don't reckon none I'd play Apache if I'm you. Thar's too much effort in bein' an Apache that a-way. I'd lay yere an' think up some joke which don't demand so much industry, an' ain't calc'lated to scare an innocent gent to death.'

"But Jaybird won't listen. He falls into admiration of his scheme; an' at last Tutt an' Jack Moore allows they'll go along an' play they's aborigines with Jaybird an' note how the tenderfoot stands the racket.

"'As long as this yere Jaybird's bound to make the play,' says Jack Moore to Enright, talkin' one side, 'it's a heap better to have the conserv'tive element represented in the deal. So I puts it up, it's a good sage move for me an' Tutts to stand in. We-alls will come handy to pull Jaybird an' this shorthorn apart if they gets their horns locked in the course of them gaities.'

"Enright takes the same view; so Jaybird an' Moore an' Tutt wanders off up the canyon a mile, an' lays in wait surreptitious to head off Todd. Jack tells me the story when him an' Tutt comes ridin' back with the corpse.

"'This is how we does,' says Jack. 'Me an' Tutt an' deceased—which last is Jaybird all right enough—is ensconced behind a p'int of rocks. Jaybird's got his blanket wropped, 'round him so he looks like a savage. It ain't long when we-alls hears the tenderfoot comin' down the canyon; it's likely he's half-mile away. He's runnin' onto us at a road-gait; an' when he's about two hundred yards off Jaybird turns out a yell to make you shiver, shakes a load or two outen his gun, goes surgin' out from 'round the p'int of rocks, an'

184

charges straight at this onthinkin' tenderfoot. It is due to trooth to say, me an' Tutt follows this Jaybird's suit, only not so voylent as to whoops.

"'Does it scare up the tenderfoot? Well, it shorely alarms him a heap. He takes Jaybird for an Injun an' makes no question; which the same is nowise strange; I'd took him for a savage myse'f, only, bein' in the deal that a-way I knows it's Jaybird. So, as I remarks, it horrifies the tenderfoot on end, an' at the first sight of Jaybird he whirls his pony an' lights out up that valley like antelope.

"'Nacherally we-alls follows; Jaybird leadin', a-whoopin', an' a- shootin', an' throwin' no end of sperit into it. It's a success, this piece of wit is, up to this juncture, an' Jaybird puts a heap of zest into it.

"'The weak spot in all this yere humor grows out of the idees this tenderfoot's been gainin', an' the improvements he's been makin', while stragglin' about in our s'ciety. I onhesitatin'ly states that if this yere joke is pulled off by Jaybird when Todd first enters our midst, it might have been the vict'ry of his life. But Jaybird defers it too long. This tenderfoot has acquired a few Western ways; enough to spoil the fun an' send pore Jaybird a-curvin' to his home on high.

"'This is what that shorthorn does which teaches me he's learnin'. While he's humpin' off up the canyon, an' me an' Jaybird an' Tutt is stampedin' along in pursoot, the fugitive throws loose his six- shooter, an' without even turnin' his head or lookin' back at us, he onhooks the entire bundle of lead our way.

"Which the worst feature of it is, this backhanded, blind shootin' is a winner. The very first shot smites Jaybird plumb through the hat, an' he goes off his pony without even mentionin' about it to either Tutt or me.

"'That's all thar is to the report. Dave an' me pulls up our broncos, abandons the joke, lays Jaybird across his saddle like a sack of corn, an' returns to state the case.'

"'Whatever did you-alls do with this frightened stranger?' asks
Enright.

"'Which we never does nothin',' says Jack. 'The last I beholds, he's flyin' up the valley, hittin' nothin' but the high places. An' assoomin' his project is to get away, he's succeedin' admirable. As he vanishes, I should jedge from his motions he's reloadin' his gun; an' from the luck he has with Jaybird, Tutt an' me is led to believe thar's no real object in followin' him no further. I don't press my s'ciety on no gent; shorely not on some locoed tenderfoot that a-way who's pulled his gun an' is done blazin' away erratic, without purpose or aim.'

"'Don't you an' Tutt know where he is at?' demands Enright.

"'Which we shorely don't,' says Jack. 'If his hoss holds, an' he don't swerve none from the direction he's p'intin' out in when he fades from view, he's goin' to be over in the San Simon country by to-morrow mornin' when we eats our grub; an' that's half way to the Borax desert. If you yearns for my impressions,' concloods Jack, 'drawn from a-seein' of him depart, I'm free to say I don't reckon you-alls is goin' to meet this yere tenderfoot none soon.'

"An' that's about the size of it. Jack calls the turn. Jaybird's last joke alarms this tenderfoot Todd plumb outen Arizona, an' thar ain't none of us ever sees ha'r, horn, nor hoof mark of him no more. An' he takes with him, this Todd does, the boss pony in our bunch."

CHAPTER XVX.

BOGGS'S EXPERIENCE.

"No; thar's nothin' prolix about Boggs. Which on the contrary, his nacher is shorely arduous that a-way. If it's a meetin' of the committee, for instance, with intent then an' thar to dwell a whole lot on the doin's of some malefactor, Boggs allers gets to a mental show-down ahead of the other gents involved. Either he's out to throw this party loose, or stretch his neck, or run him outen camp, or whatever's deemed exact jestice, long before sech slow-an'-shore people as Old Man Enright even looks at their hands. The trooth is, Boggs ain't so strong on jedgement; his long suit is instinct. An' moreover I knows from his drawin' four kyards so much in poker, Boggs is plumb emotional."

At this point in his discourse the Old Cattle man paused and put in several profound minutes in apparent contemplation of Boggs. Then he went on.

"That's it; Boggs is emotional; an' I shorely reckons which he'd even been a heap religious, only thar's no churches much on Boggs's range. Boggs tells me himse'f he comes mighty near bein' caught in some speritual round-up one time, an' I allers allows, after hearin' Boggs relate the tale, that if he'd only been submerged in what you- alls calls benigner inflooences that a-way, he'd most likely made the fold all right an' got garnered in with the sheep.

"It's just after Short Creek Dave gets to be one of them 'vangelists. Dave has been exhortin' of Wolfville to leave off its ways, over in the warehouse of the New York Store, an' that same evenin' Boggs, bein' some moved, confides in me how once he mebby half-way makes up his mind he'll be saved.

"'Leastwise,' says Boggs, when he takes me into his past that a-way, 'I allows I'll be religious in the spring after the round-up is over. But I don't; so you can't, after all, call it a religious exper'ence none; nothin' more'n a eepisode.

"'It's winter when I makes them grace-of-heaven determinations,' goes on this Boggs, 'an' the spring round-up is months away. But I allers puts it up I'd shorely filled my hand an' got plumb into the play, only it's a bad winter; an' in the spring the cattle, weak an' starved, is gettin' down an' chillin' to death about the water- holes; an' as results tharof I'm ridin' the hills, a-cussin' an' a- swearin'; an' all 'round it's that rough, an' I'm that profane an' voylent, I reckons towards April probably my soul's buried onder ten foot of cuss-words, an' that j'inin' the church in my case is mighty likely to be a bluff. An' so I passes it up.

"'You sees,' says Boggs, 'thar's no good tryin' to hold out kyards on your Redeemer. If your heart ain't right it's no use to set into the game. No cold deck goes. He sees plumb through every kyard you holds, an' nothin' but a straight deal does with Him. Nacherally, then, I thinks—bein' as how you can't bluff your way into heaven, an' recallin' the bad language I uses workin' them cattle—I won't even try. An' that's why, when resolvin' one winter to get religion mebby next June, I persists in my sinful life.

"'It's over to Taos I acquires this religious idee. I'm come new to the camp from some'ers down 'round Seven Rivers in the Pecos country, an' I don't know a gent. Which I'm by nacher gregar'ous; so not knowin' folks that a-way weighs on me; an' the first night I'm thar, I hastens to remedy this yere evil.

189

I'm the possessor of wealth to a limit,—for I shore despises bein' broke complete, an' generally keeps as good as a blue stack in my war-bags,—an' I goes projectin' 'round from dance-hall to baile, an' deciminates my dinero an' draws to me nose-paint an' friends. As thar ain't but three gin-mills, incloosive of the hurdy-gurdy, I'm goin' curvin' in them grand rounds which I institoots, on a sort of triangle.

"'Which it can't be said I don't make runnin' of it, however; I don't reckon now it's mor'n an hour before I knows all Taos, bar Mexicans an' what some folks calls "the better elements." It also follows, like its lariat does a loose pony, that I'm some organized by whiskey, not to say confused.

"'It's because I'm confused I'm misled into this yere pra'r-meetin.' Not that them exercises is due to dim my eternal game none, now nor yereafter; but as I ain't liable to adorn the play nor take proper part tharin, I'd shorely passed out an' kept on to the hurdy-gurdy if I'd knowed. As it stands, I blunders into them orisons inadvertent; but, havin' picked up the hand, I nacherally continues an' plays it.

"'It's this a-way about them religious exercises: I'm emerged from the Tub of Blood, an' am p'intin' out for the dance-hall, when I strikes a wickeyup all lighted, an' singin' on the inside. I takes it for a joint I ain't seen none as yet, an' tharupon heads up an' enters. From the noise, I allows mebby it's Mexican; which Greasers usual puts up a heap of singin' an' scufflin' an' talkin' in everythin' from monte to a bull-fight.

"'Once I'm in, I notes it ain't Mexicans an' it ain't monte. Good folks though, I sees that; an' as a passel of 'em near the door looks shocked at the sight of me, I'm too bashful to break out ag'in, but sorter aiges into the nearest seat an' stands pat.

"'I can tell the outfit figgers on me raisin' the long yell an' stampedin' round to make trouble; so I thinks to myse'f I'll fool 'em up a lot. I jest won't say a word. So I sets silent as a coyote at noon; an' after awhile the sharp who's dealin' for 'em goes on with them petitions I interrupts as I comes bulgin' in.

"'Their range-boss says one thing I remembers. It's about castin' your bread upon the waters. He allows you'll get it ag'in an' a band of mavericks with it. It's playin' white chips to win blues; that's what this sharp says.

"'It shorely strikes me as easy. Every time you does good, says this party, Fate is out to play a return game with you; an' it's written you quits winner on all the good you promulgates that a-way.

"'I sets the deal out an' gets some sleepy at it, too. But I won't leave an' scand'lize the congregation; an' as I gives up strong when the plate goes by, I ain't regarded as no setback.

"'When the contreebution-box—which she's a tin plate— comes chargin' by, I'm sorter noddin,' I'm that weary. I notes the jingle of money, an' rouses up, allowin' mebby it's a jack-pot, I reckons.

"'"How hard be you-all in?" I says to the gent next to me, who's gone to the center for a peso.

"'"Dollar," says the gent.

"'"Well," I says, "I ain't seen my hand since the draw, but I'll raise you nine blind." An' I boards a ten-dollar bill.

"'When the rest goes, I sorter sidles forth an' lines out for the dance-hall. The fact is I'm needin' what you-alls calls stimulants. But all the same it sticks in my head about castin' good deeds on the water that a-way. It sticks thar yet, for that matter.

"Bein' released from them devotions, I starts to drinkin' ag'in with zeal an' earnestness. An' thar comes a time when all my money's in my boots. Yere's how: I only takes two stacks of reds when I embarks on this yere debauch. Bein' deep an' crafty, an' a new Injun at that agency that a-way, an' not knowin' what game I may go ag'inst, I puts the rest of my bank-roll over in Howard's store. It turns out, too, that every time I acquires silver in change, I commits it to my left boot, which is high an' ample to hold said specie. Why I puts this yere silver money in my boot-laig is shore too many for me. But I feels mighty cunnin' over it at the time, an' regards it as a 'way-up play.

"'As I tells you, thar arrives an hour while I'm in the Tub of Blood when my money's all in my boot, an' thar's still licker to drink. Fact is, I jest meets a gent named Frosty, as good a citizen as ever riffles a deck or pulls a trigger, an' p'liteness demands we-alls puts the nose-paint in play. That's why I has to have money.

"'I don't care to go pullin' off my moccasins in the Tub of Blood, an' makin' a vulgar display of my wealth by pourin' the silver onto the floor. Thar's a peck of it, if thar's dos reals; an' sech an exhibition as spillin' it out in the Tub of Blood is bound to mortify me, an' the barkeep, an' Frosty, an' most

192

likely lead to makin' remarks. So I concloods I'll round up my silver outside an' then return.

"'Excuse me," I says to Frosty. "You stay right yere with the bottle, an' I'll be among you ag'in in a minute all spraddled out."

"'I goes wanderin' out back of the Tub of Blood, where it's lonesome, an' camps down by a Spanish-bayonet, an' tugs away to get my boot off an' my dinero into circ'lation.

"'An' while I'm at it, sleep an' nose-paint seizes me, an' my light goes plumb out. I rolls over behind the bayonet-bush an' raises a snore. As for that Frosty, he waits a while; then he pulls his freight, allowin' I'm too deliberate about comin' back, for him.

"'It must have made them coyotes stop an' consider a whole lot about what I be. To show you how good them coyotes is, I wants to tell you: I don't notice it ontil the next day. While I'm curled up to the r'ar of that bush they comes mighty near gnawin' the scabbard offen my gun. Fact; the leather looks like some pup has been chewin' it. But right then I ain't mindin' nothin' so oninterestin' as a coyote bitin' on the leather of my gun.

"'Now this is where that bluff about bread on the waters comes in; an' it falls so pat on the heels of them devotions of mine, it he'ps brand it on my mem'ry. While I'm layin' thar, an' mighty likely while them coyotes is lunchin' offen my scabbard that a-way, along comes a rank stranger they calls Spanish Bill.

"'I learns afterward how this Spanish Bill is hard, plumb through. He's rustled everythin' from a bunch of ponies to the mail-bags, an' is nothin' but a hold-up who needs hangin' every hour. Whatever takes him to where I lays by my bayonet-bush I never knows. He don't disclose nothin' on that p'int afterward, an' mebby he tracks up on me accidental.

"'But what informs me plain that he explores my war-bags for stuff, before ever he concloods to look after my health, is this: Later, when we gets acquainted an' I onfurls my finances onto him, he seems disapp'inted an' hurt.

"'The statistics of the barkeep of the Tub of Blood next day, goes to the effect that I'm shorely out thar four hours; an' when Spanish Bill discovers me I'm mighty near froze. Taos nights in November has a heap of things in common with them Artic regions we hears of, where them fur-lined sports goes in pursoot of that North Pole. Bein' froze, an' mebby from an over-dab of nose-paint, I never saveys about this yere Spanish Bill meetin' up with me that a-way ontil later. But by what the barkeep says, he drug me into the Tub of Blood an' allows he's got a maverick.

""Fix this yere froze gent up somethin' with teeth," says Spanish Bill to the barkeep. "I don't know his name none, but he's sufferin' an' has got to be recovered if it takes the entire check-rack."

"'Which the barkeep stands in an' brings me to. I comes 'round an' can walk some if Spanish Bill goes along steadyin' of me by the collar. Tharupon said Bill rides herd on me down to the Jackson House an' spreads me on some blankets.

"'It's daylight when I begins to be aware my name's Boggs, an' that I'm a native of Kentucky, an' little personalities like that; an' what wakes me up is this Spanish Bill.

"'"See yere," says this hold-up, "I'm goin' to turn in now, an' it's time you-all is up. Yere's what you do: Thar's five whiskey-checks on the Tub of Blood, which will he'p you to an appetite. Followin' of a s'fficient quantity of fire-water, you will return to the Jackson House an' eat. I pays for it. I won't be outen my blankets by then; but they knows that Spanish Bill makes good, 'cause I impresses it on 'em speshul when I comes in.

"'"You-all don't know me," goes on this Spanish Bill, as I sets up an' blinks at him some foggy an' blurred, "an' I don't know you"— which we-alls allows, outen p'liteness, is a dead loss to both. "But my name's Spanish Bill, an' I'm turnin' monte in the Bank Exchange. I'll be thar at my table by first-drink time this evenin'; an' if you sa'nters that a-way at that epock, we'll have a drink; an' bein' as you're busted, of course I stakes you moderate on your way."

"'It's this bluff about me not havin' money puts me in mind later that this Bill must have rustled my raiments when he finds me that time when I'm presided over by coyotes while I sleeps. When he says it, however, I merely remarks that while I'm grateful to him as mockin'-birds, money after all ain't no object with me; an', pullin' off my nigh moccasin, I pours some two pounds of specie onto the blankets.

"'"Which I packs this in my boot," I observes, "to put mysc'f in mind I've got a roll big enough to fill a nose-bag over to Howard's store."

"'"An' I'm feelin' the galiest to hear it," says this Spanish Bill; though as I su'gests he acts pained an' amazed, like a gent who's over-looked a bet.

"'Well, that's all thar is to that part. That's where Spanish Bill launches that bread of his'n; an' the way it later turns out it sorter b'ars down on me, an' keeps me rememberin' what that skyscout says at the pra'r-meetin' about the action a gent gets by playin' a good deed to win.

"'It's the middle of January, mebby two months later, when I'm over on the Upper Caliente about fifty miles back of the Spanish Peaks. I'm workin' a bunch of cattle; Cross-K is the brand; y'ear-marks a swallow-fork in the left, with the right y'ear onderhacked.'

"What's the good of a y'ear-mark when thar's a brand?" repeated the Old Cattleman after me, for I had interrupted with the question. "Whatever's the good of y'ear-marks? Why, when mixed cattle is in a bunch, standin' so close you can't see no brands on their sides, an' you-all is ridin' through the outfit cuttin' out, y'ear-marks is what you goes by. Cattle turns to look as you comes ridin' an' pesterin' among 'em, an' their two y'ears p'ints for'ard like fans. You gets their y'ear-marks like printin' on the page of a book. If you was to go over a herd by the brands, you wouldn't cut out a steer an hour. But to trail back after Boggs.

"'It's two months later, an' I'm ridin' down a draw one day,' says this Dan Boggs, 'cussin' the range an' the weather, when my pony goes to havin' symptoms. This yere pony is that sagacious that while it makes not the slightest mention of cattle when they's near, it never comes up on deer, or people in the hills, but it takes to givin' of manifestations. This is so I can squar myse'f for whatever game they opens on us.

"'As I says, me an' this yere wise pony is pushin' out into the Caliente when the pony begins to make signs. I brings him down all cautious where we can look across the valley, an'

[Illustration with caption: "Nacherally I stops an' surveys him careful]

you-all can gamble I'm some astonished to see a gent walkin' along afoot, off mebby a couple hundred yards. He sorter limps an' leans over on one side like he's hurt. Nacherally I stops an' surveys him careful. It's plenty strange he's thar at all; an' stranger still he's afoot. I looks him over for weepons; I wants to note what he's like an' how he's heeled.

"'You saveys as well as me it don't do to go canterin' out to strangers that a-way in the hills; speshully a stranger who's afoot. He might hunger for your pony for one thing, an' open a play on you with his gun, as would leave you afoot an' likewise too dead to know it.

"'I'm allers cautious that a-way, around a party who's lost his hoss. It locoes him an' makes him f'rocious; I s'pose bein' afoot he feels he'pless, an' let out an' crazy. A gent afoot is a heap easier to aggravate, too; an' a mighty sight more likely to lay for you than when he's in a Texas saddle with a pony between his knees.

"'Which is why I remarks, that I stacks up this pedestrian careful an' accurate before I goes after him.

"'As I says, he carries on like he's hurt; an' he's packin' a six-shooter. He seems familiar, too; an' while I looks him over I'm wonderin' where I cuts his trail before.

"'As I has the advantage of a Winchester, I at last rides into the open an' gives a whoopee. The party turns, comes limpin' toward me, an' whoever do you allow it is? Which it's shorely Spanish Bill; an' it's right yere he gets action on that bread on the waters he plays in when he recovers me that time in Taos.

"'To make it brief, Spanish Bill tells me that after I leaves Taos he goes over an' deals monte a bit at Wagon Mound. One night a Mexican comes caperin' in, an' Bill gives him a layout or two. At last he makes an alcy bet of fifty dollars on the queen; what the Greasers calls the "hoss." The Mexican loses; an' instead of takin' it easy like a sport should, he grabs the money.

"'As was his dooty, Spanish Bill bends his six-shooter over the
Mexican. Tharupon he searches out a knife; an' this yere so complicates the business, Bill, to simplify things, plugs the Mexican full of holes.

"'This shootin' is on the squar', an' no one takes hostile notice of it. Spanish Bill goes on layin' out his monte same as usual. Two days later, though, he gets a p'inter the Mexicans is fixin' for him. So that night he moves camp—mebby to where it's a hundred an' sixty miles from Wagon Mound, over on the Vermejo.

"'But it looks like the Greasers hangs to the trail; for the day before I tracks up on him a band of 'em hops outen a dry arroya, where they's bush-wackin' for him, an' goes to shootin'. As might be expected, Spanish Bill turns loose, free an' frequent, an' they all shorely has a high, excessive time.

"'The Mexicans downs Spanish Bill's pony, an' a bullet creases Bill's side; which last is what curves him over an' indooces him to limp when I trails up with him.

"'As Spanish Bill goes down, the Mexicans scatter. The game is too high for 'em. They was shy two people, with another plugged deep an' strong; by which you notes that Bill is aimin' low an' good.

"'After the shootin' Spanish Bill crawls over to a ranch, an', gettin' a pony an' saddle, which he easy does, he breaks back into the hills where I encounters him. It's that mornin' his pony gets tired of the deal, an' bucks him off, an' goes stampedin' back. That's why he's afoot.

"'While he's talkin' all this, I recalls how Spanish Bill rounds me up that night in Taos, so I don't hesitate. I takes him over to my camp. The next mornin' he turns his nose for Texas on my best pony; which is the last I sees or hears of Spanish Bill, onless he's the Bill who's lynched over near Eagle Pass a year later, of which I surmises it's some likely.

"'But whether Bill's lynched or not, it all brings up ag'in what that Gospel-gent says about doin' benev'lences; an' how after many days you dies an' makes a winnin', an' lives on velvet all eternity. An' don't you know this Spanish Bill pickin' me up that night, an' then in less than two months, when he's afoot an' hurt in the hills, gettin' ag'inst me an' drawin' out of the game ahead a saddle, a pony an' safety, makes it seem like that Bible-sharp is right a whole lot?

"'That's how it strikes me,' concloods Boggs. 'An' as I tells you; if so many cattle don't die that spring; an' if I don't give way so frightful in my talk, I'd shorely hunted down a congregation the next June, an' stood in.'"

CHAPTER XVIII.

DAWSON & RUDD, PARTNERS.

"Whatever's the difference between the East an' the West?" said the Old Cattleman, repeating my question rather for the purpose of consideration than from any failure to understand: "What's the difference between the East an' the West? Which, so far as I notes, to relapse into metaphor, as you-alls says, the big difference is that the East allers shoots from a rest; while the West shoots off hand.

"The West shore learns easy an' is quick to change a system or alter a play. It's plumb swift, the West is; an' what some regards as rough is mere rapidity. The West might go broke at faro-bank in the mornin', an' be rich at roulette in the afternoon; you can't tell. I knows partners in Arizona who rolls out in the gray light of breakin' day an' begins work by dissolvin' an' windin' up the firm's affairs. By dark them same gents is pards ag'in in a new enterprise complete. Folks'll fight at sun-up an' cook their chile con carne together at night, an' then sleep onder the same blankets. For which causes thar's no prophets in the West; a Western future that a-way bein' so mighty oncertain no prophet can fasten his lariat.

"Speakin' of pards an' the fog which surrounds what the same is likely to do, makes me think of the onlicensed an' onlooked-for carryin's-on of 'Doby Dawson an' Copper Queen Billy Rudd. Them two gents fosters a feud among themse'fs that splits 'em wide open an' keeps 'em pesterin' each other for years; which the doin's of them locoed people is the scandal of Wolfville while it lasts.

"It's mebby the spring after we erects the Bird Cage Op'ry House, an' Wolfville is gettin' to be considerable of a camp. We-alls is organized for a shore-'nough town, an Jack Moore is a shore-'nough marshal, with Enright for alcalde that a-way, an' thar's a heap of improvements.

"When I first tracks into Wolfville, cows is what you might call the leadin' industry, with whiskey an' faro-bank on the side. But in the days of 'Doby Dawson an' Copper Queen Billy Rudd, ore has been onearthed, the mines is opened, an' Wolfville's swelled tremendous. We-alls even wins a county-seat fight with Red Dog, wherein we puts it all over that ornery hamlet; an' we shorely deals the game for the entire region.

"As I states, it's the spring after we promotes the Bird Cage Op'ry House—which temple of amoosements is complete the fall before—that 'Doby an' Billy turns up in Wolfville. I knows she's spring, for I'm away workin' the round-up at the time, an' them gents is both thar drunk when I comes in.

"'Doby an' Billy's been pards for ten years. They's miner folks, an' 'Doby tells me himse'f one day that him an' Billy has stood in on every mine excitement from Alaska to Lower Californy. An' never once does they get their trails crossed or have a row.

"The two gents strikes at Wolfville when the mines is first opened, an' stakes out three claims; one for 'Doby, one for Billy. an' one for both of 'em. They's camped off up a draw about half a mile from town, where their claims is, an' has a little cabin an' seems to be gettin' along peaceful as a church; an' I reckons thar's' no doubt but they be.

"When 'Doby an' Billy first comes caperin' into Wolfville they's that thick an' friendly with each other, it's a shame to thieves. I recalls how their relations that a-way excites general admiration, an' Doc Peets even goes so far he calls 'em 'Jonathan an' David.' Which Peets would have kept on callin' 'em 'Jonathan an' David' plumb through, but Billy gets hostile.

"'It ain't me I cares for,' says Billy,—which he waits on Doc Peets with his gun,—'but no gent's goin' to malign 'Doby Dawson none an' alloode to him as 'Jonathan' without rebooke.'

"Seein' it pains Billy, an' as thar ain't even a white chip in mere nomenclature that a-way, of course Doc Peets don't call 'em 'Jonathan an' David' no more.

"'Doby an' Billy's been around mighty likely six months. The camp gets used to 'em an' likes 'em. They digs an' blasts away in them badger-holes they calls shafts all day, an' then comes chargin' down to the Red Light at night. After the two is drunk successful, they mutually takes each other home. An' as they lines out for their camp upholdin' an' he'pin' of each other, an' both that dead soaked in nose-paint they long before abandons tryin' to he'p themse'fs, I tells you, son, their love is a picture an' a lesson.

"'Which the way them pore, locoed sots,' says Old Man Enright one night, as 'Doby an' Billy falls outen the Red Light together, an' then turns in an' assists each other to rise,—'which the way them pore darkened drunkards rides herd on each other, an' is onse'fish an' generous that a-way, an' backs each other's play, is as good as sermons. You-all young men,' says Enright, turnin' on Jack Moore an' Boggs an' Tutt, 'you-all imatoor bucks whose character ain't really formed none yet, oughter profit plenty by their example.'

"As I remarks, 'Doby an' Billy's been inhabitin' Wolfville for mighty hard on six months when the trouble between 'em first shows its teeth. As Billy walks out one mornin' to sniff the climate some, he remarks a Mexican—which his name is Jose Salazar, but don't cut no figger nohow—sorter 'propriatin' of a mule.

"'The same,' as Billy says, in relatin' the casooalty later, 'bein' our star mule.'

"Nacherally, on notin' the misdeeds of this yere Greaser, Billy reaches inside the cabin, an' sorts out a Winchester an' plugs said culprit in among his thoughts, an tharby brings his mule-rustlin' an' his reflections to a pause some.

"It's two hours later, mebby, when the defunct's daughter— the outfit abides over in Chihuahua, which is the Mexican part of Wolfville—goes to a show-down with 'Doby an' Billy an wants to know does she get the corpse?

"'Shore,' says 'Doby, 'which we-alls has no further use for your paw, an' his remainder is free an' welcome to you. You can bet me an' Billy ain't holdin' out no paternal corpses none on their weepin' offsprings.'

"Followin' of his bluff, 'Doby goes over an' consoles with the Mexican's daughter, which her name's Manuela, an' she don't look so bad neither. Doc Peets, whose jedgement of females is a cinch, allows she's as pretty as a diamond flush, an' you can gamble Doc Peets ain't makin no blind leads when it's a question of squaws.

203

"So 'Doby consoles this yere Manuela a whole lot, while Billy, who's makin' coffee an' bakin'. powder biscuit inside, don't really notice he's doin' it. Fact is, Billy's plumb busy. The New York Store havin' changed bakin'-powder onto us the week before—the same redoocin' biscuits to a conundrum for a month after—an' that bakin'-powder change sorter engagin' Billy's faculties wholly, he forgets about deceased an' his daughter complete; that is, complete temporary. Later, when the biscuits is done an' offen his mind, Billy recalls all about it ag'in.

"'But 'Doby, who's a good talker an' a mighty tender gent that a- way, jumps in an' comforts Manuela, an' shows her how this mule her paw is stealin' is by way an' far the best mule in camp, an' at last she dries her tears an' allows in her language that she's growin' resigned. 'Doby winds up by he'pin' Manuela home with what's left of her paw.

"'Which it's jest like that 'Doby,' says Billy, when he hears of his partner packin' home his prey that a-way, an' his tones shows he admires 'Doby no limit, `which it's shorely like him. Take folks in distress, an' you-alls can bet your last chip 'Doby can't do too much for 'em.' "Billy's disgust sets in like the rainy season, however, when about two months later 'Doby ups an' weds this Mexican girl Manuela. When Billy learns of said ceremony, he declines a seat in the game, an' won't go near them nuptials nohow.

"'An' I declar's myse'f right yere,' says Billy. 'From now for'ard it's a case of lone hand with me. I don't want no more partners. When a gent with whom for ten years I've camped, trailed, an' prospected with, all the way from the Dalls to the Gila, quits me cold an' clammy for a squaw he don't know ten weeks, you can gamble that lets me plumb out. I've done got my med'cine. an' I'm ready to quit.'

"But 'Doby an' Billy don't actooally make no assignment, nor go into what you-all Eastern sharps calls liquidation. The two goes on an' works their claims together, an' the firm name still waves as 'Doby Dawson an' Copper Queen Billy Rudd,' only Billy won't go into 'Doby's new wickeyup where he's got Manuela,—not a foot.

"'Which I might have conquered my native reluctance,' says Billy, 'so to do, an' I even makes up my mind one night—it's after I've got my grub, an' you-alls knows how plumb soft an' forgivin' that a- way a gent is when his stomach's full of grub—to go up an' visit 'em a lot. But as I gets to the door I hears a noise I don't savey; an' when I Injuns up to a crack an' surveys the scene, I'm a coyote if thar ain't 'Doby, with his wife in his lap, singin' to her. That's squar'; actooally singin'; which sech efforts reminds me of ballards by cinnamon b'ars.

"'I ain't none shore,' goes on Billy, as he relates about it to me, 'but I'd stood sech egreegious plays, chargin' it general to 'Doby's gettin' locoed an' mushy; but when this yere ingrate ends his war- song, what do you-all reckon now he does? Turns in an' begins 'pologizin' for me downin' her dad. Which the old hold-up is on the mule an' goin' hell-bent when I curls him up. Well, that ends things with me. I turns on my heels an' goes down to the Red Light an' gets drunk plumb through. You recalls it; the time I'm drunk a month, an' Cherokee Hall bars me at faro-bank, allowin' I'm onconscious of my surroundin's.'

"Billy goes on livin' at their old camp, an' 'Doby an' Manuela at the new one 'Doby built. This last is mebby four hundred yards more up the draw. Durin' the day 'Doby an' Billy turns in an' works an' digs an' drills an' blasts together as of yore. The main change is that at evenin' Billy gets drunk alone; an' as 'Doby ain't along to he'p Billy home an' need Billy's he'p to get home, lots of times Billy falls by the trail an' puts in the night among the mesquite- bushes an' the coyotes impartial.

"This yere goes on for plumb a year, an' while things is cooler an' more distant between 'em, same as it's bound to be when two gents sleeps in different camps, still 'Doby an' Billy is trackin' along all right. One mornin', however, Billy goes down to the holes they's projectin' over, but no 'Doby shows up. It goes on ontil mighty likely fifth-drink time that forenoon, an' as Billy don't see no trace, sign, nor signal-smoke of his pard, he gets oneasy.

"'It's a fact,' says Billy afterward, 'thar's hours when I more'n half allows this yere squaw of 'Doby's has done took a knife, or some sech weepon, an' gets even with 'Doby, while he sleeps, for me pluggin' her paw about the mule. It's this yere idee which takes me outen the shaft I'm sinkin', an' sends me cavortin' up to 'Doby's camp. I passes a resolution on my way that if she's cashed 'Doby's chips for him that a-way, I'll shorely sa'nter over an' lay waste all Chihuahua to play even for the blow.'

"But as all turns out, them surmises of Billy's is idle. He gets mebby easy six-shooter distance from the door, when he discerns a small cry like a fox-cub's whine. Billy listens, an' the yelp comes as cl'ar on his years as the whistle of a curlew. Billy tumbles.

"'I'm a Chinaman,' says Billy, 'if it ain't a kid!'

"So he backs off quiet an' noiseless ontil he's dead safe, an' then he lifts the long yell for 'Doby. When 'Doby emerges he confirms them beliefs of Billy's; it's a kid shore-'nough.

"'Boy or girl?' says Billy.

"'Boy,' says 'Doby.'

"'Which I shorely quits you cold if it's a girl; says Billy. 'As it is, I stands by you in your troubles. I ain't none s'prised at your luck, 'Doby,' goes on Billy. ` I half foresees some sech racket as this the minute you gets married. However, if it's a boy she goes. I ain't the gent to lay down on an old-time runnin'-mate while luck's ag'in him; an' I'll still be your partner an' play out my hand.'

"Of course, 'Doby has to go back to lookout his game. An' as Billy's that rent an' shaken by them news he can't work none, he takes two or three drinks of nose-paint, an' then promulgates as how it's a holiday. Billy feels, too, that while this yere's a blow, still it's a great occasion; an' as he takes to feelin' his whiskey an' roominatin' on the tangled state of affairs, it suddenly strikes him he'll jest nacherally close up the trail by the house.

"'Women is frail people an' can't abide noises that a-way,' says Billy, ` an' 'Doby's shore lookin' some faded himse'f. I reckons, tharfore, I'll sorter stop commerce along this yere thoroughfar' ontil further orders. What 'Doby an' his squaw needs now is quietood an' peace, an' you can wager all you-alls is worth they ain't goin' to suffer no disturbances.'

"It ain't half an hour after this before Billy's got two signs, both down an' up the trail, warnin' of people to hunt another wagon- track. The signs is made outen pine boards, an' Billy has marked this yere motto onto 'em with a burnt stick

"'DOBY'S GOT A PAPOOSE, SO PULL YOUR FREIGHT."

"It ain't no time after Billy posts his warnin's, an' he's still musin' over 'em mighty reflective, when along projects a Mexican with a pair of burros he's packin' freight on. The Mexican's goin' by the notices witbout payin' the least heed tharto. But this don't do Billy, an' he stands him up.

"'Can you read?' says Billy to the Mexican, at the same time p'intin' to the signs.

"The Mexican allows in Spanish—which the same Billy saveys an' palavers liberal—that he can't read. Then he p'ints out to go by ag'in.

"'No you don't none, onless in the smoke; says Billy, an' throws a gun on him. 'Pause where you be, my proud Castilian, an' I'll flood your darkened ignorance with light by nacherally readin' this yere inscription to you a whole lot.'

"Tharupon Billy reads off the notice a heap impressive, an' winds up by commandin' of the Mexican to line out on the trail back.

"'Vamos!' says Billy. 'Which if you insists on pushin' along through yere I'll turn in an' crawl your hump some.'

"But the Mexican gets ugly as a t'ran'tler at this, an' with one motion he lugs out a six-shooter an' onbosoms the same.

"Billy is a trifle previous with a gun himse'f, an' while the Mexican is mighty abrupt, he gets none the best of Billy.

Which   the
outcome is the Mexican's shot plumb dead in his moccasins, while
Billy takes a small crease on his cheek, the same not bein' deadly.
Billy then confiscates the burros.

"'Which I plays 'em in for funeral expenses,' says Billy, an' is turnin' of 'em into the corral by his camp jest as 'Doby comes prancin' out with a six-shooter to take part in whatever game is bein' rolled.

"When 'Doby sees Billy's signs that a-way, he's 'fected so he weeps tears. He puts his hands on Billy's shoulder, an' lookin' at him, while his eyes is swimmin', he says:

"'Billy, you-all is the thoughtfullest pard that ever lived.'

"'Doby throws so much soul into it, an' him givin' 'way to emotions, it comes mighty near onhingin' Billy.

"'I knows I be,' he says, shakin' 'Doby by the hand for a minute, 'but, Old Man, you deserves it. It's comin' to you, an' you bet your life you're goin' to get it. With some folks this yere would be castin' pearls before swine, but not with you, 'Doby. You can 'preciate a play, an' I'm proud to be your partner.'

"The next few months goes on, an' 'Doby an' Billy keeps peggin' away at their claims, an' gettin' drunk an' rich about equal. Billy is still that reedic'lous he won't go up to 'Doby's camp; but 'Doby comes over an' sees him frequent. The first throw out of the box Billy takes a notion ag'in the kid an' allows he don't want no traffic with him,—none whatever.

"But 'Doby won't have it that a-way, an' when it's about six months old he packs said infant over one mornin' while Billy's at breakfast.

"'Ain't he hell!' says 'Doby, a heap gleeful, at the same time sawin' the infant onto Billy direct.

"Of course Billy has to hold him then. Which he acts like he's a hot tamale, an' shifts him about in his arms. But it's plain he ain't so displeased neither. At last the kid reaches out swift an' cinches onto Billy's beard that a-way. This delights Billy, while 'Doby keeps trackin' 'round the room too tickled to set down. All he can remark—an' he does it frequent, like it tells the entire story—is:

"'Billy, ain't he hell?'

"An' Billy ain't none back'ard admittin' he is, an' allows on hesitatin' it's the hunkiest baby in Arizona.

"'An' I've got dust into the thousands,' remarks Billy, 'which says he's the prize papoose of the reservation, an' says it ten to one. This yere offspring is a credit to you, 'Doby, an' I marvels you-all is that modest over it.'

"'You can bet it ain't no Siwash,' says 'Doby. 'It's clean strain, that infant is, if I does say it.'

"'That's whatever.' says Billy. looking the infant over an' beginnin' to feel as proud of it as 'Doby himse'f, 'that's whatever. An' I'm yere to remark, any gent who can up an' without no talk or boastin' have such a papoose as that, is licensed to plume himse'f tharon, an' put on dog over it, the same without restraint. If ever you calls the turn for the limit, pard, it's when you has this yere child.'

"At this 'Doby an' Billy shakes hands like it's a ceremony, an' both is grave an' dignified about it. 'Doby puts it up that usual he's beyond flattery, but when a gent of jedgement like Billy looks over a play that a-way, an' indorses it, you can bet he's not insensible. Then they shakes hands ag'in, an' 'Doby says:

"'Moreover, not meanin' no compliments, nor tossin' of no boquets, old pard, me an' Manuela names this young person "Willyum"; same as you-all.'

"Billy comes mighty near droppin' the infant on the floor at this, an' the small victim of his onthoughtfulness that a-way yells like a coyote.

"'That settles it,' says Billy. 'A gent who could come down to blastin' an' drillin'—mere menial tasks, as they shorely be— on the heels of honor like this, is a mighty sight more sordid than Copper Queen Billy Rudd. 'Doby, this yere is a remarkable occasion, an' we cel'brates.'

"By this time the infant is grown plumb hostile, an' is howlin' to beat the band; so 'Doby puts it up he'll take him to his mother an' afterwards he's ready to join Billy in an orgy.

"'I jest nacherally stampedes back to the agency with this yere
Willyum child,' says 'Doby, an' then we-alls repairs to the Red
Light an' relaxes.'

"They shorely does-I don't recall no sech debauch—that is, none so extreme an' broadcast—since Wolfville and Red Dog engages in them Thanksgiviin' exercises.

"Doby an' Billy, as time goes by, allers alloods to the infant as 'Willyum,' so's not to get him an' Billy mixed; an' durin' the next two years, while Billy still goes shy so far as trackin' over to 'Doby's ranch is concerned, as soon as he walks, Willyum comes down the canyon to see Billy every day.

"Oh, no, Billy ain't none onforgivin' to Manuela for ropin' up 'Doby an' weddin' him that a-way; but you see downin' her paw for stealin' the mule that time gets so it makes him bashful an' reluctant.

"'It ain't that I'm timorous neither, nor yet assoomin' airs,' this yere Billy says to me when he brings it up himse'f how he don't go over to 'Doby's, 'but I'm never no hand to set 'round an' visit free an' easy that a-way with the posterity of a gent which I has had cause to plant. This yere ain't roodness; it's scrooples,' says Billy, 'an' so it's plumb useless for me to go gettin' sociable with 'Doby's wife.'

"It's crowdin' close on two years after the infant's born when 'Doby an' Billy gets up their feud which I speaks of at the beginnin'. Yere's how it gets fulminated. Billy's loafin' over by the post- office door one evenin', talkin' to Tutt an' Boggs an' a passel of us, when who comes projectin' along, p'intin' for the New York Store, but 'Doby's wife an' Willyum. As they trails by, Willyum sees Billy—Willyum can make a small bluff at talkin' by now—an', p'intin' his finger at Billy, he sags back on his mother's dress like he aims to halt her, an' says:

"'Pop-pa! Pop-pa!' meanin' Billy that a-way; although the same is erroneous entire, as every gent in Wolfville knows.

"'Which if Willyum's forefinger he p'ints with

is a Colt's forty-four, an' instead of sayin' `Poppa!' he onhooks the same at Billy direct, now I don't reckon Billy could have been more put out. 'Doby's wife drags Willyum along at the time like he's a calf goin' to be branded, an' she never halts or pauses. But Billy turns all kinds of hues, an' is that prostrated he surges across to the Red Light an' gets two drinks alone, never invitin' nobody, before he realizes. When he does invite us he admits frank he's plumb locoed for a moment by the shock.

"'You bet!' says Billy, as he gets his third drink, the same bein' took in common with the pop'lace present, 'you bet! thar ain't a gent in camp I'd insult by no neglect; but when Willyum makes them charges an' does it publicly, it onhinges my reason, an' them two times I don't invite you-alls, I'm not responsible.'

"We-alls sees Billy's wounded, an' tharfore it's a ha'r-line deal to say anythin'; but as well as we can we tells him that what Willyum says, that a-way, bein' less'n two year old, is the mere prattle of a child, an' he's not to be depressed by it.

"'Sech breaks,' says Dan Boggs, 'is took jocose back in the States.'

"'Shore!' says Texas Thompson, backin' Boggs's play; 'them little bluffs of infancy, gettin' tangled that a-way about their progenitors, is regarded joyous in Laredo. Which thar's not the slightest need of Billy bein' cast down tharat.'

"'I ain't sayin' a word, gents,' remarks Billy, an' his tones is sad. You-alls means proper an friendly. But I warns the world at this time that I now embarks on the spree of my life. I'm goin to get drunk an' never hedge a bet; an my last requests, the same bein' addressed to the barkeep, personal,

213

is to set every bottle of bug- juice in the shebang on the bar, thar to repose within the reach of all ontil further orders.'

"It's about an hour later, an' Billy, who's filed away a quart of fire-water in his interior by now, is vibratin' between the Red Light an' the dance-hall, growin' drunk an' dejected even up. It's then he sees 'Doby headin' up the street. 'Doby hears of his son Willyum's wild play from his wife, an' it makes him hot that a-way. But he ain't no notion of blamin' Billy; none whatever.

"However, 'Doby don't have entire charge of the round-up, an' he has to figger with Billy right along.

"'Doby,' shouts Billy, as he notes his pard approachin', while he balances himse'f in his moccasins a heap difficult, "Doby, your infant Willyum is a eediot. Which if I was the parent of a fool papoose like Willyum, I'd shorely drop him down a shaft a whole lot an' fill up the shaft. He won't assay two ounces of sense to the ton, Willyum won't; an' he ain't worth powder an' fuse to work him. Actooally, that pore imbecile baby Willyum, don't know his own father.'

"Which the rage of 'Doby is beyond bounds complete. For about half a minute him an' Billy froths an' cusses each other out scand'lous, an' then comes the guns. The artillery is a case of s'prise, the most experienced gent in Wolfville not loekin' for no gun-play between folks who's been pards an' blanket-mates for years.

"However, it don't last long; it looks like both gets sorter conscience-stricken that a-way, an' lets up. Still, while it's short, it's long enough for Billy to get his laig ousted with one of 'Doby's bullets, an' it all lays Billy up for Doc Peets to fuss with for over three months.

"While Billy's stretched out, an' Doe Peets is ridin' herd on his laig, 'Doby keeps as savage as an Apache an' don't come near Billy. The same, however, ain't full proof of coldness, neither; for Billy's done give it out he'll down 'Doby if he pokes his head in the door, an' arranges his guns where he can work 'em in on the enterprise easy.

"But Willyum don't take no stand-off. The last thing Willyum's afraid of is Billy; so he comes waltzin' over each day, clumsy as a cub cinnamon on his short laigs, an' makes himse'f plumb abundant. He plays with Billy, an' he sleeps with Billy, Willyum does; an' he eats every time the nigger, who's come over from the corral to lookout Billy's domestic game while he's down, rustles some grub.

"'Doby's disgusted with Willyum's herdin' 'round with Billy that a- way, bein' sociable an' visitin' of him, an' he lays for Willyum an' wallops him. When Billy learns of it—which he does from Willyum himse'f when that infant p'ints in for a visit the day after—he's as wild as a mountain lion. Billy can't get out none, for his laig is a heap fragmentary as yet,— 'Doby's bullet gettin' all the results which is comin' that time,—but he sends 'Doby word by Peets, if he hears of any more punishments bein' meted to Willyum, he regards it as a speshul affront to him, an' holds 'Doby responsible personal as soon as he can hobble.

"'Tell him,' says Billy, 'that if he commits any further atrocities ag'in this innocent Willyum child, I'll shore leave him too dead to skin.'

"'This yere Billy's gettin' locoed entire,' says Enright, when he's told of Billy's bluff. 'The right to maul your immediate descendants that a-way is guaranteed by the constitootion, an' is one of them things we-alls fights for at Bunker Hill.

215

However, I reckons Billy's merely blowin' his horn; bein' sick an' cantankerous with his game knee.'

"Billy gets well after a while, an' him an' 'Doby sorter plans to avoid each other. Whatever work they puts in on the claim they holds in partnership, they hires other gents to do. Personal, each works the claim he holds himse'f, which keeps 'em asunder a whole lot, an' is frootful of peace.' "Deep inside their shirts I allers allows these yere persons deems high an' 'fectionate of one another right at the time they's hangin' up their hardest bluffs an' carryin' on most hostile. Which trivial incidents discloses this.

"Once in the Red Light, when a party who's new from Tucson, turns in to tell some light story of Billy,—him not bein' present none,— 'Doby goes all over this yere racontoor like a landslide, an' retires him from s'ciety for a week. An' 'Doby don't explain his game neither; jest reprimands this offensive Tucson gent, an' lets it go as it lays. Of course, we-alls onderstands it's 'cause 'Doby ain't puttin' up with no carpin' criticism of his old pard; which the same is nacheral enough.

"Don't you-all ever notice, son, how once you takes to fightin' for a party an' indorsin' of his plays, it gets to be a habit,—same, mebby, as fire-water? Which you lays for his detractors an' pulls on war for him that a-way long after you ceases to have the slightest use for him yourse'f. It's that a-way with 'Doby about Billy.

"An' this yere Billy's feelin's about 'Doby is heated an' sedulous all sim'lar. 'Doby gets laid out for a week by rheumatics, which he acquires years before—he shore don't rope onto them rheumatics none 'round Wolfville, you can gamble! said camp bein' salooberous that a-way—over on the Nevada plateaus, an' while he's treed an' can't come down to his claim, a passel of sharps ups an' mavericks it; what miners calls 'jumps it.' Whatever does Billy do? Paints for war prompt an' enthoosiastic, takes his gun, an' the way he stampedes an' scatters them marauders don't bother him a bit.

"But while, as I states, this yere trick of makin' war-med'cine which 'Doby an' Billy has, an' schedoolin' trouble for folks who comes projectin' 'round invadin' of the other's rights, mebby is a heap habit, I gleans from it the idee likewise that onder the surface they holds each other in esteem to a p'int which is romantic.

"Doby an' Billy lives on for a year after 'Doby plugs Billy in the laig, keepin' wide apart an' not speakin'. Willyum is got so he puts in most of his nights an' all of his days with Billy; which the spectacle of Billy packin' Willyum about camp nights is frequent. 'Doby never 'pears to file no protest; I reckons he looks on it as a fore-ordained an' hopeless play. However, Billy's a heap careful of Willyum's morals, an' is shorely linin' him up right.

"Once a new barkeep in the dance-hall allows he'll promote Willyum's feelin's some with a spoonful of nose-paint.

"'No, you don't,' says Billy, plenty savage; 'an' since the matter comes up I announces cold that, now or yereafter, the first gent who saws off nose-paint on Willyum, or lays for the morals of this innocent infant to corrupt 'em, I'll kill an' skelp him so shore as I packs gun or knife.'

"'Which shows,' said Dan Boggs later, when he hears of Billy's blazer, 'that this yere Billy Rudd is a mighty high-minded gent, an' you-alls can play it to win he has my regards. He can count me in on this deal to keep Willyum from strong drinks.'

"'I thinks myse'f he's right,' says Cherokee Hall. 'Willyum is now but three years old, which is shore not aged. My idee would be to raise Willyum, an' not let him drink a drop of nose-paint ever, merely to show the camp what comes of sech experiments.'

"But Billy's that pos'tive an' self-reliant he don't need no encouragement about how he conducts Willyum's habits; an', followin' his remarks, Willyum allers gets ignored complete on invitations to licker. Packin' the kid 'round that a-way shortens up Billy's booze a lot, too. He don't feel so free to get tanked expansive with Willyum on his mind an' hands that a-way.

"It's shorely a picture, the tenderness Billy lavishes on Willyum. Many a night when Billy's stayin' late, tryin' to win himse'f outen the hole, I beholds him playin' poker, or mebby it's farebank, with Willyum curled up on his lap an' shirt-front, snorin' away all sound an' genial, an' Billy makin' his raises an' callin' his draw to the dealer in whispers, for fear he wakes Willyum.

"But thar comes a time when the feud is over, an' 'Doby an' Billy turns in better friends than before. For a month mebby thar's a Mexican girl—which she's a cousin that a-way or some kin to 'Doby's wife—who's been stayin' at 'Doby's house, sorter backin' their play.

"It falls out frequent this Mexican girl, Marie, trails over to Billy's, roundin' up an' collectin' of Willyum to put another shirt onto him, or some sech benefit. Billy never acts like he's impressed by this yere girl, an', while he relinquishes

Willyum every time, he growls an' puts it up he's malev'lent over it.

"But the seniorita is game, an' don't put no store by Billy's growls. She ropes up Willyum an' drags him away mighty decisive. Willyum howls an' calls on Billy for aid, which most likely is pain to Billy's heart; but he don't get it none. The senorita harnesses Willyum into a clean shirt, an' then she throws Willyum loose on the range ag'in, an' he drifts back to Billy.

"It's the general view that Billy never once thinks of wedlock with the senorita if he's let alone. But one day Doc Peets waxes facetious.

"'In a month,' says Peets to Billy, while we-alls is renooin' our sperits in the Red Light, 'this yere Marie'll quit comin' over for Willyum.'

"'Why?' says Billy, glarin' at Peets s'picious.

"'Cause,' replies Peets, all careless, "cause you ups an' weds her by then. I sees it in your eye. Then, when she's thar for good, I reckons she nacherally quits comin' over.'

"'Oh, I don't know,' says Texas Thompson, who's takin' in Doc Peets' remark; ' I don't allow Billy's got the nerve to marry this yere Marie. Not but what she's as pretty as an antelope. But think of 'Doby. He jest never would quit chewin' Billy's mane if he goes pullin' off any nuptial ceremonies with his wife's relative that a- way.'

"Billy looks hard as granite at this. He ain't sayin' nothin', but he gets outside of another drink in a way which shows his mind's made up, an' then he goes p'intin' off towards his camp, same as a gent who entertains designs.

"'I offers three to one,' says Cherokee Hall, lookin' after Billy sorter thoughtful that a-way, 'that Billy weds this yere Mexican girl in a week; an' I'll go five hundred dollars even money he gets her before night.'

"'An' no takers,' says Doc Peets, 'for I about thinks you calls the turn.'

"An' that's what happens. In two hours after this impulsive Billy prances out of the Red Light on the heels of Texas Thompson's remarks about how hostile 'Doby would be if he ever gets Marie, he's done lured her before the padre over in Chihuahua, an' the padre marries 'em as quick as you could take a runnin'-iron an' burn a brand on a calf.

"'Which this is not all. Like they was out to add to the excitement a whole lot, I'm a Mohave if 'Doby an' his wife don't turn loose an' have another infant that same day.

"'I never sees a gent get so excited over another gent's game as
Billy does over 'Doby's number two. He sends his new wife up   to
'Doby's on the run, while he takes Willyum an' comes pirootin'   back
to the Red Light to brace up. Billy's shore nervous an' needs it.

"'My pore child,' says Billy to Willyum about the third drink— Willyum is settin' on a monte-table an' payin' heed to Billy a heap decorous an' respectful for a three-year-old— 'my pore child,' says Billy that a-way, 'you-all is ag'in a hard game up at your paw's. This yere is playin' it plumb low on you, Willyum. It looks like they fills a hand ag'in you, son, an' you ain't in it no more at 'Doby's; who, whatever is your fool claims on that p'int a year ago, is still your dad ondoubted. But you-all knows me, Willyum. You knows that talk in Holy Writ. If your father an' mother shakes you, your Uncle Billy takes you up. I'm powerful 'fraid, Willyum, you'll have to have action on them promises."

"Willyum listens to Billy plenty grave an' owly, but he don't make no observations on his luck or communicate no views to Billy except that he's hungry. This yere ain't relevant none, but Billy at once pastures him out on a can of sardines an' some crackers, while he keeps on bein' liberal to himse'f about whiskey.

"'I don't feel like denyin' myse'f nothin',' he says. 'Yere I gets married, an' in less'n an hour my wife is ravaged away at the whoop of dooty to ride herd on another gent's fam'ly,; leavin' me, her husband, with that other gent's abandoned progeny on my hands. This yere's gettin' to be a boggy ford for Billy Rudd, you bet.'

"But while Billy takes on a heap, he don't impress me like he's hurt none after all. When Doc Peets trails in from 'Doby's, where he's been in the interests of science that a-way, Billy at once drug him aside for a pow-wow. They talks over in one corner of the Red Light awhile, then Billy looks up like one load's offen his mind, an' yells:

" 'Barkeep, it's another boy. Use my name freely in urgin' drinks on the camp.'

"Then Billy goes on whisperin' to Doc Peets an' layin' down somethin', like his heart's sot on it. At last Doc says:

"'The best way, Billy, is for me to bring 'Doby over.' With this   Doc
Peets gets onto his pony at the door an' goes curvin' back to 'Doby's.

"'It's a boy,' says Billy to the rest of us after Doc Peets lines out, `an' child an' mother both on velvet an' winnin' right along.'

"These yere events crowdin' each other that a-way—first a weddin' an' then an infant boy—has a brightenin' effect on public sperit. It makes us feel like the camp's shorely gettin' a start. While we- alls is givin' way to Billy's desire to buy whiskey, Peets comes back, bringin' 'Doby.

"Thar's nothin' what you-alls calls dramatic about 'Doby an' Billy comin' together. They meets an' shakes, that's all. They takes a drink together, which shows they's out to be friends for good, an' then Billy says:

"'But what I wants partic'lar, 'Doby, is that you makes over to me your son Willyum. He's shore the finest young-one in Arizona, an' Marie an' me needs him to sorter organize on.'

"'Billy,' says 'Doby, 'you-all an' me is partners for years, an' we're partners yet. We has our storm cloud, an' we has also our eras of peace. Standin' as we do on the brink of one of said eras, an' as showin' sincerity, I yereby commits to you my son Willyum. Yereafter, when he calls you "Pop," it goes, an' the same will not be took invidious.'

"'Doby,' replies Billy, takin' him by the hand, 'this yere day 'lustrates the prophet when he says: "In the midst of life we're in luck." If you-all notes tears in my eyes I'm responsible for 'em. Willyum's mine. As I r'ars him it will be with you as a model. Now you go back where dooty calls you. When you ceases to need my wife, Marie, send her back to camp, an' notify me tharof. Pendin' of which said notice, however,' concloods Billy, turnin' to us after 'Doby starts back, 'Willyum an' me entertains.'"

CHAPTER XIX.

MACE BOWMAN, SHERIFF.

"And so you think the trouble lies with the man and not with the whiskey?" I said.

The Old Cattleman and I were discussing "temperance."

"Right you be. This yere whiskey-drinkin'," continued the old gentleman as he toyed with his empty glass, "is a mighty cur'ous play. I knows gents as can tamper with their little old forty drops frequent an' reg'lar. As far as hurtin' of 'em is concerned, it don't come to throwin' water on a drowned rat. Then, ag'in, I've cut gents's trails as drinkin' whiskey is like playin' a harp with a hammer. Which we-alls ain't all upholstered alike; that's whatever. We don't all show the same brands an' y'earmarks nohow: What's med'cine for one is p'isen for t'other; an' thar you be.

"Bein' a reg'lar, reliable drunkard that a-way comes mighty near bein' a disease. It ain't no question of nerve, neither. Some dead- game gents I knows—an' who's that obstinate they wouldn't move camp for a prairie-fire—couldn't pester a little bit with whiskey.

"Thar's my friend, Mace Bowman. Mace is clean strain cl'ar through, an' yet I don't reckon he ever gets to a show-down with whiskey once which he ain't outheld. But for grim nerve as'll never shiver, this yere Bowman is at par every time.

"Bowman dies a prey to his ambition. He starts in once to drink all the whiskey in Wolfville. By his partic'lar request most of the white male people of the camp stands in on the deal, a-backin' his play for to make Wolfville a dry camp. At the close of them two lurid weeks Mace lasts, good jedges, like Enright an' Doc Peets, allows he's shorely made it scarce some.

"But Wolfville's too big for him. Any other gent but Mace would have roped at a smaller outfit, but that wouldn't be Mace nohow. If thar's a bigger camp than Wolfville anywhere about, that's where he'd been. He's mighty high-hearted an' ambitious that a-way, an' it's kill a bull or nothin' when he lines out for buffalo.

"But the thirteenth day, he strikes in on the big trail, where you never meets no outfits comin' back, an' that settles it. The boys, not havin' no leader, with Mace petered, gives up the game, an' the big raid on nose-paint in Wolfville is only hist'ry now.

"When I knows Bowman first he's sheriff over in northeast New Mexico. A good sheriff Mace is, too. Thar ain't nothin' gets run off while he's sheriff, you bet. When he allows anythin's his dooty, he lays for it permiscus. He's a plumb sincere offishul that a-way.

"One time I recalls as how a wagon-train with households of folks into it camps two or three days where Mace is sheriff. These yere people's headin' for some'ers down on the Rio Grande, aimin' to settle a whole lot. Mebby it's the third mornin' along of sun-up when they strings out on the trail, an' we-alls thinks no more of 'em. It's gettin' about third-drink time when back rides a gent, sorter fretful like, an' allows he's done shy a boy.

"'When do you-all see this yere infant last?' says Mace.

"'Why,' says the gent, 'I shorely has him yesterday, 'cause my old woman done rounds 'em up an' counts.'

"'What time is that yesterday?'

"'Bout first-drink time,' says the bereaved party.

"'How many of these yere offsprings, corral count, do you-all lay claim to anyway?' asks Mace.

"'Which I've got my brand onto 'leven of 'em,' says the pore parent, beginnin' to sob a whole lot. 'Of course this yere young-one gettin' strayed this a-way leaves me short one. It makes it a mighty rough crossin', stranger, after bringin' that boy so far. The old woman, she bogs right down when she knows, an' I don't reckon she'll be the same he'pmeet to me onless I finds him ag'in.'

"'Oh, well,' says Mace, tryin' to cheer this bereft person up, 'we lose kyards in the shuffle which the same turns up all right in the deal; an' I reckons we-alls walks down this yearlin' of yours ag'in, too. What for brands or y'earmarks, does he show, so I'll know him.'

"'As to brands an' y'earmarks,' says the party, a-wipin' of his eye, 'he's shy a couple of teeth, bein' milk-teeth as he's shed; an' thar's a mark on his for'ard where his mother swipes him with a dipper, that a-way, bringin' him up proper. That's all I remembers quick.'

"Mace tells the party to take a cinch on his feelin's, an' stampedes over to the Mexican part of camp, which is called Chilili, on a scout for the boy. Whatever do you-all reckon's become of him, son? I'm a wolf if a Mexican ain't somehow cut him out of the herd an' stole him. Takes him in, same as you mavericks a calf. Why in the name of hoss-stealin' he ever yearns for that young-one is allers too many for me.

"When the abductor hears how Mace is on his trail, which he does from other Mexicans, he swings onto his bronco an' begins p'intin' out, takin' boy an' all. But Mace has got too far up on him, an' stops him mighty handy with a rifle. Mace could work a Winchester like you'd whirl a rope, an' the way he gets a bullet onder that black-an'-tan's left wing don't worry him a little bit. The bullet tears a hole through his lungs, an' the same bein' no further use for him to breathe with, he comes tumblin' like a shot pigeon, bringin' the party's offspring with him.

"Which this yere is almighty flatterin' to Mace as a shot, an' it plumb tickles the boy's sire. He allows he's lived in Arkansaw, an' shorely knows good shootin', an' this yere's speshul good. An' then he corrals the Greaser's skelp to take back with him.

"'It'll come handy to humor up the old woman with, when I gets back to camp,' he says; so he tucks the skelp into his war-bags an' thanks Mace for the interest he takes in his household.

"'That's all right,' says Mace; 'no trouble to curry a little short hoss like that.'

"He shakes hands with the Arkansaw gent, an' we-alls rounds   up   to Bob Step's an' gets a drink.

"But the cat has quite a tail jest the same. A Mexican that a-way is plenty oncertain. For instance: You're settin' in on a little game of monte all free an' sociable, an' one of 'em comes crowdin' 'round for trouble, an' you downs him. All good enough, says you. No other Mexican seems like he wants to assoome no pressure personal; no one goes browsin' 'round to no sheriff; an' thar you be deluded into theeries that said killin's quit bein' a question. That's where you- all is the victim of error.

"Which in this case the Mexican Mace stretches has uncles or somethin' down off Chaperita. Them relatives is rich. In a week—no one never saveys how—everybody knows that thar's five thousand dollars up for the first party who kills Mace. I speaks to him about it myse'f, allowin' he'd oughter be careful how he goes spraddlin' about permiscus. Mebby, when he's lookin' north some time, somebody gets him from the south.

"'I ain't worryin' none,' says Mace; 'I ain't got no friends as would down me, nohow; an' my enemies ain't likely none to think it's enough dinero. Killin' me is liable to come mighty high.'

"After which announcements he goes romancin' along in his cheerful, light-hearted way, drinkin' his whiskey an' bein' sheriff, mingled, an' in a week or so we-alls begins to forget about them rewards. One day a little Mexican girl who Mace calls Bonita—she'd shorely give a hoss for a smile from him any time—scouts over an' whispers to Mace as how three Greasers from down around Anton Chico is in camp on a hunt for his ha'r. Them murderers is out for the five thousand; they's over in Chilili right then.

"'Whereabouts in Chilili be them Mexicans?' asks Mace, kinder interested.

"'Over camped in old Santa Anna's dance. hall, a-drinkin' of mescal an' waitin' for dark,' says the girl.

"'All right,' says Mace; 'I'll prance over poco tiempo, an' it's mighty likely them aliens from Anton Chico is goin' to have a fitful time.'

"Mace kisses the little Bonita girl, an' tells her not to chirp nothin' to no Mexican; an' with the caress that a-way her black eyes gets blacker an' brighter, an' the red comes in her cheek, an' bats could see she'd swap the whole Mexican outfit for a word from Mace, an' throw herse'f in for laniyap.

"Mace p'ints out to get another gun; which is proper enough, for he's only one in his belt, an' in a case like this yere he's mighty likely to need two a lot.

"'Some of us oughter go over with Mace, I reckons,' says a party named Benson, sorter general to the crowd. 'What do you-alls think yourse'fs?'

"'Go nothin'!' retorts a gent who's called Driscoll, an' who's up to the hocks into a game of poker, an' don't like to see it break up an' him behind. 'The hand Mace holds don't need no he'p. If Mace is out after two or three of the boys now, it would be plenty different; but whoever hears of a white man's wantin' he'p that a- way to down three Greasers, an' him to open the game? Mace could bring back all the skelps in Chilili if he's that f'rocious an' wants to, an' not half try.'

"This seems to be the general idee, an', aside of some bets which is made, no one takes no interest. Bob Short puts it up he'd bet a hundred dollars even Mace gets one of 'em; a hundred to two hundred he gets two, an' a hundred to five hundred he gets 'em all; an' some short-kyard sharp who's up from Socorro, after figgerin' it all silent to himse'f, takes 'em all.

"'Now I don't reckon, stranger,' says Benson, sorter reproachful, to the short-kyard party, 'you knows Mace Bowman mighty well? If you- all did you wouldn't go up ag'in a shore thing like that.'

"We never gets anythin' but Mace's story for it. He tells later how he sa'nters into Santa Anna's an' finds his three Anton Chico felons all settin' alone at a table. They knows him, he says, an' he camps down over opp'site an' calls for a drink. They's watchin' Mace, an' him doin' sim'lar by them. Final, he says, one of 'em makes a play for his gun, an', seein' thar's nothin' to be made waitin', Mace jumps up with a six-shooter in each hand, an' thar's some noise an' a heap of smoke, an' them three Mexicans is eliminated in a bunch.

"When he plays his hand out Mace comes back over to us— no other Mexicans allowin' for to call him—an' relates how it is, an' nacheral we says it's all right, which it shorely is. I asks old Santa Anna for the details of the shake-up later, but he spreads his hands, an' shrugs his shoulders, an' whines

"'No quien sabe.'

"An', of course, as I can't tell, an' as Santa Anna don't, I gives' up askin'."

CHAPTER XX.

A WOLFVILLE THANKSGIVING.

It was in the earlier days of autumn. Summer had gone, and there was already a crisp sentiment of coming cold in the air. The Old Cattleman and I had given way to a taste for pedestrianism that had lain dormant through the hot months. It was at the close of our walk, and we were slowly making our way homeward.

"An' now the year's got into what hoss-folks calls the last quarter," remarked the old gentleman musingly. "You can feel the frost in the atmosphere; you can see where it's bit the leaves a lot, an' some of 'em's pale with the pain, an' others is blood-red from the wound. "Which I don't regard winter much, say twenty years ago. Thar's many a night when I spreads my blankets in the Colorado hills, flakes of snow a-fallin' as soft an' big an' white as a woman's hand, an' never heeds 'em a little bit. But them days is gone. Thar's no roof needed in my destinies then. An' as for bed, a slicker an' a pair of hobbles is sumptuous.

"When a gent rounds up seventy years he's mighty likely to get a heap interested in weather. It's the heel of the hunt with him then, an' he's worn an' tired, and turns nacherally to rest an' fire."

We plodded forward as he talked. To his sage comments on the seasons, and as well the old age of men, I offered nothing. My silence, however, seemed always to meet with his tacit approval; nor did he allow it to impede his conversational flow.

"Well," observed the old fellow, after a pause, "I reckons I'll see the winter through all right; likewise the fall. I'm a mighty sight like that old longhorn who allows he's allers noticed if he lives through the month of March he lives through the rest of the year; so I figgers I'll hold together that a-way ontil shorely March comin'. Anyhow I regards it as an even break I does.

"Thar's one thing about fall an' winter which removes the dreariness some. I alloods to them festivals sech as Thanksgivin' an' Christmas an' New Year. Do we-alls cel'brate these yere events in Wolfville? Which we shorely does. Take Christmas: You-all couldn't find a sober gent in Wolfville on that holy occasion with a search-warrant; the feelin' to cel'brate is that wide-spread an' fervid.

"Thanksgivin' ain't so much lotted on; which for one thing we frequent forgets it arrives that a-way. Thar's once, though, when we takes note of its approach, an' nacherally, bein' organized, we ketches it squar' in the door. Them Thanksgivin' doin's is shorely great festivities that time. It's certainly a whirl.

"Old Man Enright makes the first break; he sorter arranges the game. But before all is over, the food we eats, the whiskey we drinks, an' the lies we tells an' listens to, is a shock an' a shame to Arizona.

"Thar's a passel of us prowlin' 'round in the Red Light one day, when along comes Enright. He's got a paper in his hand, an' from the air he assooms it's shore plain he's on the brink of somethin'.

"'What I'm thinkin' of, gents, is this,' says Enright, final. 'I observes to-morrow to be Thanksgivin' by this yere paper

Old Monte packs in from Tucson. The Great Father sets to-morrow for a national blow-out, a-puttin' of it in his message on the broad ground that everybody's lucky who escapes death. Now, the question is, be we in this? an' if so, what form the saturnalia takes?'

What's the matter of us hoppin' over an' shootin' up Red Dog?" says Dan Boggs. 'That bunch of tarrapins ain't been shook up none for three months.'

"'Technical speakin',' says Doc Peets—which Peets, he shorely is the longest-headed sharp I ever sees, an' the galiest—'shootin' up Red Dog, while it's all right as a prop'sition an' highly creditable to Boggs, is not a Thanksgivin' play. The game, turned strict, confines itse'f to eatin', drinkin', an' lyin'.'

"'Thar's plenty of whiskey in camp,' says Jack Moore, meditative- like, 'whereby that drinkin' part comes easy.'

"'I assooms it's the will of all to pull off a proper Thanksgivin' caper,' says Enright, 'an' tharfore I su'gests that Doc Peets and Boggs waits on Missis Rucker at the O. K. restauraw an' learns what for a banquet she can rustle an' go the limit. Pendin' the return of Peets an' Boggs I allows the balance of this devoted band better imbibe some. Barkeep, sort out some bottles.'

"The committee comes back after a little, an' allows Missis Rucker reports herse'f shy on viands on account of the freighters bein' back'ard comin' in.

"'But,' says Peets, 'she's upholstered to make a strong play on salt hoss an' baked beans, with coffee an' biscuits for games on the side.'

"'That's good enough for a dog,' says Jack Moore, 'to say nothin' of mere people. Any gent who thinks he wants more is the effect victim of whims.'

"While we-alls is discussin' the ground plans for this yere feast, thar's a clatter of pony-hoofs an' a wild yell outside, an' next thar's a big, shaggy-lookin' vagrant, a-settin' on his hoss in front of the Red Light's door.

"'Get an axe, somebody,' he shouts, 'an' widen this yere portal some. I aims to come in on my hoss.'

"'Hands up, thar!' says Jack Moore, reachin' for his six-shooter. 'Hands up! I'll jest fool you up about comin' in on your hoss. You work in one wink too many now, an' I puts a hole in your face right over the eye.'

"'Go slow, Jack,' says Enright. 'Who may you-all be?' he goes on to the locoed man on the hoss.

"'Me?' says the locoed man. 'I'm Red Dog Bill. Tell that sot,' he continues, p'intin' at Jack, ' to put down his gun an' not offer it at me no more. He's a heap too vivid with that weepon. Only I'm a white-winged harbinger of peace, I shore ups an' makes him eat the muzzle offen it.'

"'Well, whatever be you thirstin' for, anyhow?' says Enright. 'You comes ridin' in yere like you ain't got no regards for nothin'. Is this a friendly call, or be you present on a theery that you runs the town?'

"'I'm the Red Dog committee on invitations,' he says. 'Red Dog sends its comps, an' asks Wolfville to bury the hatchet for one day in honor of to-morrow bein' Thanksgivin', an' come feed with us.'

"'Let's go him,' says Dan Boggs.

"'Now stand your hand a second,' says Enright, 'don't let's overlook no bets. Whatever has you Red Dog hold-ups got to eat, anyhow?'

"'Ain't got nothin' to eat much—maybe some can stuff—what you-alls calls air-tights,' says the Red Dog man. 'But we has liquid, no limit.'

"'Got any can tomatters?' says Boggs.

"'Can tomatters we-alls is 'speshul strong on,' says the Red Dog man. 'It's where we-alls lives at; can tomatters is.'

"'I tells you what you-all do,' says Enright, 'an' when I speaks, I represents for this yere camp.'

"'Which he shore does,' says Jack. 'He's the Big Gray Wolf yere, you can gamble. If he don't say "go slow" when you comes a-yellin' up, your remains would a-been coverin' half an acre right now. It would look like it's beef-day at this yere agency, shore.'

"'You-all go back to Red Dog,' says Enright, payin' no notice to Jack's interruptions, 'an' tell 'em we plants the war-axe for one day, an' to come over an' smoke ponies with us, instead of we-alls come thar. We're goin' to have baked beans an' salt hoss, an' we looks for Red Dog in a body. Next Thanksgivin' we eats in Red Dog. Does this yere go?'

"'It goes,' says the Red Dog gent; 'but be you-alls shore thar's s'fficient whiskey in your camp? Red Dog folks is a dry an' burnin' outfit an' is due to need a heap.'

"'The liquid's all right,' says Boggs. 'If you alls wants to do yourse'f proud, freight in a hundred-weight of them can tomatters. Which we runs out entire.'

The next day Missis Rucker sets tables all over her dinin'-room an' brings on her beans. Eighteen Red Dog gents is thar, each totin' of a can of tomatters. An' let me impart right yere, son, we never has a more free an' peacefuller day than said Thanksgivin'.

"'Them beans is a little hard, ain't they?' says Doc Peets, while we-alls is eatin', bein' p'lite an' elegant like. 'Mebby they don't get b'iled s'fficient?'

"'Them beans is all right,' says the War Chief of the Red Dogs. 'They be some hard, but you can't he'p it none. It's the altitood; the higher up you gets, the lower heat it takes to b'ile water. So it don't mush up beans like it should.'

"'That's c'rrect every time,' says Enright; 'I mind bein' over back of Prescott once, an' up near timber-line, an' I can't b'ile no beans at all. I'm up that high the water is so cold when it b'iles that ice forms on it some. I b'iles an' b'iles on some beans four days, an' it don't have no more effect than throwin' water on a drowned rat. After persistent b'ilin', I skims out a hand. ful an' drops 'em onto a tin plate to test 'em, an' it sounds like buckshot. As you says, it's the altitood.'

"'Gents,' says the boss of Red Dog, all of a sudden, an' standin' up by Enright, 'I offers the toast: "Wolfville an' Red Dog, now an' yereafter."'

"Of course we-alls drinks, an' Doc Peets makes a talk. He speaks mighty high of every gent present; which compliments gets big action in sech a game. The Red Dog chief—an' he's a mighty civilized- lookin' gent—he talks back, an' calls Wolfville an' Red Dog great commercial centers, which they sore be. He says, 'We-alls is friendly to-day, an' fights the rest of the year,' which we-alls agrees to cordial. He says fightin'. or, as he calls it, 'a generous rivalry,' does camps good, an' I reckons he's right, too, 'cause it shore results in the cashin' in of some mighty bad an' disturbin' elements. When he sets down, thar's thunders of applause.

"It's by this time that the drinkin' becomes frequent an' common. The talk gets general, an' the lies them people evolves an' saws off on each other would stampede stock.

"Any day but Thanksgivin' sech tales would shore lead to reecriminations an' blood; but as it is, every gent seems relaxed an' onbuckled that a-way in honor of the hour, an' it looks like lyin' is expected.

"How mendacious be them people? If I recalls them scenes c'rrectly, it's Texas Thompson begins the campaign ag'in trooth.

"This yere Texas Thompson tells, all careless-like, how 'way back in the forties, when he's a boy, he puts in a Thanksgivin' in the Great Salt Lake valley with Old Jim Bridger. This is before the Mormons opens their little game thar.

"'An' the snow falls to that extent, mebby it's six foot deep,' says Texas. 'Bridger an' me makes snow-shoes an' goes slidin' an' pesterin' 'round all fine enough. But the pore animals in the valley gets a rough time.

"'It's a fact; Bridger an' me finds a drove of buffalos bogged down in the snow,—I reckons now thar's twenty thousand of 'em,—and never a buffalo can move a wheel or turn a kyard.

Thar they be planted in the snow, an' only can jest wag their y'ears an' bat their eyes.

"'Well, to cut it brief, Bridger an' me goes projectin' 'round an' cuts the throats of them twenty-thousand buffalo; which we-alls is out for them robes a whole lot. Of course we don't skin 'em none while they's stuck in the snow; but when the snow melts in the spring, we capers forth an' peels off the hides like shuckin' peas. They's froze stiff at the time, for the sun ain't got 'round to thaw the beef none yet; an' so the meat's as good as the day we downs 'em.

"'An' that brings us to the cur'ous part. As fast as we-alls peels a buffalo, we rolls his carcass down hill into Salt Lake, an' what do you-alls reckons takes place? The water's that briny, it pickles said buffalo-meat plumb through, an' every year after, when Bridger an' me is back thar—we're trappin' an' huntin' them times,—all we has to do is haul one of them twenty thousand pickled buffalos ashore an' eat him.

"'When the Mormons comes wanderin' along, bein' short on grub that a-way, they nacherally jumps in an' consooms up the whole outfit in one season, which is why you-alls don't find pickled buffalo in Salt Lake no more.

"'Bridger an' me starts in, when we learns about it, to fuss with them polygamists that a-way for gettin' away with our salt buffalos. But they's too noomerous for us, an' we done quits 'em at last an' lets it go.'

"Nobody says much when Texas Thompson is through. We merely sets 'round an' drinks. But I sees the Red Dog folks feels mortified. After a minute they calls on their leadin' prevaricator for a yarn. His name's Lyin' Jim Riley, which the people who baptizes him shorely tumbles to his talents.

239

"This yere Lyin' Jim fills a tin cup with nose-paint, an' leans back listless-like an' looks at Enright.

"'I never tells you-alls,' he says, 'about how the Ratons gets afire mighty pecooliar, an' comes near a-roastin' of me up some, do I? It's this a-way: I'm pervadin' 'round one afternoon tryin' to compass a wild turkey, which thar's bands of 'em that Fall in the Ratons a-eatin' of the pinyon-nuts. I've got a Sharp's with me, which the same, as you-alls knows, is a single-shot, but I don't see no turks, none whatever. Now an' then I hears some little old gobbler, 'cross a canyon, a-makin' of sland'rous remarks about other gobblers to some hen he's deloodin', but I never manages a shot. As I'm comin' back to camp—I'm strollin' down a draw at the time where thar's no trees nor nothin'—thar emanates a black-tail buck from over among the bushes on the hill, an' starts to headin' my way a whole lot. His horns is jest gettin' over bein' velvet, an' he's feelin' plenty good an' sassy. I sees that buck—his horns eetches is what makes him—jump eighteen feet into the air an' comb them antlers of his'n through the hangin' pine limbs. Does it to stop the eetchin' an' rub the velvet off. Of course I cuts down on him with the Sharp's. It's a new gun that a-way, an' the sights is too coarse—you drags a dog through the hind sights easy—an' I holds high. The bullet goes plumb through the base of his horn, close into the ha'r, an' all nacheral fetches him sprawlin'. I ain't waitin' to load my gun none, which not waitin' to load, I'm yere to mention, is erroneous. I'm yere to say thar oughter be an act of Congress ag'in not loadin' your gun. They oughter teach it to the yearlin's in the schools, an' likewise in the class on the Sabbath. Allers load your gun. Who is that sharp, Mister Peets, who says, "Be shore you're right, then go ahead"? He once ranches some'ers down on the Glorieta. But what he oughter say is: "Be shore your gun's loaded, then go ahead."'"

"'That's whatever!' says Dan Boggs, he'pin' himse'f an' startin' the bottle; 'an' if he has a lick of sense, that's what he would say.'

"'Which I lays down my empty gun,' goes on this Lyin' Jim, ' an' starts for my buck to bootcher his neck a lot. When I gets within ten feet he springs to his hoofs an' stands glarin'. You can gamble, I ain't tamperin' 'round no wounded buck. I'd sooner go pesterin' 'round a widow woman.'

"'I gets mingled up with a wounded buck once,' says Dave Tutt, takin' a dab of paint, 'an' I nacherally wrastles him down an' lops one of his front laigs over his antlers, an' thar I has him; no more harm left in him than a chamber-maid. Mine's a white-tailed deer over on the Careese.'

"'This yere's a black-tail, which is different; says Lyin' Jim; 'it's exactly them front laigs you talks of so lightly I'm 'fraid of.

"'The buck he stands thar sorter dazed an' battin' of his eyes. I ain't no time to go back for my Sharp's, an' my six-shooter is left in camp. Right near is a high rock with a steep face about fifteen feet straight up an' down. I scrambles on to this an' breathes ag'in, 'cause I knows no deer is ever compiled yet who makes the trip. The buck's come to complete by now, an' when he observes me on the rock, his rage is as boundless as the glory of Texas.'

"'Gents, we-alls takes another cow-swaller, right yere,' shouts Texas Thompson. 'It's a rool with me to drink every time I hears the sacred name of Texas.'

"When we-alls conceals our forty drops in the usual place, Lyin' Jim proceeds:

241

"'When this buck notes me, he's that frenzied he backs off an' jumps ag'in the face of the rock stiff-laiged, an' strikes it with them hoofs of him. Which he does this noomerous times, an' every hoof cuts like a cold-chisel. It makes the sparks go spittin' an' flyin' like it's a blacksmith-shop.

"'I'm takin' it ca'm enough, only I'm wonderin' how I'm goin' to fetch loose, when I notices them sparks from his hoofs sets the pine twigs an' needles a-blazin' down by the base of the rock.

"'That's what comes to my relief. In two minutes this yere spreads to a general conflagration, and the last I sees of my deer he's flyin' over the Divide into the next canyon with his tail a-blazin' an' him utterin' shrieks. I has only time to make camp, saddle up, an' line out of thar, to keep from bein' burned before my time.

"'This yere fire rages for two months, an' burns up a billion dollars worth of mountains, I'm a coyote if some folks don't talk of lawin' me about it.'

"'That's a yarn which has the year-marks of trooth, but all the same it's deer as saves my life once,' says Doc Peets, sorter trailin' in innocent-like when this Lyin' Jim gets through; 'leastwise their meat saves it. I'm out huntin' same as you is, this time to which I alloods.

"'I'm camped on upper Red River; up where the river is only about twelve feet wide. It ain't deep none, only a few inches, but it's dug its banks down about four feet. The river runs along the center of a mile-wide valley, which they ain't no trees in it, but all cl'ar an' open. It's snowin' powerful hard one, evenin' about 3 o'clock when I comes back along the ridge towards my camp onder the pines. While I'm ridin' along I crosses the trail of nineteen deer. I takes it too quick, 'cause I needs deer in my business, an' I knows these is close or their tracks would be covered, the way it snows.

"'I runs the trail out into the open, headin' for the other ridge. The snow is plenty deep out from onder the pines, but I keeps on. Final, jest in the mouth of a canyon, over the other side where the pines begins ag'in, up jumps a black. tail from behind a yaller-pine log, and I drops him.

"'My pony's plumb broke down by now, so I makes up my mind to camp. It's a 'way good site. Thar's water comin' down the canyon; thar's a big, flat floor of rocks—big as the dance-hall floor—an' all protected by a high rock-faced bluff, so no snow don't get thar none; an' out in front, some twelve feet, is a big pitch-pine log. Which I couldn't a-fixed things better if I works a year.

"'I sets fire to the log, cuts up my deer, an' sorter camps over between the log an' bluff, an' takes things as ba'my as summer. I has my saddle-blanket an' a slicker, an' that's all I needs.

"'Thar ain't no grass none for the little hoss, but I peels him about a bushel of quakin'-ash bark, an' he's doin' well 'nough. Lord! how it snows outside! When I peers out in the mornin' it scares me. I saddles up, 'cause my proper camp is in the pines t'other side of this yere open stretch, an' I've got to make it.

"'My pony is weak, an' can only push through the snow, which is five feet deep. I'm walkin' along all comfortable, a-holdin' of his tail, when "swish" he goes plumb outen sight. I peers into the orifice which ketches him, an' finds he's done slumped off that four-foot bank into Red River, kerslop!

243

Which he's at once swept from view; the river runnin' in onder the snow like a tunnel.

"That settles it; I goes pirootin' back. I lives in that canyon two months. It snows a heap after I gets back, an' makes things deeper'n ever. I has my deer to eat, not loadin' my pony with it when I starts, an' I peels some sugar-pines, like I sees Injuns, an' scrapes off the white skin next the trees, an' makes a pasty kind of bread of it, an' I'm all right.

"'One mornin', jest before I gets out of meat, I sees trouble out in the snow. Them eighteen deer—thar's nineteen, but I c'llects one, as I says—comes sa'nterin' down my canyon while I'm asleep, an' goes out an' gets stuck in the snow. I allows mebby they dresses about sixty pounds each, an' wallers after 'em with my knife an' kills six.

"'This yere gives me meat for seventy-two days—five pounds a day, which with the pine bark is shore enough, The other twelve I turns 'round an' he'ps out into the canyon ag'in, an' do you know, them deer's that grateful they won't leave none? It's a fact, they simply hangs 'round all the time I'm snowed in.

"'In two months the snow melts down, an' I says adios to my twelve deer an' starts for camp. Which you-alls mebby imagines my s'prise when I beholds my pony a-grazin' out in the open, saddle on an' right. Yere's how it is: He's been paradin' up an' down the bed of Red River onder that snow tunnel for two months. Oh! he feeds easy enough. Jest bites the yerbage along the banks. This snow tunnel is four feet high, an' he's got plenty of room.

"'I'm some glad to meet up with my pony that a-way, you bet! an' ketches him up an' rides over to my camp. An' I'm followed by my twelve deer, which comes cavortin' along all genial an' cordial an' never leaves me. No, my hoss is sound, only his feet is a little water-soaked an' tender; an' his eyes, bein' so long in that half. dark place onder the snow, is some weak an' sore.'

"As no one seems desirous to lie no more after Doc Peets gets through, we-alls eats an' drinks all we can, an' then goes over to the dance-hall an' whoops her up in honor of Red Dog. Nothin' could go smoother.

"When it comes time to quit, we has a little trouble gettin' sep'rate from 'em, but not much. We-alls starts out to 'scort 'em to Red Dog as a guard of honor, an' then they, bustin' with p'liteness, 'scorts us back to Wolfville. Then we-alls, not to be raised out, sees 'em to Red Dog ag'in, an' not to have the odd hoss onto 'em in the matter, back they comes with us.

"I don't know how often we makes this yere round trip from one camp to t'other, cause my mem'ry is some dark on the later events of that Thanksgivin'. My pony gets tired of it about the third time back, an' humps himse'f an' bucks me off a whole lot, whereupon I don't go with them Red Dog folks no further, but nacherally camps down back of the mesquite I lights into, an, sleeps till mornin'. You bet! it's a great Thanksgivin'.'

CHAPTER XXL.

BILL HOSKINS'S COON.

"Now I thoroughly saveys," remarked the Old Cattleman reflectively, at a crisis in our conversation when the talk turned on men of small and cowardly measure, "I thoroughly saveys that taste for battle that lurks in the deefiles of folk's nacher like a wolf in the hills Which I reckons now that I, myse'f, is one of the peacefullest people as ever belts on a weepon; but in my instincts—while I never jestifies or follows his example—I cl'arly apprehends the emotions of a gent who convenes with another gent all sim'lar, an' expresses his views with his gun. Sech is human nacher onrestrained, an' the same, while deplorable, is not s'prisin'.

"But this yere Olson I has in my mem'ry don't have no sech manly feelin's as goes with a gun play. Olson is that cowardly he's even furtive; an' for a low-flung measly game let me tell you-all what Olson does. It's shorely ornery.

"It all arises years ago, back in Tennessee, an' gets its first start out of a hawg which is owned by Olson an' is downed by a gent named Hoskins—Bill Hoskins. It's this a-way.

"Back in Tennessee in my dream-wreathed yooth, when livestock goes projectin' about permiscus, a party has to build his fences 'bull strong, hawg tight, an' hoss high,' or he takes results. Which Hoskins don't make his fences to conform to this yere rool none; leastwise they ain't hawg tight as is shown by one of Olson's hawgs.

"The hawg comes pirootin' about Hoskins's fence, an' he goes through easy; an' the way that invadin' animal turns

246

Bill's potatoes bottom up don't hinder him a bit. He shorely loots Bill's lot; that's whatever.

"But Bill, perceivin' of Olson's hawg layin' waste his crop, reaches down a 8-squar' rifle, 30 to the pound, an' stretches the hawg. Which this is where Bill falls into error. Layin' aside them deeeficiencies in Bill's fence, it's cl'ar at a glance a hawg can't be held responsible. Hawgs is ignorant an' tharfore innocent; an' while hawgs can be what Doc Peets calls a' CASUS BELLI,' they can't be regarded as a foe legitimate.

"Now what Bill oughter done, if he feels like this yore hawg's done put it all over him, is to go an' lay for Olson. Sech action by Bill would have been some excessive,—some high so to speak; but it would have been a line shot. Whereas killin' the hawg is 'way to one side of the mark; an' onder.

"However, as I states, Bill bein' hasty that a-way, an' oncapable of perhaps refined reasonin', downs the pig, an' stands pat, waitin' for Olson to fill his hand, if he feels so moved.

"It's at this pinch where the cowardly nacher of this yere Olson begins to shine. He's ugly as a wolf about Bill copperin' his hawg that a-way, but he don't pack the nerve to go after Bill an' make a round-up of them grievances. An' he ain't allowin' to pass it up none onrevenged neither. Now yere's what Olson does; he 'sassinates Bill's pet raccoon.

"That's right, son, jest massacres a pore, confidin' raccoon, who don't no more stand in on that hawg-killin' of Bill's, than me an' you,—don't even advise it.

"Which I shorely allows you saveys all thar is to know about a raccoon. No? Well, a raccoon's like this: In the first place he's plumb easy, an' ain't lookin' for no gent to hold out kyards or ring a cold deck on him. That's straight; a raccoon is simple-minded that a-way; an' his impressive trait is, he's meditative. Besides bein' nacherally thoughtful, a raccoon is a heap melancholy,—he jest sets thar an' absorbs melancholy from merely bein' alive.

"But if a raccoon is melancholy or gets wropped in thought that a- way, it's after all his own play. It's to his credit that once when he's tamed, he's got mountainous confidence in men, an' will curl up to sleep where you be an' shet both eyes. He's plumb trustful; an' moreover, no matter how mournful a raccoon feels, or how plumb melancholy he gets, he don't pester you with no yarns.

"I reckons I converses with this yere identical raccoon of Bill's plenty frequent; when he feels blue, an' ag'in when he's at his gailiest, an' he never remarks nothin' to me except p'lite general'ties.

"If this yere Olson was a dead game party who regards himse'f wronged, he'd searched out a gun, or a knife, or mebby a club, an' pranced over an' rectified Bill a whole lot. But he's too timid an' too cowardly, an' afraid of Bill. So to play even, he lines out to bushwhack this he'pless, oninstructed raccoon. Olson figgers to take advantage of what's cl'arly a loop-hole in a raccoon's constitootion.

"Mebby you never notices it about a raccoon, but once he gets interested in a pursoot, he's rigged so he can't quit none ontil the project's a success. Thar's herds an' bands of folks an' animals who's fixed sim'lar. They can start, an' they can't let up. Thar's bull-dogs: They begins a war too easy; but the c'pacity to quit is left out of bull-dogs entire. Same about nose-paint with gents I knows. They capers up to whiskey at the beginnin' like a kitten to warm milk; an' they never does cease no more. An' that's how the kyards falls to raccoons.

"Knowin these yere deefects in raccoons, this Olson plots to take advantage tharof; an' by playin' it low on Bill's raccoon, get even with Bill about that dead hawg. Which Bill wouldn't have took a drove of hawgs; no indeed! not the whole Fall round-up of hawgs in all of West Tennessee, an' lose that raccoon.

"It's when Bill's over to Pine Knot layin' in tobacker, an' nose- paint an' corn meal, an' sech necessaries, when Olson stands in to down Bill's pet. He goes injunnin' over to Bill's an' finds the camp all deserted, except the raccoon's thar, settin', battin' his eyes mournful an' lonesome on the doorstep. This Olson camps down by the door an' fondles the raccoon, an' strokes his coat, an' lets him search his pockets with his black hands ontil he gets that friendly an' confident about Olson he'd told him anythin'. It's then this yere miscreant, Olson, springs his game. "H's got a couple of crawfish which he's fresh caught at the Branch. Now raccoons regards crawfish as onusual good eatin'. For myse'f, I can't say I deems none high of crawfish as viands, but raccoons is different; an' the way they looks at it, crawfish is pie.

"This Olson brings out his two crawfish an' fetchin' ajar of water from the spring, he drops in a crawfish an' incites an' aggravates Zekiel—that's the name of Bill's raccoon—to feel in an' get him a whole lot.

"Zekiel ain't none shy on the play. He knows crawfish like a gambler does a red chip; so turnin' his eyes up to the sky, like a raccoon does who's wropped in pleasant anticipations that a-way, he plunges in his paw an' gets it.

"Once Zekiel acquires him, the pore crawfish don't last as long as two-bits at faro-bank. When Zekiel has him plumb devoured he turns his eyes on Olson, sorter thankful, an' 'waits developments.

"Olson puts in the second crawfish, an' Zekiel takes him into camp same as t'other. It's now that Olson onfurls his plot on Zekiel. Olson drops a dozen buckshot into the jar of water. Nacherally, Zekiel, who's got his mind all framed up touchin' crawfish, goes after the buckshot with his fore foot. But it's different with buck- shot; Zekiel can't pick 'em up. He tries an' tries with his honest, simple face turned up to heaven, but he can't make it. All Zekiel can do is feel 'em with his foot, an' roll 'em about on the bottom of the jar.

"Now as I remarks prior, when a raccoon gets embarked that a-way, he can't quit. He ain't arranged so he can cease. Olson, who's plumb aware tharof, no sooner gets Zekiel started on them buckshot, than knowin' that nacher can be relied on to play her hand out, he sa'nters off to his wickeyup, leavin' Zekiel to his fate. Bill won't be home till Monday, an' Olson knows that before then, onless Zekiel is interrupted, he'll be even for that hawg Bill drops. As Olson cones to a place in the trail where he's goin' to lose sight of Bill's camp, he turns an' looks back. The picture is all his revenge can ask. Thar sets Zekiel on the doorstep, with his happy countenance turned up to the dome above, an' his right paw elbow deep in the jar, still rollin' an' feelin' them buckshot 'round, an' allowin' he's due to ketch a crawfish every moment.

"Which it works out exactly as the wretched Olson figgers. The sun goes down, an' the Sunday sun comes up an' sets again; an' still pore Zekiel is planted by the jar, with his hopeful eyes on high, still feelin' of them buckshot. He can't quit no more'n if he's loser in a poker game; Zekiel can't. When Bill rides up to his door about second-drink time Monday afternoon, Olson is shorely even on that hawg. Thar lays Zekiel, dead. He's jest set thar with them buck-shot an' felt himse'f to death.

"But speakin' of the sapiency of Bill Hoskins's Zekiel," continued the old gentleman as we lighted pipes and lapsed into desultory puffing, "while Zekiel for a raccoon is some deep, after all you-all is jest amazed at Zekiel 'cause I calls your attention to him a whole lot. If you was to go into camp with 'em, an' set down an' watch 'em, you'd shorely be s'prised to note how level-headed all animals be.

"Now if thar's anythin' in Arizona for whose jedgement I don't have respect nacheral, it's birds. Arizona for sech folks as you an' me, an' coyotes an' jack-rabbits, is a good range. Sech as we-alls sorter fits into the general play an' gets action for our stacks. But whatever a bird can find entrancin' in some of them Southwestern deserts is allers too many for me.

"As I su'gests, I former holds fowls, who of free choice continues a residence in Arizona, as imbeciles. Yet now an' then I observes things that makes me oncertain if I'm onto a bird's system; an' if after all Arizona is sech a dead kyard for birds. It's possible a gent might be way off on birds an' the views they holds of life. He might watch the play an' esteem 'em loser, when from a bird's p'int of view they's makin' a killin', an' even callin' the turn every deal.

"What he'ps to open my eyes a lot on birds is two Road Runners Doc Peets an' me meets up with one afternoon

251

comin' down from Lordsburg. These yere Road Runners is a lanky kind of prop'sition, jest a shade off from spring chickens for size. Which their arrangements as to neck an' laigs is onrestricted an' liberal, an' their long suit is runnin' up an' down the sun-baked trails of Arizona with no object. Where he's partic'lar strong, this yere Road Runner, is in waitin' ontil some gent comes along, same as Doc Peets an' me that time, an' then attachin' of himse'f said cavalcade an' racin' along ahead. A Road Runner keeps up this exercise for miles, an' be about the length of a lariat ahead of your pony's nose all the time. When you- all lets out a link or two an' stiffens your pony with the spur, the Road Runner onbuckles sim'lar an' exults tharat. You ain't goin' to run up on him while he can wave a laig, you can gamble your last chip, an' you confers favors on him by sendin' your pony at him. Thar he stays, rackin' along ahead of you ontil satiated. Usual thar's two Road Run. ners, an' they clips it along side by side as if thar's somethin' in it for 'em; an' I reckons, rightly saveyed, thar is. However, the profits to Road Runners of them excursions ain't obvious, none whatever; so I won't try to set 'em forth. Them journeys they makes up an' down the trail shorely seems aimless to me.

"But about Doc Peets an' me pullin' out from Lordsburg for Wolfville that evenin': Our ponies is puttin' the landscape behind 'em at a good road-gait when we notes a brace of them Road Runners with wings half lifted, pacin' to match our speed along the trail in front. As Road Runners is frequent with us, our minds don't bother with 'em none. Now an' then Doc an' me can see they converses as they goes speedin' along a level or down a slope. It's as if one says to t'other, somethin' like this yere

"'How's your wind, Bill? Is it comin' easy?'

"'Shore,' it would seem like Bill answers. 'Valves never is in sech shape. I'm on velvet; how's your laigs standin' the pace, Jim?'

"'Laigs is workin' like they's new oiled,' Jim replies back; 'it's a plumb easy game. I reckons, Bill, me an' you could keep ahead of them mavericks a year if we-alls feels like it.'

"'Bet a blue stack on it,' Bill answers. ' I deems these yere gents soft. Before I'd ride sech ponies as them, I'd go projectin' 'round some night an' steal one.'

"'Them ponies is shorely a heap slothful,' Jim answers.

"'At this mebby them Road Runners ruffles their feathers an' runs on swifter, jest to show what a slow racket keepin' ahead of me an' Peets is. An' these yere locoed birds keeps up sech conversations for hours.

"Mind I ain't sayin' that what I tells you is what them Road Runners really remarks; but I turns it over to you-all the way it strikes me an' Doc at the time. What I aims to relate, however, is an incident as sheds light on how wise an' foxy Road Runners be.

"Doc Peets an' me, as I states, ain't lavishin' no onreasonable notice on these yere birds, an' they've been scatterin' along the trail for mebby it's an hour, when one of 'em comes to a plumb halt, sharp. The other stops likewise an' rounds up ag'inst his mate; an' bein' cur'ous to note what's pesterin 'em, Peets an' me curbs to a stand-still. The Road Runner who stops first—the same bein' Bill— is lookin' sharp an' interested-like over across the plains.

"'Rattlesnake,' he imparts to his side partner.

"'Where's he at?' says the side partner, which is Jim, 'where's this yere snake at, Bill? I don't note no rattlesnake.'

"'Come round yere by me,' Bill says. 'Now on a line with the top of yonder mesa an' a leetle to the left of that soap-weed; don't you- all see him quiled up thar asleep?'

"'Which I shorely does,' says Jim, locatin' the rattlesnake with his beady eye, 'an' he's some sunk in slumber. Bill, that serpent is our meat.'

"'Move your moccasins easy,' says Bill, 'so's not to turn him out.
Let's rustle up some flat cactuses an' corral him.'

"Tharupon these yere Road Runners turns in mighty diligent; an' not makin' no more noise than shadows, they goes pokin' out on the plains ontil they finds a flat cactus which is dead; so they can tear off the leaves with their bills. Doc Peets an' me sets in our saddles surveyin' their play; an' the way them Road Runners goes about the labors of their snake killin' impresses us it ain't the first bootchery of the kind they appears in. They shorely don't need no soopervisin'.

"One after the other, Jim an' Bill teeters up, all silent, with a flat cactus leaf in their beaks, an' starts to fence in the rattlesnake with 'em. They builds a corral of cactus all about him, which the same is mebby six-foot across. Them engineerin' feats takes Jim an' Bill twenty minutes. But they completes 'em; an' thar's the rattlesnake, plumb surrounded.

"These yere cactuses, as you most likely saveys, is thorny no limit; an' the spikes is that sharp, needles is futile to 'em. Jim an' Bill knows the rattlesnake can't cross this thorny corral.

"He don't look it none, but from the way he plays his hand, I takes it a rattlesnake is sensitive an' easy hurt onder the chin.

"An' it's plain to me an' Peets them Road Runners is aware of said weaknesses of rattlesnakes, an' is bankin' their play tharon. We- alls figgers, lookin' on, that Jim an' Bill aims to put the rattlesnake in prison; leave him captive that a-way in a cactus calaboose. But we don't size up Jim an' Bill accurate at all. Them two fowls is shorely profound.

"No sooner is the corral made, than Jim an' Bill, without a word of warnin', opens up a warjig 'round the outside; flappin' their pinions an' screechin' like squaws. Nacherally the rattlesnake wakes up. The sight of them two Road Runners, Jim an' Bill, cussin' an' swearin' at him, an' carryin' on that a-way scares him.

"It's trooth to say Bill an' Jim certainly conducts themse'fs scand'lous. The epithets they heaps on that pore ignorant rattlesnake, the taunts they flings at him, would have done Apaches proud.

The rattlesnake buzzes an' quils up, an' onsheaths his fangs, an' makes bluffs to strike Bill an' Jim, but they only hops an' dances about, thinkin' up more ornery things to say. Every time the rattlesnake goes to crawl away—which he does frequent—he strikes the cactus thorns an' pulls back. By an' by he sees he's elected, an' he gets that enraged he swells up till he's big as two snakes; Bill an' Jim maintainin' their sass. Them Road Runners is abreast of the play every minute, you can see that.

"At last comes the finish, an' matters gets dealt down to the turn. The rattlesnake suddenly crooks his neck, he's so plumb locoed with rage an' fear, an' socks his fangs into himse'f. That's the fact; bites himse'f, an' never lets up till he's dead.

"It don't seem to astound Jim an' Bill none when the rattlesnake 'sassinates himse'f that a-way, an' I reckons they has this yere sooicide in view. They keeps pesterin' an' projectin' about ontil the rattlesnake is plumb defunct, an' then they emits a whirlwind of new whoops, an' goes over to one side an' pulls off a skelp dance. Jim an' Bill is shorely cel'bratin' a vic'try.

"After the skelp dance is over, Bill an' Jim tiptoes over mighty quiet an' sedate, an' Jim takes their prey by the tail an' yanks it. After the rattlesnake's drug out straight, him an' Bill runs their eyes along him like they's sizin' him up. With this yere last, however, it's cl'ar the Road Runners regards the deal as closed. They sa'nters off down the trail, arm in arm like, conversin' in low tones so Peets an' me never does hear what they says. When they's in what they takes to be the c'rrect p'sition, they stops an' looks back at me an' Peets. Bill turns to Jim like he's sayin':

"'Thar's them two short-horns ag'in. I wonders if they ever aims to pull their freight, or do they reckon they'll pitch camp right yere?'"

CHAPTER XXII.

OLD SAM ENRIGHT'S "ROMANCE."

"It mebby is, that romances comes to pass on the range when I'm thar," remarked the Old Cattleman, meditatively, "but if so be, I never notes 'em. They shorely gets plumb by me in the night."

The old gentleman had just thrown down a daily paper, and even as he spoke I read on the upturned page the glaring headline: "Romance in Real Life." His recent literature was the evident cause of his reflections.

"Of course," continued the Old Cattleman, turning for comfort to his inevitable tobacco pipe, "of course, at sech epocks as some degraded sharp takes to dealin' double in a poker game, or the kyards begins to come two at a clatter at faro-bank, the proceedin's frequent takes on what you-all might call a hue of romance; an' I admits they was likely to get some hectic, myse'f. But as I states, for what you-all would brand as clean. strain romance, I ain't recallin' none."

"How about those love affairs of your youth?" I ventured.

"Which I don't deny," replied the old gentleman, between puffs, "that back in Tennessee, as I onfolds before, I has my flower- scented days. But I don't wed nothin', as you-all knows, an' even while I'm ridin' an' ropin' at them young female persons, thar's never no romance to it, onless it's in the fact that they all escapes.

"But speakin' of love-tangles, Old Man Enright once recounts a story; which the same shows how female fancy is rootless an' onstable that a-way.

"'Allers copper a female.' says Cherokee Hall, one day, when Texas Thompson is relatin' how his wife maltreats him, an' rounds up a divorce from him down at Laredo. 'Allers play 'em to lose. Nell, yere,' goes on Cherokee, as he runs his hand over the curls of Faro Nell, who's lookout for Cherokee, 'Nelly, yere, is the only one I ever meets who can be depended on to come winner every trip.'

"'Which females,' says Old Man Enright, who's settin' thar at the time, ' an' partic'lar, young females, is a heap frivolous, nacheral. A rainbow will stampede most of 'em. For myse'f, I'd shorely prefer to try an' hold a bunch of five hundred ponies on a bad night, than ride herd on the heart of one lady. Between gent an' gent that a-way, I more'n half figger the 'ffections of a female is migratory, same as buffaloes was before they was killed, an' sorter goes north like in the spring, an' south ag'in in the winter.'

"'As for me; says Texas Thompson, who's moody touchin' them divorce plays his wife is makin', 'you-alls can gamble I passes all females up. No matter how strong I holds, it looks like on the showdowns they outlucks me every time. Wherefore I quits 'em cold, an' any gent who wants my chance with females can shorely have the same.'

"'Oh, I don't know!' remarks Doc Peets, gettin' in on what's a general play, 'I've been all through the herd, an' I must say I deems women good people every time; a heap finer folks than men, an' faithfuller.'

259

"'Which I don't deny females is fine folks,' says Texas, 'but what I'm allowin' is, they's fitful. They don't stay none. You-alls can hobble an'sideline'em both at night; an' when you rolls out in the mornin', they's gone.'

"'What do you-all think, Nell?' says Doc Peets to Faro Nell, who's perched up on her stool by Cherokee's shoulder. 'What do you-all reckon now of Texas yere, a-malignin' of your sex? Why don't you p'int him to Dave Tutt an' Tucson Jennie? Which they gets married, an' thar they be, gettin' along as peaceful as two six-shooters on the same belt.'

"'I don't mind what Texas says, none,' replies Faro Nell. 'Texas is all right, an' on the square". I shouldn't wonder none if this yere Missis Thompson does saw it off on him some shabby, gettin' that sep'ration, an' I don't marvel at his remarks. But as long as Cherokee yere thinks I'm right, I don't let nobody's views pester me a little bit, so thar.'

"'It's what I says awhile back,' interrupts Enright. 'Texas Thompson's wife's motives mighty likely ain't invidious none. It's a heap probable if the trooth is known, that she ain't aimin' nothin' speshul at Texas; she only changes her mind. About the earliest event I remembers,' goes on Enright, 'is concernin' a woman who changes her mind. It's years ago when I'm a yearlin'. Our company is makin' a round-up at a camp called Warwhoop Crossin', in Tennessee, organizin' to embark in the Mexican war a whole lot, an' thin out the Greasers. No one ever does know why I, personal, declar's myse'f in on this yere imbroglio. I ain't bigger 'n a charge of powder, an' that limited as to laigs I has to clamber onto a log to mount my pony.

"'But as I'm tellin', we-alls comes together at Warwhoop to make the start. I reckons now thar's five hundred people thar.

`'Which the occasion, an' the interest the public takes in the business, jest combs the region of folks for miles about.

"'Thar's a heap of hand-shakin' an' well-wishin' goin' on; mothers an' sisters, an' sweethearts is kissin' us good-bye; an' while thar's some hilarity thar's more sobs. It's not, as I looks back'ard, what you-alls would call a gay affair.

"'While all this yere love an' tears is flowin', thar's a gent—he's our Captain—who's settin' off alone in his saddle, an' ain't takin' no hand. Thar's no sweetheart, no mother, no sister for him.

"'No one about Warwhoop knows this yere party much; more'n his name is Bent. He's captain with the Gov'nor's commission, an' comes from 'way-off yonder some'ers. An' so he sets thar, grim an' solid in his saddle, lookin' vague-like off at where the trees meets the sky, while the rest of us is goin' about permiscus, finishin' up our kissin'.

"'"Ain't he got no sweetheart to wish goodbye to him?" asks a girl of me. "Ain't thar no one to kiss him for good luck as he rides away?"

"'This yere maiden's name is Sanders, an' it's a shore fact she's the prettiest young female to ever make a moccasin track in West Tennessee. I'd a-killed my pony an' gone afoot to bring sech a look into her eyes, as shines thar when she gazes at the Captain where he's silent an' sol'tary on his hoss.

"'No," I replies, "he's a orphan, I reckons. He's plumb abandoned that a-way, an' so thar's nobody yere to kiss him, or shake his hand."

"'This yere pretty Sanders girl—an' I'm pausin' ag'in to state she's a human sunflower, that a-way—this Sanders beauty, I'm sayin', looks at this party by himse'f for a moment, an' then the big tears begins to well in her blue eyes. She blushes like a sunset, an' walks over to this yere lone gent.

"'Mister Captain," she says, raisin' her face to him like a rose, "I'm shore sorry you ain't got no sweetheart to say 'good-bye;' an' bein' you're lonesome, that a-way, I'll kiss you an' say adios myse'f."

"'Will you, my little lady?" says the lonesome Captain, as he swings from his saddle to the ground by her side; an' thar's sunshine in his eyes.

"'I'll think of you every day for that,"he says, when he kisses her, "an' if I gets back when the war's done, I'll shorely look for you yere."

"'The little Sanders girl—she is shorely as handsome as a ace full on kings—blushes a heap vivid at what she's done, an' looks warm an' tender. Which, while the play is some onusual an' out of line, everybody agrees it's all right; bein' that we-alls is goin' to a war, that a-way.

"'Now yere,' goes on Enright, at the same time callin' for red-eye all 'round, ' is what youalls agrees is a mighty romantic deal. Yere's a love affair gets launched.'

"'Does this yere lone-hand gent who gets kissed by the Sanders lady outlive the war?' asks Texas Thompson, who has braced up an' gets mighty vivacious listenin' to the story.

"'Which he shorely outlives that conflict,' replies Enright. 'An' you can gamble he's in the thick of the stampede, too, every time. I will say for this yere Captain, that while I ain't with him plumb through, he's as game a sport as ever fought up hill. He's the sort which fights an goes for'ard to his man at the same time. Thar's no white feathers on that kind; they's game as badgers. An' bad.'

"'Which if he don't get downed none,' says Texas Thompson, 'an' hits Tennessee alive, I offers ten to one he leads this yere Sanders female to the altar.'

"'Which you'd lose, a whole lot,' says Enright, at the same time raisin' his whiskey glass.

"'That's what I states when I trails out on this yere romance. Females is frivolous an' plumb light of fancy. This Captain party comes back to Warwhoop, say, it's two years an' a half later, an' what do you-alls reckon? That Sanders girl's been married mighty nigh two yzars, an' has an infant child as big as a b'ar cub, which is beginnin' to make a bluff at walkin.'

"'Now, on the squar', an' I'm as s'prised about it as you be— I'm more'n s'prised, I'm pained—I don't allow, lookin' over results an' recallin' the fact of that b'ar-cub infant child, that for all her blushin', an' all her tears, an' kissin' that Captain party good-by that a-way, that the Sanders girl cares a hoss-h'ar rope for him in a week. An' it all proves what I remarks, that while females ain't malev'lent malicious, an' don't do these yere things to pierce a gent with grief, their 'ffections is always honin' for the trail, an' is shorely prone to move camp. But, bless 'em! they can't he'p it none if their hearts be quicksands, an' I libates to 'em ag'in.'

"Whereat we-alls drinks with Enright; feelin' a heap sim'lar.

"'Whatever becomes of this yerc pore Captain party?' asks Faro Nell.

"'Well, the fact about that Captain,' replies Enright, settin' down his glass, 'while the same is mere incident, an' don't have no direct bearin' on what I relates; the fact in his case is he's wedded already. Nacherally after sayin' "howdy!" to the little Sanders girl, an' applaudin' of her progeny—which it looks like he fully endorses that a-way—this yere Captain gent hits the trail for Nashville, where his wife's been keepin' camp an' waitin' for him all the time.'"

CHAPTER XXIII.

PINON BILL'S BLUFF.

"This narrative is what you-all might call some widespread," said the Old Cattleman, as he beamed upon me, evidently in the best of humors. "It tells how Pinon Bill gets a hoss on Jack Moore; leaves the camp bogged up to the saddle-girths in doubt about who downs Burke; an' stakes the Deef Woman so she pulls her freight for the States.

"Pinon Bill is reckoned a hard game. He's only in Wolfville now an' then, an' ain't cuttin' no figger in public calc'lations more'n it's regarded as sagacious to pack your gun while Pinon Bill's about.

"No; he don't down no white men no one ever hears of, but thar's stories about how he smuggles freight an' plunder various from Mexico, an' drives off Mexican cattle, an' once in awhile stretches a Mexican himse'f who objects to them enterprises of Pinon Bill's; but thar's nothin' in sech tales to interest Americans, more'n to hear 'em an' comment on 'em as plays.

"But while Pinon Bill never turns his talents to American, them liberties he takes with Greasers gives him a heap of bad repoote, as a mighty ornery an' oneasy person; an' most of us sorter keeps tab on him whenever he favors Wolfville with his presence.

"'This time he collides with Jack Moore, an' so to speak, leaves the drinks on Jack, he's been trackin' 'round camp mebby it's six weeks.

"'Likewise thar's an old longhorn they calls the 'Major'; he's been hangin' about for even longer yet. Don't go to figgerin' on no hostilities between this Pinon Bill an' the Major, for their trails never does cross once. Another thing' Pinon Bill ain't nacheraliy hostile neither; ain't what you-all calls trailin' trouble; whereas the Major's also a heap too drunk to give way to war, bein' tanked that a-way continuous.

"Which I don't reckon thar's the slightest doubt but the Major's a bigger sot than Old Monte, though the same is in dispoote; Cherokee Hall an' Boggs a-holdin' he is; an' Doc Peets an' Tutt playin' the other end; Enright an' Jack Moore, ondecided.

"Peets confides in me of an' concernin' the Major that thar's a time—an' no further up the trail than five years—when the Major is shore-'nough a Major; bein' quartermaster or some sech bluff in the army.

"But one day Uncle Sam comes along an' wants to cash in; an' thar this yere crazy-hoss Major is with ten times as many chips out as he's got bank-roll to meet, an' it all fatigues the gov'ment to that extent the Major's cashiered, an' told to vamos the army for good.

"I allers allows it's whiskey an' kyards gets the Major's roll that time. Peets says he sees him 'way back once over some'ers near the Mohave Desert—Wingate, mebby—an' whiskey an' poker has the Major roped; one by the horns, the other by the hoofs; an' they jest throws him an' drug him, an' drug him an' throws him, alternate. The Major never shakes loose from the loops of them vices; none whatever.

"An' that's mighty likely, jest as I says, how the Major finds himse'f cashiered an' afoot; an' nothin' but disgrace to get rid of an' whiskey to get, to fill the future with.

"So it comes when I trails up on the Major he's a drunkard complete, hangin' 'round with a tin-horn an' a handful of dice, tryin' to get Mexicans or Chinamen to go ag'in 'em for any small thing they names.

"It's on account of this yere drunkard the Major that the Deef Woman comes stagin' it in with Old Monte one day. Got a papoose with her, the Deef Woman has, a boy comin' three, an' it's my firm belief, which this view is common an' frequent with all Wolfville, as how the Deef Woman's the Major's wife.

"It ain't no cinch play that this female's deef, neither; which it's allers plain she hears the most feeblesome yelp of that infant, all the way from the dance-hall to the O. K. House, an' that means across the camp complete.

"Boggs puts it up she merely gives it out she's deef that a-way to cut off debate with the camp, an' decline all confidences goin' an' comin'.

"Thar's no reason to say the Deef Woman's the Major's wife, more'n she tumbles into camp as onlooked for as Old Monte sober, an' it's easy to note she s'prises an' dismays the Major a lot, even drunk an' soaked with nose paint as he shorely is.

"The Deef Woman has a brief pow-wow with him alone over at the O. K. House, followin' of which the Major appears the whitiest an' the shakiest I ever beholds him—the last bein' some strong as a statement—an' after beggin' a drink at the Red Light, p'ints out afoot for Red Dog, an' is seen no more.

"What the Deef Woman says to the Major, or him to her; or what makes him hit the trail for Red Dog that a-way no one learns. The Deef Woman ain't seemin' to regard the Major's jumpin' the outfit as no loss, however. Wherein she's plenty accurate, for that Major shorely ain't worth ropin' to brand.

"After he's gone—an' the Major's moccasin track ain't never seen in Wolfville no more, he's gone that good—the next we-alls hears of the deal, this yere Deef Woman's playin' the piano at the dance- hall.

"Doc Peets an' Enright, likewise the rest, don't like this none whatever, for she don't show dance-hall y'ear marks, an' ain't the dance-hall brand; but it looks like they's powerless to interfere.

"Peets tries to talk to her, but she blushes an' can't hear him; while Enright an' Missis Rucker—which the last bein' a female herse'f is rung in on the play—don't win out nothin' more. Looks like all the Deef Woman wants is to be let alone, while she makes a play the best she can for a home-stake.

"I pauses to mention, however, that durin' the week the Deef Woman turns her game at the piano—for she don't stay only a week as the play runs out—she comes mighty near killin' the dance-hall business. The fact is this were Deef Woman plays that remarkable sweet no one dances at all; jest nacherally sets'round hungerin' for them melodies, an' cadences to that extent they actooally overlooks drinks.

"That's right; an' you can gamble your deepest chip when folks begins to overlook drinks, an' a glass of whiskey lasts energetic people half an hour, they's shorely some rapt.

"Even the coyotes cashes in an' quits their howls whenever the Deef Woman drug her chair up to that piano an' throws loose. An' them coyotes afterward, when she turns up her box an' stops dealin', gets that bashful an' taciturn they ain't sayin' a word; but jest withholds all yells entire the rest of the night.

"But thar's no use talkin' hours about the Deef Woman's music. It only lasts a week; even if Wolfville does brag of it yet.

"It's this a-way: It's while Pinon Bill is romancin' round the time I mentions, that we-alls rolls outen our blankets one mornin' an' picks up a party whose name's Burke. This yere Burke is shot in the back; plumb dead, an' is camped when we finds him all cold an' stiff out back of the New York store.

"The day before, Burke, who's a miner, diggin' an' projectin' 'round over in the Floridas, is in camp layin' in powder an' fuse a whole lot, with which he means to keep on shootin' up the he'pless bosoms of the hills like them locoed miner people does.

"At night he's drunk; an' while thar's gents as sees Burke as late, mebby it's two hours after the last walse at the dance-hall, thar's nobody who ups an' imparts how Burke gets plugged. All Wolfville knows is that at first-drink time in the mornin', thar this Burke is plumb petered that a-way.

"An' the worst feature shorely is that the bullet goes in his back, which makes it murder plain. Thar ain't a moccasin track to he'p tell who drops this yere Burke. Nacrerally, everybody's deeply taken to know who does it; for if thar's a party in camp who's out to shoot when your back's turned, findin' of him an' hangin' him can't be too pop'lar an' needful as a play. But, as I remarks, we're baffled, an' up ag'inst it absoloote. No one has the least notion who gets this yere Burke. It's money as is the object of the murder, for Burke's war-bags don't disclose not a single centouse when the committee goes through 'em prior to the obsequies.

"It's two days the camp is talkin' over who does this crime, when Texas Thompson begins to shed a beam of light. This last was onlooked for, an' tharfore all the more interestin'.

"Texas Thompson is a jedge of whiskey sech as any gent might tie to. He's a middlin' shot with a Colt's .44 an' can protect himse'f at poker. But nobody ever reckons before that Texas can think. Which I even yet deems this partic'lar time a inspiration, in which event Texas Thompson don't have to think.

"It's over in the Red Light the second after. noon when Texas turns loose a whole lot.

"'Enright,' he says, 'I shore has a preemonition this yere Burke gets plugged by Pinon Bill.'

"'How does the kyards run so as to deal s'picions on Pinon Bill?' says Enright.

"'This a-way,' says Texas, some confident an' cl'ar; 'somebody downs Burke; that's dead certain. Burke don't put that hole in the middle of his back himse'f; no matter how much he reckons it improves him. Then, when it's someone else who is it? Now,' goes on Texas, as glib as wolves, 'yere's how I argues: You-all don't do it; Peets don't do it; Boggs don't do it; thar's not one of us who does it. An' thar you be plumb down to Pinon Bill. In the very nacher of the deal, when no one else does it an' it's done, Pinon Bill's got to do it. I tells you as shore as my former wife at Laredo's writin' insultin' letters to me right now, this yere Pinon Bill's the party who shoots up that miner gent Burke.'

"What Texas Thompson says makes an impression; which it's about the first thoughtful remark he ever makes, an' tharfore we're prone to give it more'n usual attention.

"We imbibes on it an' talks it up an' down, mebby it's half an hour; an' the more we drinks an' the harder we thinks, the cl'arer it keeps gettin' that mighty likely this yere Texas has struck the trail. At last Jack Moore, who's, as I often says, prompt an' vig'lant that a-way, lines out to hunt this yere Pinon Bill.

"Whyever do they call him Pinon Bill? Nothin' much; only once he comes into camp drunk an' locoed; an' bein' in the dark an' him hawg-hungry, he b'iles a kettle of pinon-nuts, a-holdin' of 'em erroneous to be beans, an' as sech aimin' to get some food outen 'em a whole lot. He goes to sleep while he's pesterin' with 'em, an' when the others tumbles to his game in the mornin', he's branded as 'Pinon Bill' ever more.

"When Jack hops out to round-up Pinon Bill, all he does is go into the street. The first thing he notes is this yere Pinon Bill's pony standin' saddled over by the O. K. House, like he plans to pull his freight.

"'Which that bronco standin' thar,' says Jack to Enright, 'makes it look like Texas calls the turn with them surmises.' An' it shorely does.

"This pony makes Jack's play plenty simple; all he does now is to sa'nter 'round the pony casooal like an' lay for Pinon Bill.

"Jack's too well brought up to go surgin' into rooms lookin' for

Pinon Bill, where Jack's eyes comin' in outen the sun that a-way,

can't see for a minute nohow, an' where Pinon Bill has advantages.

It's better to wait for him outside.

"You-all saveys how it's done in the West. When a gent's needed you allers opens the game with a gun-play.

"'Hold up your hands!' says you, sorter indicatin' a whole lot at your prey with a gun.

"Which, by the way, if he don't enter into the sperit of the thing prompt an' p'int his paws heavenward an' no delay, you-all mustn't fall into no abstractions an' forget to shoot some. When you observes to a fellow-bein' that a-way

'Hold up your hands!' you must be partic'lar an' see he does it. Which if you grows lax on this p'int he's mighty likely to put your light out right thar.

"An' jest as Jack Moore tells me once when we're puttin' in some leesure hours an' whiskey mingled, you don't want to go too close to standup your gent. Over in the Gunnison country, Jack says, a marshal he knows gets inadvertent that a-way, an' thoughtless, an' goes up close.

"'Throw up your hands' says this yere marshal.

"His tone shows he's ennuied; he has so many of these yere blazers to run; that's why he's careless, mebby. When the party throws up his hands, he is careful an knocks the marshal's gun one side with his left hand, bein' he's too close as I says, at the same time pullin' his own wherewith he then sends that marshal to the happy huntin' grounds in one motion. Before ever that Gunnison offishul gets it outen his head that that sport's holdin' up his hands, he's receivin' notice on high to hustle 'round an' find his harp an' stand in on the eternal chorus for all he's worth.

"'Which the public,' says Jack Moore, the time he relates about this yere Gunnison marshal bein over-played that time, 'takes an' hangs the killer in a minute. An' he's shorely a bad man.

"'Does you-all want to pray?" says one of the gents who's stringin' of him.

"'No, Ed," he says that a-way, "prayin's a blind trail to my eyes an' I can't run it a inch."

"'"What for a racket," says this yere Ed, "would it be to pick out a sport to pray for you a whole lot; sorter play your hand?"

"'"That's all right," says this culprit. "Nominate your sharp an' tell him to wade in an' roll his game. I reckons it's a good hedge, an' a little prayin' mebby does me good."

"'Tharupon the committee puts for'ard a gent who's a good talker; but not takin' an interest much, he makes a mighty weak orison, that a-way. Thar's nohody likes it, from the culprit, who's standin' thar with the lariat 'round his neck, to the last gent who's come up. This party blunders along, mebby it's a minute, when the culprit, who's plumb disgusted, breaks in.

""""That's a hell of a pra'r," he says, "an' I don't want no more of it in mine. Gimme a drink of whiskey, gents, an' swing me off."

"'The committee, whose sympathies is all with this yere party who's to hang, calls down the gent a heap who's prayin', gives the other his forty drops, an' cinches him up some free of the ground; which the same bein' ample for strang'lation.

"'But,' concloods Jack, 'while they hangs him all right an' proper, that don't put off the funeral of the marshal none, who gets careless an' goes too close.' An' you bet Jack's right.

"But goin' back: As I remarks, Jack stands round loose an' indifferent with his eye on the pony of Pinon Bill's, which it looks now like this yere Bill is aware of Jack's little game. He comes out shore-'nough, but he's organized. He's got his gun in his hand; an' also he's packin' the Deef Woman's yearlin' in front of his breast an' face.

"Jack gives him the word, but Pinon Bill only laughs. Then Jack makes a bluff with his gun like he's goin' to shoot Pinon Bill, the infant, an' all involved tharin. This yere last move rattles Pinon Bill, an' he ups an' slams loose at Jack. But the baby's in his way as much mebby as it is in Jack's, an' he only grazes Jack's frame a whole lot, which amounts to some blood an' no deep harm.

"'Down his pony, Jack!' shouts Dave Tutt, jumpin' outen the Red
Light like he aims to get in on the deal.

"But this yere Pinon Bill shifts the cut on 'em.

"'If one of you-alls so much as cracks a cap,' he says, 'I blows the head offen this yere blessed child.'

"An' tharupon he shoves his gun up agin that baby's left y'ear that a-way, so it shore curdles your blood. He does it as readily as if it's grown-up folks. It shore sends a chill through me; an' Dan Boggs is that 'fected he turns plumb sick. Boggs ain't eatin' a thing, leastwise nothin' but whiskey, for two days after he sees Pinon Bill do it.

"'That's on the level,' says this Pinon Bill ag'in.—The first vestich of a gun-play I witnesses, or if any gent starts to follow me ontil I'm a mile away, I'll send this yearlin' scoutin' after Burke. An' you-alls hears me say it.'

"Thar it is; a squar' case of stand-off. Thar ain't a gent who's game to make a move. Seein' we ain't got a kyard left to play, this yere Pinon Bill grins wide an' satisfactory, an' swings into the saddle.

"All this time—which, after all, it ain't so long—the baby ain't sayin' nothin', and takes the deal in plumb silence. But jest as Pinon Bill lands in the saddle it onfurls a yell like a wronged panther. That's what brings the Deef Woman stampedin' to the scene. She don't hear a morsel of all this riot Jack an' Tutt an' Pinon Bill kicks up; never even gets a hint of Pinon Bill's six-shooter. But with the earliest squeak of that infant that a-way, you bet! she comes a-runnin'.

"The second she sees where her baby's at, up in the saddle along with Pinon Bill, she makes a spring for the whole outfit. We-alls stands lookin' on. Thar ain't one of us dares crook a finger, for this Pinon Bill is cool an' ca'm plumb through. He's still got the drop on the kid, while he's holdin' baby an' bridle both with the other arm an' hand. His sharp eyes is on the Deef Woman, too.

"She springs, but she never makes it. Pinon Bill jumps his pony sideways out of her reach, an' at that the Deef Woman c'lapses on her face an' shoulder in a dead swoon.

"'Adios!' says Pinon Bill, to the rest of us, backin' an' sidlin' his pony up the street so he don't lose sight of the play. 'Ten minutes from now you-alls finds this yere infant a mile from camp as safe an' solid as a sod house.'

"'Bill,' says Enright, all at once, 'I makes you a prop'sition. Restore the baby to me, an' thar ain't a gent in camp who follows you a foot. I gives you the word of Wolfville.'

"'Does that go?' demands Pinon Bill, turnin to Jack, who's shakin' the blood offen his fingers where it runs down his arm.

"'It goes,' says Jack; 'goes wherever Enright sets it. I makes good his bluffs at all times on foot or in the stirrups.'

"'An' I takes your promise,' says Pinon Bill with a laugh, 'an' yere's the baby. Which now I'm goin', I don't mind confidin' in you- alls,' goes on this Pinon Bill, 'that I never intends to hurt that infant nohow.'

"Enright gets the child, an' in no time later that Pinon Bill is fled from sight. You can believe it; it takes a load offen the public mind about that infant when the kyards comes that a-way.

"Which the story's soon told now. It's three days later, an', seein' it's refreshed in our thoughts, Enright an' the rest of us

277

is resoomed op'rations touchin' this Deef Woman, about gettin' her outen camp, an' she's beginnin' to recover her obduracy about not sayin' or hearin' nothin', when in comes a package by Old Monte an' the stage. It's for Enright from that hoss. thief, Pinon Bill. Thar's a letter an' Soo for the baby.

"'Tell that Decf Woman,' says this yere Pinon Bill, 'that I has an even thousand dollars in my war-bags, when I stacks in her offspring ag'inst the camp to win; an' I deems it only squar' to divide the pot with the baby. The kid an' me's partners in the play that a-way, an' the enclosed is the kid's share. Saw this yere dinero off on her somehow; an' make her pull her freight. Wolfville's no good place to raise that baby.'

"'Which this Pinon Bill ain't so bad neither,' says Dan Boggs, when he hears it. 'Gents, I proposes the health of this outlaw. Barkeep, see what they takes in behalf of Pinon Bill.'

"The letter an' the money's dead straight, an' the Deef Woman can't dodge or go 'round. All of which Missis Rucker takes a day off an' beats it into her by makin' signs. It's like two Injuns talkin'. It all winds up by the Deef Woman p'intin' out on her way some'ers East, an' thar ain't one of us ever sees the Major, the Deef Woman, the kid, nor yet this Pinon Bill, no more. Which this last, however, is not regarded as food for deep regrets,"

CHAPTER XXIV.

CRAWFISH JIM.

"Don't I never tell you the story of the death of Crawfish Jim?"

The Old Cattleman bent upon me an eye of benevolent inquiry. I assured him that the details of the taking off of Crawfish Jim were as a sealed book to me. But I would blithely listen.

"What was the fate of Crawfish Jim?"I asked. The name seemed a promise in itself.

"Nothin' much for a fate, Crawfish's ain't," rejoined the Old Cattleman. "Nothin' whatever compared to some fates I keeps tabs onto. It was this a-way: Crawfish Jim was a sheep-man, an' has a camp out in the foothills of the Tres Hermanas, mebby it's thirty miles back from Wolfville. This yere Crawfish Jim was a pecooliar person; plumb locoed, like all sheep-men. They has to be crazy or they wouldn't pester 'round in no sech disrepootable pursoots as sheep.

You-all has seen these yere gents as makes pets of snakes. Mebby it's once in a thousand times you cuts the trail of sech a party. Snakes is kittens to him, an' he's likely to be packin' specimens 'round in his clothes any time.

"That's the way with this Crawfish Jim. I minds talkin' to him at his camp one day when I'm huntin' a bunch of cattle. The first I notes, snake sticks his head outen Crawfish's shirt, an' looks at me malev'lent and distrustful. Another protroods its nose out up by Crawfish's collar.

"'Which you shore seems ha'nted of snakes?' I says, steppin' back an' p'intin' at the reptiles.

"'Them's my dumb companions,' says Crawfish Jim. 'They shares my solitood.'

"'You-all do seem some pop'lar with 'em,' I observes, for I saveys at once he's plumb off his mental reservation; an' when a party's locoed that a-way it makes him hostile if you derides his little game or bucks his notions.

"I takes grub with Crawfish that same day; good chuck, too; mainly sheep-meat, salt-hoss, an' bakin'-powder biscuit. I watches him some narrow about them snakes he's infested with; I loathin' of 'em, an' not wantin' 'em to transfer no love to me, nor take to enlivenin' my secloosion none.

"Well, son, this yere Crwafish Jim is as a den of serpents. I reckons now he has a plumb dozen mowed away in his raiment. Thar's no harm in 'em; bein' all bull-snakes, which is innocuous an' without p'ison, fangs, or convictions.

"When Crawfish goes to cook, he dumps these folks oaten his clothes, an' lets 'em hustle an'play'round while grub's gettin'.

"'These yere little animals,' he says, 'likes their reecreations same as humans, so I allers gives 'em a play-spell while I'm busy round camp.'

"'Don't they ever stampede off none?' I asks.

"'Shorely not,' says Crawfish. 'Bull-snakes is the most domestical snake thar is. If I'd leave one of these yere tender creatures ere over night he'd die of homesickness.'

"When Crawfish gets ready to bile the coffee, he tumbles the biggest bullsnake I'd seen yet outen the coffee-pot onto the grass. Then he fills the kettle with water, dumps in the coffee, an' sets her on the coals to stew.

"'This yere partic'lar snake,' says Crawfish, 'which I calls him Julius Caesar, is too big to tote 'round in my shirt, an' so he lives in the coffee-pot while I'm away, an' keeps camp for me.'

"'Don't you yearn for no rattlesnakes to fondle?' I inquires, jest to see what kyard he'd play.

"'No,' he says, 'rattlesnakes is all right—good, sociable, moral snakes enough; but in a sperit of humor they may bite you or some play like that, an' thar you'd be. No; bull-snakes is as 'fectionate as rattles, an' don't run to p'ison. You don't have no inadvertencies with 'em.'

"'Can't you bust the fangs outen rattlesnakes?' I asks.

"'They grows right in ag'in,' says Crawfish, same as your finger- nails. I ain't got no time to go scoutin' a rattlesnake's mouth every day, lookin' up teeth, so I don't worry with 'em, but plays bull-snakes straight. This bein' dentist for rattlesnakes has resks, which the same would be foolish to assoom.'

"While grub's cookin' an' Crawfish an' me's pow-wowin', a little old dog Crawfish has—one of them no-account nce-dogs—comes up an' makes a small uprisin' off to one side with Julius Caesar. The dog yelps an' snaps, an' Julius Caesar blows an' strikes at him, same as a rattle. snake. However, they ain't doin' no harm, an' Crawfish don't pay no heed.

"'They's runnin' blazers on each other,' says Crawfish, 'an' don't mean nothin'. Bimeby Caribou Pete—which the same is the dog—will go lie down an' sleep; an' Julius Caesar will quile up ag'in him to be warm. Caribou, bein' a dog that a-way, is a warm-blood animal, while pore Julius has got cold blood like a fish. So he goes over an' camps on Caribou, an' all the same puts his feet on him for to be comfortable.'

"Of course, I'm a heap interested in this yere snake knowledge, an' tells Crawfish so. But it sorter coppers my appetite, an' Crawfish saves on sheep-meat an' sow-belly by his discourse powerful. Thinkin' an' a-lookin' at them blessed snakes, speshul at Julius Cmsar, I shore ain't hungry much. But as you says: how about Crawfish Jim gettin' killed?

"One day Crawfish allows all alone by himse'f he'll hop into Wolfville an' buy some stuff for his camp,—flour, whiskey, tobacker, air-tights, an' sech.

"What's air-tights? Which you Eastern shorthorns is shore ignorant.
Air-tights is can peaches, can tomatters, an' sim'lar bluffs.

"As I was sayin', along comes pore old Crawfish over to Wolfville; rides in on a burro. That's right, son; comes loafin' along on a burro like a Mexican. These yere sheep-men is that abandoned an' vulgar they ain't got pride to ride a hoss.

"Along comes Crawfish on a burro, an' it's his first visit to Wolfville. Yeretofore the old Cimmaron goes over to Red Dog for his plunder, the same bein' a busted low-down camp on the Lordsburg trail, which once holds it's a rival to Wolfville. It ain't, however; the same not bein' of the same importance, commercial, as a prairie-dog town.

283

"This time, however, Crawfish pints up for Wolfville. An' to make himse'f loved, I reckons, whatever does he do but bring along Julius Caesar.

"I don't reckon now he ever plays Julius Caesar none on Red Dog. Mighty likely this yere was the bull-snake's first engagement. I clings to this notion that Red Dog never sees Julius Caesar; for if she had, them drunkards which inhabits said camp wouldn't have quit yellin' yet. Which Julius Caesar, with that Red Dog whiskey they was soaked in, would have shore given 'em some mighty heenous visions. Fact is, Crawfish told Jack Moore later he never takes Julius Caesar nowhere before.

"But all the same Crawfish prances into camp on this yere occasion with Julius bushwacked 'way 'round back in his shirt, an' sech vacant spaces about his person as ain't otherwise occupied a- nourishin' of minor bull-snakes plenty profuse.

"Of course them snakes is all holdin' back, bein', after all, timid cattle; an' so none of us s'spects Crawfish is packin' any sech s'prises. None of the boys about town knows of Crawfish havin' this bull-snake habit but me, nohow. So the old man stampedes'round an' buys what he's after, an' all goes well. Nobody ain't even dreamin' of reptiles.

"At last Crawfish, havin' turned his little game for flour, air-tights, an' jig-juice, as I says, gets into the Red Light, an' braces up ag'in the bar an' calls for nose-paint all 'round. This yere is proper an' p'lite, an' everybody within hearin' of the yell lines up.

"It's at this crisis Crawfish Jim starts in to make himse'f a general fav'ritc. Everybody's slopped out his perfoomcry, an'

284

Dan Boggs is jest sayin': 'Yere's lookin' at you, Crawfish,' when that crazy-boss shepherd sorter swarms 'round inside his shirt with his hand, an' lugs out Julius Cesar be the scruff of his neck, a- squirmin' an' a-blowin', an' madder'n a drunken squaw. Once he gets Julius out, he spreads him 'round profuse on the Red Light bar an' sorter herds him with his hand to keep him from chargin' off among the bottles.

"'Gents,' says this locoed Crawfish, 'I ain't no boaster, but I offers a hundred to fifty, an' stands to make it up to a thousand dollars in wool or sheep, Julius Caesar is the fattest an' finest serpent in Arizona; also the best behaved.'

"Thar ain't no one takin' Crawfish's bet. The moment he slams Julius on the bar, more'n ten of our leadin' citizens falls to the floor in fits, an' emerges outen one par'xysm only to slump into another. Which we shorely has a general round-up of all sorts of spells.

"'Whatever's the matter of you-all people?' says Crawfish, lookin' mighty aghast. 'Thar's no more harm in Julius Caesar than if he's a fullblown rose.'

"Jack Moore, bein' marshal, of course stands his hand. It's his offishul dooty to play a pat hand on bull-snakes an' danger in all an' any forms. An' Jack does it.

"While Crawfish is busy recountin' the attainments of Julius Caesar, a-holdin' of his pet with one hand, Jack Moore takes a snap shot at him along the bar with his six-shooter, an' away goes Julius Caesar's head like a puff of smoke. Then Moore rounds up Crawfish, an', perceivin' of the other bull-snakes, he searches 'em out one by one an' massacres 'em.

"'Call over Doc Peets,' says Jack Moore final, 'an' bring Boggs an' Tutt an' the rest of these yere invalids to.'

"Doc Peets an' Enright both trails in on the lope from the New York Store. They hears Moore's gun-play an' is cur'ous, nacheral 'nough, to know who calls it. Well, they turns in an' brings the other inhabitants outen their fits; pendin' which Moore kills off the last remainin' bull-snake in Crawfish's herd.

"Son, I've seen people mad, an' I've seen 'em gay, an' I've seen 'em bit by grief. But I'm yere to remark I never runs up on a gent who goes plumb mad with sadness ontil I sees Crawfish that day Jack Moore immolates his bull-snake pets. He stands thar, white, an' ain't sayin' a word. Looks for a minute like he can't move. Crawfish don't pack no gun, or I allers allowed we'd had notice of him some, while them bullsnakes is cashin' in.

"But at last he sorter comes to, an' walks out without sayin' nothin'. They ain't none of us regardin' of him much at the time; bein' busy drinkin' an' recoverin' from the shock.

"Now, what do you s'pose this old Navajo does? Lopes straight over to the New York Store—is ca'm as a June day about it, too—an' gets a six-shooter.

"The next information we gets of Crawfish, 'bang!' goes his new gun, an' the bullet cuts along over Jack Moore's head too high for results. New gun that a-way, an' Crawfish not up on his practice; of course he overshoots.

"Well, the pore old murderer never does get a second crack. I reckons eight people he has interested shoots all at once,

286

an' Crawfish Jim quits this earthly deal unanimous. He stops every bullet; eight of 'em, like I says.

"'Thar ain't a man of us who don't feel regrets; but what's the use? Thar we be, up ag'inst the deal, with Crawfish clean locoed. It's the only wagon-track out.

"'I shore hopes he's on the hot trail of them bull-snakes of his'n,' says Dan Boggs, as we lays Crawfish out on a monte-table. 'Seems like he thought monstrous well of 'em, an' it would mighty likely please him to run up on 'em where he's gone.'

"Whatever did we do? Why, we digs a grave out back of the dance-hall an' plants Crawfish an' his pets tharin.

"'I reckons we better bury them reptiles, too,' says Doc Peets, as we gets Crawfish stretched out all comfortable in the bottom. 'If he's lookin' down on these yere ceremonies it'll make him feel easier.'

"Doc Peets is mighty sentimental an' romantic that a-way, an' allers thinks of the touchin' things to do, which I more'n once notices likewise, that a gent bein' dead that a-way allers brings out the soft side of Peets's nacher. You bet! he's plumb sympathetic.

"We counts in the snakes. Thar's 'leven of 'em besides Julius Caesar; which we lays him on Crawfish's breast. You can find the grave to-day.

"Shore! we sticks up a headboard. It says on it, the same bein' furnished by Doc Peets—an' I wants to say Doc Peets is the best eddicated gent in Arizona-as follows

287

SACRED TO THE MEMORY OF CRAWFISH JIM, JULIUS CAESAR AND ELEVEN OTHER BULL SNAKES, THEY MEANT WELL, BUT THEY MISUNDERSTOOD EXISTENCE AND DIED.

THIS BOARD WAS REARED BY AN ADMIRING CIRELE OF FRIENDS WHO WAS WITH DECEASED TO THE LAST.

"An' don't you-all know, son, this yere onfortunate weedin' out of pore Crawfish that a-way, sorter settles down on the camp an' preys on us for mighty likely it's a week. It shorely is a source of gloom. Moreover, it done gives Dan Boggs the fan-tods. As I relates prior, Boggs is emotional a whole lot, an' once let him get what you-all calls a shock—same, for instance, as them bull-snakes—its shore due to set Boggs's intellects to millin'. An' that's what happens now. We-alls don't get Boggs; bedded down none for ten days, his visions is that acoote.

"'Which of course,' says Boggs, while we-all s settin' up administerin' things to him, 'which of course I'm plumb aware these yere is mere illoosions; but all the same, as cl'ar as ever I notes an ace, no matter where I looks at, I discerns that Julius Caesar serpent a-regardin' me reproachful outen the atmospher. An' gents, sech spectacles lets me out a heap every time. You-alls can gamble, I ain't slumberin' none with no snake-spook that a-way a-gyardin' of my dreams.'

"That's all thar is to the death of Crawfish Jim. Thar ain't no harm in him, nor yet, I reckons, in Julius Caesar an' the rest of Crawfish's fam'ly. But the way they gets tangled up with Wolfville, an' takes to runnin' counter to public sentiment an' them eight six- shooters, Crawfish an' his live-stock has to go."

Made in the USA
Lexington, KY
14 March 2018